The bite of gravel at his bare feet irritated as much as curiosity and conscience plagued Gray's mind, encouraging him to be quick. Upon opening the passenger door, he saw that the van was designed for commercial purposes. There was only the shell of the truck and little else. A suitcase, sleeping bag and pillow were stacked neatly behind the driver's seat. Anna Diaz was traveling light.

Leaning over the passenger seat, he spotted a black leather purse on the floorboard. Without the slightest twinge of guilt, he lifted out her wallet. Flipping open the buttery-soft flap, he eyed the Louisiana license, then tilted the thing back and forth to get a better look at her photo. No, it wasn't glare on the plastic that made it so unclear, he realized. The photo was scratched.

His unease growing, he checked the rest of the wallet. All of the credit card slots were empty, and there were no other photos; however, what had him exhaling in a low whistle was the amount of cash she was carrying.

He found yet another stash of bills in a different compartment in the bag. Maybe, he thought with growing bitterness, he would also find the reason for her to have such resources. Simple logic was beginning to offer a few conclusions.

Gray shoved the purse back in place...possibly a bit too roughly because it tipped over. As he reached to straighten it, his fingertips brushed against something in the seat pocket.

Frowning, he eased his hand inside and closed his fingertips around smooth steel. He drew out a Smith & Wesson .9 mm automatic—not the kind of thing a simple working girl relocating toted around with her...unless her work was dangerous.

Helen R. Myers

FINAL STAND

MIRA

ISBN 1-55166-878-5

FINAL STAND

Copyright © 2002 by Helen R. Myers.

MIRA and the Star Colophon are trademarks used under license and registered in Australia, New Zealand, Philippines, United States Patent and Trademark Office and in other countries.

Visit us at www.mirabooks.com

Printed in U.S.A.

To Ethan Ellenberg

Acknowledgments

While suspense novels are always and foremost marketed as entertainment, it's not wholly my approach to writing. Fortunately, I have an agent who both challenges me as he encourages, while I try to transfer today's social and political issues into scenarios where the Jane and John Does of the world can associate. It was he who pointed out as I developed *Final Stand* that I'd managed to create the contemporary version of one of his favorite stories, the Western classic *High Noon*. Seeing the themes of justice and honor, I immediately recognized that we all have mini "high noons" in our lives. To have the opportunity to tell the story with a woman in the courageous role that Gary Cooper made so memorable was both intimidating as it was irresistible.

As usual, Sasha's nemesis, Melor Borodin, came as a result of disturbing newspaper headlines. That my dialogue with my agent occurred shortly after a fascinating discussion I'd had regarding the Russian Mafia and their growing presence as a result of the World Trade Treaty seemed to me one of those innumerable "gifts" that guide a writer's way.

In many ways this is once again a personal story. It speaks to a part of my ancestry, and so I'm particularly grateful to my aunt, Pauline Serpas, affectionately known as "The Duchess" by those who have spent any time with her. Without her generosity of sharing her insights into the Russian culture, I couldn't have gotten beyond my own recollections and textbook agendas. *Spasibo, Tante.*

Thank you, "Gator," for being researcher, tour guide and bodyguard as I realized the need to hunt the right location for this story. When you finish building that plane, I want to fly into Sonora with you and watch the field light up.

Gail Reed, you came to my rescue and made the world of the veterinarian a little more clear to this animal lover. Whenever I need a laugh, I will think of the antibiotics line.

Karen Kelley, friend and author, your EMS background was invaluable, even when you had me muttering.

And to Lynette Bagley, who sent the timely bit of inspiration in the epilogue when your own world's axis was doing a tilt. Once again we learn that timing, intent and heart mean everything.

Readers, please be assured that any inaccuracies that slipped through are completely my error.

Finally, and always, to my friends and family—most of all Robert, for getting us through that five-day, six-hour-and-ten-minute stint without electricity after the ice storm—my love and thanks.

In memory of Jake, who made the title Final Stand *literal.*

GLOSSARY

Baba	grandmother, older woman
blat	influence, connections, networking
blini	pancake
borsch	beet soup
da	yes
defitstny	deficit goods
doróga	road, path, way
do svidaniya	till we meet again
górod	city, town
gospodin	lord, master; gentleman; equivalent to Sir or Mr.
knout	heavy whip
lyuks	luxury
nichevo	nothing; don't let it bother you
nyet	no
po blay	by connections (i.e. networking)
po dusham	heart-to-heart
pojalsta	please
póle	field, ground
sabaka	dog
spasibo	thank you
spekulyanty	speculators
stukachi	informer
ti mne i ya tebe	you for me and me for you
vzyatka	"the take"
zakurski	hors d'oeuvres

Here I stand. I can do no other.
God help me.
Amen.
—Martin Luther

_____ Prologue _____

Bitters, Texas
Thursday, August 24, 2000
10:30 p.m. CST

With a sharp strike against the small box's score, the match ignited. A flash of light, a ghostly puff of smoke, the nose-stinging scent of sulfur, and it was done. The arsonist's ragged emotions were set free. Instantly, any doubt or anxiety about this decision vanished, replaced by righteous conviction.

The flame stayed steady and bright as it was lowered to the mass of dry wood piled on the board stairs leading to the church's vestibule. Whole lengths of browned evergreen branches and other dead vegetation had been easy to collect, thanks to the wild terrain and yet another year of drought.

As expected, the brittle debris caught quickly. Flowing like liquid, the flames spread, advanced and climbed. It wouldn't be long before they gave birth to a torch, a pyre, a veritable shaking fist against this serene night, this star-studded summer sky, luminous and wide, unmarred by the slightest hint of a cloud. This silent witness to everything.

Soon the vestibule doors would catch, and then…maybe the interior. It was possible if help was slow to respond.

Tossing the box of matches into the intensifying blaze, escape became the next focus. There might not be anyone on this remote highway tonight, but there was always the chance an alert trucker on I–10, or worse, a state trooper, would spot the distant glow and mention it on his radio, initiating an alarm too soon. However, the arsonist's escape vehicle was parked facing the road; even that had been thought through. What hadn't been was the unreliable nature of the vehicle itself.

It took try after terrifying try, but just as the smell of gasoline could be detected, the engine finally roared to life and the arsonist peeled out of the lot making a skidding turn west onto the unlit single-lane highway.

1

"No!"

The dog came out of nowhere, a streak of black, darker than the night, cutting across the single-lane highway, directly into the path of the van. The driver hit the brakes, but in that surreal instant, the young woman noticed that the animal was hobbling along on only three legs. The poor creature didn't stand a chance.

Tires protested in a high-pitched squeal as she pulled at the steering wheel in an instinctive attempt to direct the vehicle away from catastrophe, and the van slid across the double yellow line. Luckily there was no other traffic on the dark, unlit road. Fully expecting the sickly thud of impact, out of the corner of her eye she caught the brief, amazing glimpse of the black mass hurling itself into a ditch. For a few seconds, she almost got to savor relief—until logic returned with stomach-roiling bitterness.

She may not be responsible for killing the dog, but that survivalist's dive had probably finished the poor thing. Even if it hadn't, maimed as it was, it wouldn't last much longer out here. Either way, she couldn't let herself care. It was imperative that she keep going.

But no sooner did the van come to a full stop than she shifted into Reverse and backed up. She angled off to the shoulder, all the way until her headlights found the animal.

A pair of glowing amber eyes watched her from the deepest part of a shallow draw.

"Damn it."

The dog had to have a cat or two in its family tree. Just her luck, since staying in one spot for any length of time was nothing short of an invitation for trouble. She should have taken the chance and gotten on the interstate.

With a sharp, angry yank, the woman shifted into Park, set the emergency brake and turned on the flashers. This surge of compassion was as unwelcome as it was risky. Here she was prepared to kill, and what was she doing? Playing nursemaid. On the other hand, if it was her lying out there...

"Bet it was born crippled," she muttered as she fumbled in the dark for a flashlight.

Her fingers brushed against the gun that would be hidden in the litterbag and covered with trash should police lights flash in the rearview mirror. For a moment she debated whether to take the automatic, too, but decided against it. The dog might be someone's pet and known as the friendliest thing since Lassie; however, she'd had enough experience with canines to know they tended to react negatively to firearms, wild or not. Hopefully, this one wasn't. But better to end up with a tooth tattoo than to disrupt the calm night with a gunshot this close to town.

The dog didn't budge as she approached it. As she drew nearer, she understood why, and whatever resentment she'd been feeling vanished.

"Oh, hell. Who else did you have a run-in with tonight?"

The woman winced at the sight of the pup that she now guessed was no more than four or five months old. A retriever mix...female, she determined as the dog rolled submissively onto her back. Starved, and scared out of her wits, she concluded as she came close enough to see how the animal was trembling.

Pointing the light beam off to the side so as not to frighten her any more than necessary, the woman crouched beside her. "Hey, little one," she crooned. "Good girl. I'm going to see how bad things are. No fast moves or rough handling on my part, so no hostility on yours, deal? I'm giving you fair warning—I have a reputation for biting back, and that's when I'm in a good mood. This isn't one of those times."

With a whimper, the dog offered a paw.

"Nice to meet you, too."

The woman's crooked smile vanished as she noticed the deep, bloody scratches around the dog's face, and worse, the torn flesh on the inside of the left back leg. There was a long gash that stretched halfway along the abdomen, and she couldn't quite hold back a sympathetic groan at the sight of the ugly wound. A gash like that couldn't be from a run-in with another vehicle; the unfortunate pooch must have been on the losing end of a fight. The question was, with what?

"Who's the bully in your neighborhood? Some older sibling, or was it a coyote or bobcat?"

The wounds looked fresh, and that had the woman scanning her unfamiliar surroundings with new unease. She should have brought the gun after all. From what she'd determined, this was a wild section of southwest Texas and sparsely inhabited. The town she'd just passed through had been called Bitters of all things, population a whopping three hundred eleven, a road sign had announced. A block-long testament to ghost towns, the sign would have been memorable regardless because of the notation some wise guy had added in spray paint: *And dropping.* In fact, she'd been thinking of the fitting editorial, which is the other reason for her near miss with the dog. This was challenging land, the geography no less dramatic than what she'd been driving through most of the day—minimal vegetation, rolling terrain interspersed with craggy draws meandering across the prairie and sudden stark outcroppings of weather-and-man-chiseled rock. More than once she'd wondered what people did to survive. The only industry aside from oil-field services appeared to be ranching. Exotic-game farming seemed a particularly profitable investment, meaning there was no necessity for extraneous guessing about what was lurking out in the denser shadows.

All the more reason to get going. There was nothing she could do here. But as she accepted that sad fact, the dog offered her paw again…and again. It was as though it, *she,* was trying to delay her…or more. Adding to the awkward and grim situation, this time when the pup whimpered, the entreaty sounded human, too similar to "Please."

Although she eased her hand forward to be sniffed, the woman sighed with regret. "Yes, you're a sweetheart, but you chose the wrong person, Miss Mess."

The dog stuck out the tip of her tongue and cautiously licked her fingers.

"Nice try, but my days as a soft touch are behind me."

Nevertheless, she gently stroked the dog under the chin and glanced over her shoulder. That vet clinic was a mere minute or two drive back into town. She remembered the old timber-framed sign at the entrance because it happened to be right next to the police station.

The dog shifted onto her side again and nudged the woman's stilled hand with her scratched nose.

"Nothing subtle or shy about you, is there?" the

woman murmured. "That's okay. I prefer the direct approach myself."

Maybe she could get help and be on the road without losing too much time. There hadn't been any nightlife to speak of in town, except for the twenty-four-hour convenience store by the service road. There was no round-the-clock patrolling, and the fire department was a volunteer unit. In fact, it had been the lack of traffic that had allowed her to spot the well-lit house behind the vet's office. Surely veterinarians were on call at all hours, the same as medical doctors?

"I'm not going to lie to you," she said to the watchful mongrel. "I'm not wild about this idea, and you may end up hating it, but it's the best that I can do. You're the one warning me that you don't stand a chance otherwise, right?"

The dog shifted to lay her head on the woman's jogging shoe. Her prolonged sigh sounded as though the weight of the world was on her under-nourished back.

"You and me both, kiddo. Are you going to let me pick you up? Come on, sweetie. Up. *Ti mne i ya tebe.* Understand? 'You for me and me for you.' Show me that you can stand, or let me lift you. Up, up, up."

The dog did attempt to stand, but at the cost of most of her remaining energy. In fact, she would have fallen again if the woman hadn't quickly scooped her into her arms. That's when her rescuer realized how seriously undernourished the pup was.

"If it wasn't for the dirt and bugs, you'd weigh less than my sneakers. When was the last time you had a good meal, hmm?"

The dog simply rested her head on the woman's shirtsleeve and stared off into space.

As skinny as the animal was, the climb up the slope to the van was a challenge and the woman was glad to settle her burden on the passenger seat. "Just don't get any ideas," she said. "You may have convinced me to do this, but this arrangement is temporary."

Carefully shutting the door, she hurried around and climbed in on the driver's side. She took a moment to check the signal on her cellular phone, only to grimace when she saw it still didn't register one. Her anxiety deepened when, just as she shifted into Drive, the engine stalled.

Swearing under her breath, she keyed it once, then again. After a slight pause, she tried a third time.

Not now.

On the fourth attempt, the engine started. Exhaling shakily, the woman completed as neat a U-turn as the narrow road allowed.

About to reach over to give the dog a reassuring pat, a light in the rearview mirror drew her gaze. The eastern sky was getting brighter...but it wasn't even midnight yet.

As she continued to keep one eye on the strange orange-amber glow, headlights appeared, momentarily obliterating everything but glare. She immediately flipped the mirror tab down to cut the sharp light, her heart pounding with new dread.

It was just a vehicle, she told herself, and coming from the wrong direction. Nothing to be worried about. But to give herself peace of mind, she eased off the accelerator to force the driver to overtake her.

Not only didn't the tailgater do that, the vehicle backed off. All right, she reasoned, fair enough. She wouldn't jump to conclusions. People often disliked passing slower traffic at night. But could it be determined that she was a woman traveling alone? The back-window curtains didn't allow for much of a view, and the lack of streetlights had to help. That was why she'd been traveling by night as much as possible. At the same time, the farther east she came, the more she prepared herself for the "redneck syndrome" to kick in. She'd hoped this nondescript commercial-type van would draw less attention to her. It was painted a green the military would reject, and no woman with an ounce of taste would be caught dead driving. Had she subjected herself to this for nothing?

She glanced in the rearview mirror again. Keeping a respectable distance, the vehicle followed her the rest of the way into town. As a precaution, in case it was a cop looking for an excuse to pull her over, the woman turned on her blinker in plenty of time to warn she was turning into the animal clinic's lot. Only when the other vehicle continued by did she finally relax.

It was a pickup. If the invisible hand around her throat didn't have such a tight squeeze around her voice box, she would have laughed out loud. A junker! No wonder it hadn't passed her.

The scare did, however, reinforce her doubts about what she was doing. "That settles it," she told her wide-eyed passenger. "No offense, but I'm dropping you off and getting out of Dodge, *pardner.*"

She drove around the unlit clinic to the light brick ranch-style house tucked between a barn and stock pen on the left, and a separate garage on the right. Parking by the house's front door, she experienced another moment of doubt because there were now fewer lights on than she remembered from before.

"Looks as though they've gone to bed. Prepare yourself for a less than cheerful reception," she told the dog.

After her initial knock on the front door, she spotted the bell behind an overgrown branch of red crepe myrtle, and pressed the glowing button. Beyond the sheer drapes, she could see a picture light on in the living room, but that was all.

She waited a good half minute, and when no one

responded, she pressed the bell again. "Hello! Can somebody help me, please?"

A moment after that something changed. She didn't hear or see anything per se, but suddenly she felt a presence. Instinctively, she shifted her hand to her right hip and glanced around, only to remember what she was reaching for wasn't there. Nevertheless, she knew the feeling—she was being watched—and followed the gut instincts that had kept her alive so far. She stepped off the stoop and toward the van, ready to dive for cover or drive if necessary. Then her gaze settled on the security hole.

That had to be it, she thought. But whoever was inside watching through the viewer sizing her up, he or she had to be one intense person, because the hairs on her arms had yet to quit tickling.

Finally, she heard a dead bolt turning. As the door opened, she drew a stabilizing breath...only to have it lock in her throat.

2

She stared...and he stared back.

This was the vet? she wondered. Couldn't be.

"Yes?" the man asked.

Baritone-voiced and bare-chested, he filled the entryway almost as completely as the weathered wooden door had. It was, however, his face that triggered stronger doubts. She'd seen less disturbing mug shots. His eyes were at once eerily light and yet sunken in a way that made her think of utter exhaustion if not long-term illness. Neither of which, she reminded herself, was her problem. What's more, she'd just added to her already loaded plate.

She cleared her throat. "I found an injured dog."

The unsmiling giant stepped out onto the stoop into the glow of a yellow insect light that probably had done little for her appearance and certainly didn't make him any easier on the nerves. Although barefoot, he was the size of a piece of Stonehenge. Unfortunately, the stoop wasn't more than an inch above the packed clay, sand and gravel she stood on. Even face-to-face she wouldn't reach his scarred chin. The thought of having to grapple with him for control over a weapon convinced her to take another cautionary step backward.

"Back or front?" he asked.

His jeans were unbuttoned and negligently zipped. While he was hardly her first exhibitionist, she was willing to give the guy the benefit of the doubt. After all, this was the boonies and it was an ungodly hour even for a social call—and he didn't look like someone who was given to many of those. He could have forgotten to zip up in his haste to get to the door. On the other hand, he hadn't hurried, and his bloodshot eyes looked too intelligent to make a case for early senility.

When he caught her looking, she expected him to excuse himself and step behind the door, or at least turn away to correct the situation. Instead, he brushed past her.

"While you're sight-seeing, I'll find out for myself."

Thank goodness for the unmistakable scent of scotch. It deep-sixed her self-consciousness and snapped her back into full wariness. Drunks were always a problem, big ones could be dangerous, angry ones could be lethal. The poor pooch, she thought with sympathy. Rescued from one predator only to be placed at the mercy of another.

"Front," she said at the same moment that he glanced through the passenger window.

Bringing up the rear, she wasn't surprised that the pup cowered at the sight of him. "Easy does it, sweetie," she crooned. "Believe it or not, this is the cavalry."

Stonehenge shot her a sidelong look as he opened the door. "What's its name?"

"Feel free to pick something. But…I believe it's a she."

As he began examining the animal, she found herself hoping he wasn't one of those incompetents who got into a profession because a parent or spouse had decided it was lucrative. Of course, the thought of his parentage then triggered the wry speculation as to which landmass he'd been excavated from. Moments later she had to acknowledge guilty admiration when she noticed his deft and surprisingly gentle inspection.

"She's filthy. I can't believe you put her in your van."

Charming he wasn't, however. "Me neither. But considering her condition, I doubted she could handle running tied to the sideview mirror."

He cast her a brief, but unamused glance. "How old is she?"

"Are we having a hearing problem here or a language one? She ran in front of my car not ten minutes ago on the edge of town."

"People always say that when they bring in a

hurt animal they want to get rid of. Thing is, most don't have the nerve to try that when it's in as bad a shape as this one.''

If his intent was to intimidate, the man should have stuck with a stern bedside manner. All he'd succeeded in doing was to push her buttons. "Doctor, one more time…this is not my pet."

The vet tilted his head toward the wary dog. "And I'm taking her word for it. She keeps looking at you for reassurance as to whether or not she should trust me."

"Can you blame her?" The blunt response was out before she could edit it, the result of a fatigue brought on by too many hours behind the wheel and stress from too much concern over survival. "What I mean is—"

"Never mind. I'm prone to bluntness myself these days. And you're right, I do look like hell, and my manners are worse."

He seemed ready to say something else, but the dog, possibly reacting to a gentling of his gruff tone, edged over onto her back, exposing her belly as she had earlier. Frowning, he took new interest in the creature.

"That's a nasty gash. Doesn't quite look like an HBC, though. Hit by car," he added at her blank look.

"If I hadn't braked in time, you could have been looking at that, too. Whatever happened, it couldn't have been long ago, could it?"

"No, my guess is a confrontation with a raccoon, or else she didn't quite make a clean pass through barbed wire."

"Can you help her?"

"I'll need better light to examine her more thoroughly. Come on. You'll have to help."

"Excuse me?" She stared in disbelief as he scooped the animal into his arms and started toward the clinic. Help how? Slamming the van door, she called, "Wait. Hey!"

He kept walking.

"What do you mean help?" she demanded at his retreating back.

"Assist."

"Not me. I'm no nurse."

"You'll do for this job."

"But I have to go."

"Don't even think about it."

To avoid raising her voice any more than necessary, she ran after him. "Look, undoubtedly you've put in a long day and would much prefer being in bed right now. So would I for that matter. Which is why I suspect we're not communicating well. What I don't think you're grasping is that I'm not acquainted with, or in any way, shape or form connected to this dog."

"I heard you the first time."

"Then you understand that I'm not taking her with me after you treat her?"

"Did you read that sign out front?"

She was sure she had, but her usually reliable memory failed her. At the moment she couldn't remember if his name was Sawyer, Sanders or... What did the smaller print say under Animal Clinic?

"What's your point?"

"I don't run an animal shelter, that's up at Sonora. I'll do what I can for her, but after that she's your responsibility...and so is the bill."

She couldn't believe it. She was trying to perform a simple act of goodwill and he was going to stick it to her? No doubt charge overtime rates, too.

"No way!"

"You brought her in, she's your responsibility. It's either that or I'll be forced to put her down straight off. Take your pick."

As he said that, the dog whimpered and twisted in his arms with increased anxiety, not unlike an infant terrified that it was being abandoned to a stranger. The woman tried not to notice while struggling to figure a way out of her own dilemma.

This was what she deserved for not following training, let alone instincts. Granted, leaving the animal where she'd found it would have bothered her, but there wasn't a day that went by when she didn't see worse. It was the price you paid in her line of work. Now all she'd done was shift the pup from one kind of trouble into another. And there was no option of taking her with her; the dog would be miserable even if she hadn't been in such poor condition, and in just as much jeopardy. Possibly more.

"Doctor, really—"

"The name's Slaughter, first name Gray. Try to resist any impulses at humor if you don't mind. I probably heard most of the nicknames before you were out of braces."

It wasn't the name that had her lifting her eyebrows. One of the first writers her father had introduced her to when the children's section at the library had become boring, was surgeon-novelist Frank Slaughter. What startled her was the vet's obvious misconception about the difference in their ages.

"Dr. Slaughter, I've been out of braces longer than you think, and I'm not about to—"

"Can you get the key?"

He'd stopped at the door and half turned toward her. She followed his glance downward, but only briefly.

"Now who's being the comedian?"

"You interrupt a man when he's trying to have a quiet drink in the privacy of his bedroom, you get what you get. Come on. This critter might be starving, but she's still heavier than a feather pillow, and however old you are, I'm too much of a hard case for you to bother trying for a virginal blush."

She gave him an arctic smile. Her looks had been a problem for her as long as she could remember, and although there was nothing she could do if he wanted to see her as some kind of vamp, he would be wise not to test whether she would defend herself.

About to say as much, to tell him what he could do with his key, she heard sirens. A fire truck, she concluded, with at least one patrol car. No, here came a second one. Damn. Exactly the kind of commotion she didn't need. That kind of racket in a community this small was going to rouse the whole town.

"You okay?"

Ignoring him, she weighed her options against her predicament. She didn't want to stay here a minute longer than necessary, but being on the road now could be a bigger mistake. Chances were no one here knew anything about her—yet—and she might slip through, but if asked tomorrow or the next day, how many details would people remember? Their answers could endanger more than her.

Resigned, she muttered, "Which pocket?"

"Right."

She leaned from the waist, saw the half moon of a key ring and plucked out the small handful of keys. They sounded like wind chimes in the renewed silence—or a fleeting, mocking laugh. "Which is it?"

"The medium-size silver one with the flattened edge."

Aware of his scrutiny, she unlocked the door and

flipped on the switch just inside. The long line of fluorescent lights burned her travel-weary eyes and, blinking, she stepped aside to let him pass. He turned left at the first room, switching on those lights with his elbow, illuminating a fully equipped examination-operating room.

In the merciless brilliance, his five o'clock shadow added to his haggard, neglected appearance, and she wondered exactly how many drinks he'd already consumed. Was he even in any condition to do what had to be done for the dog?

"Come hold her," the vet directed as he set the wounded animal on the examination table. He must have seen her hesitation for he sighed. "Look, I've been out on a call that took the better part of the day and I only got home a half hour before you arrived. I'm beat, ticked over losing an animal and I can't remember my last meal. So I apologize if I'm short on manners. Try not to take it personally."

If what he said about his day was true, she owed him an apology in return. But she'd also met enough barflies to know they were perfectly capable of achieving a considerable buzz in less time than that. So she simply nodded and did as he asked, focusing on keeping the dog calm. It didn't take much. The pup was remarkably docile and gave every indication that regardless of her pain, she felt safer with them than where she'd been.

Gray worked from nose to wound. "Eyes don't

indicate shock," he noted. "Gums are a decent pink, so there hasn't been considerable blood loss. Makes sense. The wound isn't as deep as I first thought. Let me take a blood sample, and if things look okay, we'll start an IV and get to work."

He retreated to the sink and began washing up. With each movement the muscles along his back flexed. Although he was no bodybuilder, his waist tapered and his hips were trim. For a guy who acted as if he went through life on cruise control, he sure didn't give any indication that he was heading for Flab City.

"You're not from around here," he said, slipping on gloves.

She put aside her own speculation. "No." What she wasn't going to tell him was that she didn't exactly feel the place she'd come from was "home" either.

"Didn't think I detected a Texas accent."

"Which reinforces my claim that this can't be my dog." She willed the animal not to start licking her hand as she'd done earlier.

"You're consistent, I'll give you that."

For the next minute or two he worked in silence. He took the blood sample and withdrew to the adjacent room. There she heard a steady series of movements, things being switched on and off and slid around. Finally he returned and she couldn't help but notice that, while his feet remained bare, he had slipped on a blue lab coat. He had also fastened the jeans.

"So?" she asked.

"She's surprisingly strong. Probably hasn't been on her own for over a week or so. No sign of heartworm. Except for needing a heap of good food, she's a healthy enough dog. Do we continue?"

The question startled her. "Of course. That's why I backtracked, why I came to you."

He turned away and began collecting all kinds of paraphernalia. "Let's get her on lactated Ringers before we get her cleaned up a bit."

"Sorry?"

"An IV." As he moved around the room, he asked, "So what do I call you?"

"Whatever you'd like. I think we can both agree this isn't going to be a long relationship."

He grunted, and the sound could have passed as a brief chuckle. "Fine, I'll entertain myself by guessing until I see your check or credit card."

"I'll be paying cash."

His slight hesitation, a tightening around his mouth, told her that she'd made a mistake. She didn't yet know how much his fee would be.

"The name's Ann," she said, mentally kicking herself.

"As in Ann Doe? No, that would have to be Jane."

It took an effort not to grit her teeth. "Anna Diaz."

"Oh, *Anna*, not Ann."

"My friends tend to shorten it."

"Not very good ones. Anna is a beautiful name. Diminish the name, next they're diminishing the person."

"Moonlight as a shrink, Doc?"

"Just another student of life. I guessed you were of Spanish or Welsh descent. Your complexion's too fair for Mexican, lacks the olive tones for Italian. Could be—"

"In a hurry." She nodded at the dog. "Couldn't you put her under for whatever it is you're going to do? I'll get your money and—"

"You step out of this room and I'll call the cops."

Anna stiffened. It wasn't often that she heard such a threat delivered in a voice so calm and assured. The man knew how to catch a person off guard.

"The cops. Isn't that a bit drastic?"

"You strike me as too eager to leave, which tells me that either you have no intention of paying me, or else you're hiding something."

He couldn't be more right—and wrong. The urge to laugh, or run, grew. "That's ridiculous. If I wanted to avoid responsibility or hide anything, I would be thirty miles down the road by now."

"Then wash up while I put in this IV, and slip on those gloves I set out for you. I'm also going to remove some of these ticks and clean her as much as I can. We don't need anything crawling inside her while I'm sewing her shut.''

Grateful that at least he showed some concern for the animal, she did as he directed. After soaping her hands, she ran cold water on her wrists to calm down her racing pulse.

"How long is this going to take?" She wrestled with the gloves as she returned to the table. Spotting the jar of blood-swollen insects floating in what she guessed was alcohol, she grimaced.

"Not very, but you can forget about her traveling tonight. We'll see how she is in the morning."

Not "we," she amended silently. By morning, she planned to be hundreds of miles from here. And the first thing she would be doing was looking for a change of vehicles.

Gray closed the lid on the container and deposited it and the tweezers he'd been using in the sink. When he returned he had another injection prepared.

"What's that?" Anna asked, eyeing the yellowish liquid.

"Sodium Pentothal. Lidocaine would probably do, but she's been through a lot. Better to go with the general anesthetic."

Once he appeared satisfied that the drug had taken effect, he went to work. He'd completed several neat sutures before asking, "So what do you do?"

He didn't look up, and since they had only the

examination table between them, Anna was glad. "I'm...between jobs."

"Good."

"Why do you say that?"

"This way you won't have to feel guilty in the morning for being groggy on the job. Healing, whether it's man or beast, requires time."

No doubt, but she took from his sudden chattiness that he was softening her up, fishing for more information. She had no intention of taking the bait. She did, however, approve of how he worked, with speed and efficiency.

"Holding up okay?" he asked midway through.

"Well enough." And for good reason—she was trying not to look. The last time Anna had been in an emergency room, it was to hold the hand of a kid getting her forehead sewn together. Blood had never bothered her before, but, maybe because the patient was a kid, the room had spun like a carousel gone out of control, almost costing her what remained of a six-hour-old lunch. Somehow this poor pooch brought that all back.

"I'm impressed. Would have bet twenty you'd be hanging over the edge of the sink by now."

As she tried to ignore what her peripheral vision was picking up, she countered, "Does that mean I get a discount?"

"It means I'm grateful that the sight of a half-gutted creature doesn't make you faint...or worse."

"Then maybe skipping that grilled chicken salad was my one smart move today."

The gaze he shot her from under stark eyebrows, though brief, was sweeping and all-encompassing. His eyes, she realized, were neither aquamarine blue nor silver, but the color of the coldest January skies.

"Don't tell me you diet." When she failed to respond, he murmured, "Ah, the profundity of the uncommunicative woman. But you're right, I've ventured out of line again."

He didn't speak after that, working with such focus Anna almost believed he forgot about her. After knotting the last stitch, he snipped the end, then swabbed the area with what she suspected was another antiseptic. Then he prepared another injection.

"Penicillin," he explained. "You'll want to pay special attention to keeping the sutures dry and the area clean. She also needs as quiet an environment as possible. Don't let her chase any squirrels or rabbits." He administered the injection. "Otherwise, the stitches can be removed in about a week."

Anna shook her head, not at all happy with what she was hearing again. "You don't really expect me to take her in a moving van?"

"Not tonight, no...at least not for a long trip. The motion is liable to upset her stomach more than the wound. How much farther do you have to go?''

She countered with, ''What would it cost for you to nurse her back to health and see that she finds a good home?''

He made a face. ''Honey, you could tie a hundred-dollar bill to this mutt's tail and there wouldn't be any takers.''

Talk about blunt! She took a moment to consider the listless dog and tried to see her from the perspective of a child. ''She'd be a cute pet once she was cleaned up.''

''Then you'd better head in a direction where they've had rain in the last four months because no one around here has the patience or funds to find out.''

It wasn't his sarcasm that got to her—she'd heard far worse—but the thought of being responsible for another life right now, even if it was a stray dog that no one else on the planet gave a spit about. ''Why did you bother sewing her up then? I thought vets were supposed to help animals.''

''I did,'' Gray intoned, pointing toward the door. ''Do you know how often people dump their problems on me? Almost every week I find something or other in one of the outside kennels, or litters left by the front door. Occasionally some get out of their boxes and end up on the street. Are you catching my drift? And not just dogs, it's cats, rabbits—''

"What if I pay for her to be spayed?" she asked, not wanting to hear any more.

"She's too weak for that. Have your family vet do it in the next month or two."

"I don't *have* a— Why are you being difficult about this?" Anna used her forearm to wipe the moisture from her brow. It wasn't just her agitated state that was getting to her, the man must shut down the air-conditioning when he locked up every night; it was as hot and steamy as a sauna in here. "I've never been on that highway before today, and you said yourself that you didn't recognize me."

"I also don't believe a woman traveling alone at this hour would pull over and pick up a strange dog out of a ravine. Animals don't like to be touched when they're hurting, especially not by strangers in the middle of the night."

"There! Testimony to my personality. If the dog trusts me, why can't you?"

The look he shot her with those frosty eyes had her closing her own.

"Fine. Whatever. The fact remains that I have to leave, so if you'll help me get her back in the van, I'll pay you."

"And I told you that's risky."

"Believe me, that's the least of my problems."

He started to reply, but another sound, that of the back door opening, stopped him.

"Slaughter! You in there?"

3

The sharp query yielded a strange reaction in the doctor, an odd stillness and deeper resentment. If that was possible, Anna thought, not exactly happy with the idea of company herself.

"Yeah." After the curt reply, Gray added to her, "You have a complaint to make? Here's your chance. That's your so-called 'cavalry.'"

"I don't understand."

"The Law."

Before she could recover from that jarring announcement, their visitor appeared in the doorway.

"Well, well." The man in the summer blues of Bitters's police department leaned back against the doorjamb, one hand on his hip, the other on the gun strapped to his belt. A slow grin spread across his wide mouth. "What do we have here?"

"Take a wild guess," Gray replied. "Better yet, tell me what you want since I know better than to think it was concern for my safety that brings you over."

The sarcasm only made the cop grow more cheerful. He was a ripcord-lean man, surprisingly fair-skinned for someone in this part of the country, yet the muscles on his arms suggested rawhide toughness. Contrasting that were sunny blue eyes as curious and mischievous as a boy's, framed by hair the color of chili powder and just long enough to curl with its own hint of devilry. He was, she decided, Shakespeare's Puck grown up. Then his gaze moved over her with the laconic speed of cooled molasses and she knew to abandon the amusing analogies. This man hadn't been a harmless charmer for decades—maybe not ever.

"Did you happen to hear the sirens earlier?" he asked them.

Gray remained focused on the dog, but allowed, "You know Pike's not one to be a quiet hero. He sounds those alarms on the truck driving through town after a wash."

"Well, this was no polishing party. Somebody torched Assembly of Souls Church."

"Arson...you're sure?"

"What else would you make of a bonfire built on the front steps? Fortunately, Pike was having a smoke outside the station and spotted the glow. They caught it fairly early on. Only lost the porch. Well, maybe the front wall, too."

Frowning, Gray carried his instruments to the sterilizing container. "Bitters as the center of hate in Sutton County...that'll be an interesting sell."

"Racism is nothing to joke about."

"What racism? There isn't one black person in

twenty miles, and the Mexicans the mayor and half of your business owners have working in their homes and at their ranches are Catholic. They don't care about not being welcome at Assembly of Souls. They're also making more money here in a month than all year at home. Racism...give me a break.''

Instead of answering, Elias switched his gaze back to Anna. ''I noticed your Texas plates, but I don't believe I've had the pleasure.''

Wishing she could be anywhere but here, Anna was grateful that at least she was wearing surgical gloves and didn't have to shake hands. ''Diaz. Anna Diaz.''

''I'm Frank Elias.''

''Congratulations, Frank,'' Gray drawled. ''You managed to resist adding your title. He's the chief,'' he explained to her. ''Meaning that if there's any *racism* to be exercised around here, he claims first rights.''

Elias's glance was cutting, but he let the dig pass.

Anna remained silent, too, preferring to wait for the point to all of this.

''That your dog?'' the lawman finally asked.

She shook her head.

''What did I do, Slaughter, interrupt a hot date? Just when I thought you'd never get back into circulation. But it's a helluva time to try to impress a lady with your professional skills.''

What on earth was going on? Anna thought, her unease growing.

Gray tossed the bloody bandages into the marked receptacle. "Get to the point, or better yet, get out before I'm tempted to assume you're here to get something tucked and snipped yourself."

Sensing that whatever was between them went deeper than a simple misunderstanding, Anna decided she wanted no part of it. "Dr. Slaughter kindly helped out after I happened across this injured dog up the road," she interjected in the hopes of keeping things from getting uglier.

"Whereabouts?"

She glanced around remembering the layout of the building in conjunction to the street and then pointed east. "That way."

"You're sure? How far?"

"Maybe a mile."

To her surprise, the two men exchanged glances. After a second, Gray merely shrugged.

"Get as far as the church?" Chief Elias asked.

"No, it was mostly woods where I stopped."

"The church isn't far beyond the city limits sign. Pretty hard to miss."

"Then apparently I didn't get there."

"Visiting kin in the area?"

"No."

He waited for her to continue. She didn't.

"Just passing through?"

"That's right."

"Not exactly safe times for a woman to be driving alone, particularly at this hour."

The heat Anna was trying to ignore manifested into a trickle of sweat streaking down her back. It was no less uncomfortable than the droplets condensing between her breasts, but she did her best to keep her tone and expression calm. "Probably not."

"So where are you heading?"

"East."

"Did you happen to see any other vehicles?"

"No...wait. Yes. Someone came up behind me once I started back to town. And come to think of it, there was a bright glow in the sky." Preoccupied with her own problems, she hadn't connected the two images until he'd brought it to her attention.

"A bright glow like...streetlights or another vehicle?"

"I honestly didn't give it much thought. I was concerned with the dog."

"Right." Frank nodded, all agreeableness. "Tell me what you can about the vehicle."

"There's not much. It stayed behind me all the way back to town. I kept hoping it would pass me—"

"Why?"

"For exactly the reasons you mentioned. Also, I didn't want to be forced to drive in a way that might cause the dog more pain."

"This dog that you've never seen before tonight?"

Gray smirked. "You think I'm a hard case," he told her, "when he's bored, he plucks the legs off crickets and grasshoppers for entertainment."

"Not everybody sees sticking your hand up a cow's butt as a religious experience," Elias replied, crossing his arms over his chest. To Anna he added, "You were saying?"

She shrugged. "It continued on by as I pulled in here. It was a white pickup truck."

"A pickup, wouldn't you know it," the chief drawled. "The one thing we have more of in Texas, aside from beautiful women and bullshit."

Once again she found herself losing ground to the day, to its demands and dangers, only to be provoked by Frank Elias's snide tone. "I could say it was a Rolls, but that *would* be some of that bullshit that you insinuated."

The laughter vanished from Elias's blue eyes. "How would you like to walk next door with me and try being cute over there?"

"Calm down, Frank." Shooting Anna a cautioning glance, Gray passed between them to get to the waste container. "It's not her fault that you don't have any clues, let alone suspects."

The chief rubbed his knuckles against his jutting jaw. "Who says I don't? Maybe my numero uno suspect is staring me right in the face, eh, Ms. *Diaz?*"

"I hope that's your idea of a joke," Gray said quietly.

"Hey, I have every right to be suspicious, not to mention a little sore, when someone brings trouble to my town."

"You should suggest the chamber of commerce use that on a billboard," Anna said, recognizing the man for what he was—a full-blown, narrow-minded redneck. "'The town where the only trouble is the tourists.'"

Frank straightened and assumed his initial pose. "Yeah, I think you'd better come with me."

Anna eyed the hand on the holster. "Are you arresting me?"

"Did I say that? No, all I'm saying is that a change of environment will help you answer the rest of my questions."

"What kind of questions?"

"For one thing I'll want to know where you can be reached should we need your testimony in the future."

"I don't have a permanent address yet."

"You said you knew where you were heading."

God, Anna thought, this was getting worse by the minute. If only she'd kept her mouth shut. "Generally, not specifically. I'm in the process of relocating."

"Do you hear that, Slaughter?"

Gray shrugged. "Most people see moving as a constitutional right."

"God bless the U.S.A. So, in that case," the chief continued to Anna, "we'll take down your statement, get some cellular-phone number or a relative's address, whatever you have, and you'll be back on your way in no time at all. Sound good?"

Only if you were a fresh-hatched chick. She didn't believe him and wouldn't trust him until she had his office, this entire town, in her rearview mirror. But she was reassured by the "we" part. That must mean more staff would be at the station due to the fire. Reassured, she drew a stabilizing breath and, pulling off her gloves, said to Gray, "Doctor, it appears that I have to impose on your kindness a while longer."

4

Moths executed jet-fighter maneuvers in the blinding floodlights outside the back of the clinic, but their erratic movements were nothing compared to what was happening behind Anna's ribs. She wondered what she was heading into. The temptation to risk making a run for it couldn't be entirely ignored.

I've told so many lies, how many more should I risk?

"Whereabouts in Texas do you live?"

Though spoken matter-of-factly, Anna knew there was nothing casual about the question, just as there was nothing innocent about the way Chief Elias maneuvered around her so that she was on his left. It was the opposite side of his gun.

"I don't live in Texas."

"That's what the plates on your van indicate."

How close had he gotten to the vehicle? Not close enough to have looked inside, she assured herself, otherwise she would be cuffed by now. But she regretted not having taken the time to lock up the way she usually did. Gray Slaughter hadn't given her the chance.

"They're Texas plates because I started having transmission trouble and traded in my old car before I ended up stranded," she replied. It wasn't the truth, but it was a logical explanation.

"Smart girl. Mechanics always rip you off for that kind of work, and once a transmission is shot, you might as well ditch the vehicle. So where are you from?"

Anna knew she had to give him something. "Louisiana."

"You don't say? Huh. Still don't hear an accent."

"I've been out West for several years."

He studied her profile, all of it, as they walked. "You an actress?"

She focused on the building they were approaching and the single patrol car parked before it. "A failed one."

"I bet you're just being modest."

The compliment would have been easier to stomach with less oil soaking it. "No, embarrassingly honest."

She could feel his curiosity intensifying, and tried to tolerate that by getting a better feel for her surroundings, what little there was. Not only was the town small, it was deserted. She'd missed the sign for the health-food store across the street next to the supermarket. Not surprisingly, there was a

For Rent sign in the window. Next to that was a non-franchise hardware store.

"Married? Involved?"

"Not interested."

He grinned, exposing strong, square teeth. "Doesn't hurt to ask."

No doubt he asked often, Anna thought gloomily, and with enough success to think women liked his brand of flirtation.

"Did you shoot down Slaughter, too?"

They stopped before the glass door of the station where all that was written was the white lettering for an evening number in case of emergencies. What she didn't see beyond the door bothered her as much as his question, making her slow to answer. "Pardon?"

"Are you going to pretend that I didn't sense a little chemistry going on between you and the doc when I came in?"

Here we go again, she thought. Never mind that she'd hidden her hair under a baseball cap most of the day and it had to be a mess, or that she felt windblown and dust-caked from driving with the window down because the van *was* a rip-off and the air conditioner was trying to die on her.

"Whatever you think you sensed," she said, frowning into the dark building, "you're wrong."

He didn't reply, merely reached over and opened the front door. But his arm came so close to brushing against her breasts, it was as good as a spoken taunt.

In that instant, Anna knew two things: she wasn't going to get out of here tonight without a confrontation with Frank Elias...and he was low enough to use his badge as leverage.

5

Pissed didn't begin to describe Gray's mood as he carried the drugged dog to a cage in the otherwise empty kennel area. He eased her into one of the larger units, setting her on top of a thick towel he'd placed there a moment ago. His movements were mechanical, like a teacher delivering rote lessons for the umpteenth time, but for a change he appreciated that. He didn't want to think about the pitiful animal, didn't want to concern himself with what she'd been through to end up in this fix, or consider the fate likely awaiting her. As he'd tried to make clear to Anna Diaz, he'd seen too many animals like this, and too much rejection in his life. He was coming to the conclusion that the only thing people neglected worse than the pets they claimed to love was each other.

God, he was tired. And thanks to the woman and this mangy mutt, even if he returned to the house right now, he would need another shower before crawling into bed, and it was already closing in on midnight. But that wasn't going to happen because he had to wait for her to finish next door. Waiting also gave him too much time to think...about how much of what she'd told him was a lie, and how, despite those doubts, for the first time in over a year he'd learned he wasn't dead from the waist down. Most of all, he had time to think of the expression on her face as Frank had led her away.

Was she worth the strong impulse he was getting to go after them? No way did he believe she was simple Anna Diaz merely passing through town. The woman had secrets. Big ones. But did that make her Frank's firebug? He couldn't buy it. On the other hand, he knew Frank.

There had to be answers in her van.

Making up his mind, Gray rechecked the examination-operating room and shut off all but the night-light he kept plugged in the hallway for these kind of occurrences. Then he locked up the building.

The van remained where she'd parked it. A glance over at the police station indicated that he still had time; they were over there all right. He could tell by the beam of light spilling out from the front door and window, further illuminating the street. That the beam looked pretty weak compared to what it should be if all the lights were turned on left a bad taste in his mouth. Then again, Frank knew to keep costs down, to not strain the town's ever-tightening budget.

The bite of gravel at his bare feet irritated as much as curiosity and conscience plagued Gray's mind, encouraging him to be quick. Upon opening the passenger door, he saw that the van was designed for commercial purposes. There was only the shell of the truck and little else. A suitcase, sleeping bag and pillow were stacked neatly behind the driver's seat. Anna Diaz was traveling light and the sleeping bag explained why she didn't want that flea-and-tick-infested dog traveling with her.

Meaning what—that she'd been truthful about only happening upon the dog? The idea sat better with him than believing she'd let the poor beast degenerate into such a pitiful condition. But something still didn't feel right.

Leaning over the passenger seat, he spotted a black leather purse on the floorboard. Without the slightest twinge of guilt, he lifted out her wallet. Like the purse, it was made of quality hide. Flipping open the buttery-soft flap, he eyed the Louisiana license for Anna Diaz and discovered that her thirtieth birthday was only a few months away. Then he tilted the thing back and forth to get a better look at her photo. No, it wasn't glare on the plastic that made it so unclear, he realized. The photo was scratched.

His unease growing, he checked the rest of the wallet. All of the credit card slots were empty, and there were no other photos; however, what had him exhaling in a low whistle was the amount of cash she was carrying. The lady wasn't going to starve this month, or for a while if she didn't indulge in too many four-star establishments.

He found yet another stash of bills in a different compartment in the bag. Maybe, he thought with growing bitterness, he would also find the reason for her to have such resources. Simple logic was beginning to offer a few conclusions.

Gray shoved the purse back in place...possibly a bit too roughly because it tipped over. As he reached to straighten it, his fingertips brushed against something in the seat pocket.

Frowning, he eased his hand inside and closed his fingers around smooth steel. He drew out a Smith & Wesson .9mm automatic—not the kind of thing a simple working girl relocating toted around with her...unless her work was dangerous.

Determined to find out what else he could, Gray unlocked the side door, slid it open and climbed into the back of the van. There he unzipped the navy blue weekender-style bag and sifted through the neatly folded, but minimal assortment of clothes. All of it was casual—jeans, a few T-shirts and denim shirts, like what she was wearing. The underwear was no less understated—white cotton. But considering the body on the woman, not even that blandness would disappoint. What pulled his mind away from the unwelcome fantasy of seeing her in it was that most of the stuff either still had tags or remained in their wrappers. The suitcase looked new, too.

Otherwise there was little else...a few toiletry items—soap, toothpaste, toothbrush, mouthwash and a bundle of pocket-size tissue packets. What was missing was makeup. Okay, he allowed, with her exotic features and dramatic coloring, she didn't need much. But where were the dozen bottles and tubes of hair-care products, the variety of perfumes and body creams, the nail polish if not for her fingernails, then her toes? What planet had this luscious Barbie doll descended from that she packed with the restraint of a special ops commando?

Replacing everything, he checked a zippered compartment and took out a manila envelope. "Bingo," he murmured as a treasure trove of documents fell out. He sifted through a second license, a birth certificate and a few photos...and froze as he opened a small leather billfold.

"Well, I'll be damned."

After browsing through everything, Gray repacked it all, but with far less care than before. Closing up behind himself, he loped toward Frank's office, this time oblivious to the sting of the stones.

A neat brick building, Bitters's police station remained locked tight more often than it was occupied, partly due to the town's inability to fund more than a staff of two including Frank, with a part-time night patrolman for weekends, holidays and emergencies. Day Officer Kenny Plummer's patrol car was undoubtedly parked in his driveway. "Murph" Cox wouldn't use his vehicle until Friday night, but he was allowed to keep it at his place in case of heretofore-nonexistent emergencies. Gray knew better than most what a dubious department the trio made. Fortunately, until now, this blink-and-miss town hadn't needed much in the way of law enforcement. They didn't draw much traffic off of I–10 to worry about crime waves, even with the convenience store–gas station being the only fuel for ten miles.

The news he now possessed could change that, and he wasn't certain Frank Elias was the one to pass it over to. Frank clung hard to his reckless and irreverent ways with a stubbornness Gray would find difficult to stomach without the bad blood between them. Nevertheless, as he entered the station, he was willing to put that aside. More important at the moment was justice, and making sure the law hadn't been abused. What he saw across the dimly lit room, however, thrust that into the back of his mind.

Across the room Frank was all over Anna Diaz like latex on a professional wrestler. What's more, the way his hands were groping her had nothing to do with an official body search.

"*Elias.*"

Gray stormed across the room, grabbed a handful of the startled man's collar and yanked him off her.

"What the fuck—Slaughter, get your hands off me!"

Gray obliged by shoving the cop toward his desk. Frank missed his chair and went sprawling beneath the table. "You don't get enough willing tail, you have to resort to this?"

"She was trying to escape."

"He's lying!" Anna turned, but needed the wall to keep standing. With shaking hands, she closed the snaps on her denim shirt. "He attacked me."

Frank snorted as he rose. "Yeah, and you were fighting so hard. Admit it, you wanted it."

"Is that why her cheek's rubbed raw from that wall?" Gray demanded. He shook his head in disgust. "You're a pig."

This was Frank's weakness—keeping his hands to himself, discretion, *respect,* especially when it came to women. Even knowing that his past behavior had cost him the one person he claimed to love, as well as his boyhood friendship with Gray. The man hadn't learned a damn thing after all these years.

"Stick it up your ass." Scrambling to his feet, Frank settled on the edge of his desk. "What are you doing here, anyway?"

As far as Gray was concerned, what he had come to say was no longer Frank's business. If guilty of something, *Anna Diaz* could take it up with someone who deserved to wear a badge.

"It's late and I have to get up early," he replied. "I wanted to settle Ms. Diaz's account and call it a day. Instead I find this. Do you realize how deep a shithole you've dug for yourself this time?''

"I was interviewing her. She went out of control. You heard her pushing it earlier."

"You were provoking me." Anna clenched her hands at her sides. "There's nothing else to say. At least not what you want to hear."

Some of his bravado was returning and Frank smiled smugly. "The night's young and the doc here turns in early. Want to keep trying?''

Gray got the gist of what was going on. "You asked for a witness statement. Did you get it?''

"I think she's lying."

"You *asked* for a statement.''

"And I'm telling you that she may be our arsonist.''

"Based on what evidence?''

"She's too anxious to get away from here.''

Gray could only stare at him. "Do you know the person you've just described? Anyone with an IQ over Pike's brother's after spending more than ten minutes in your presence. Anyway, guilty or not, you've denied her her rights.''

As the old animosity between them heated to its new combustion point, a feathery twitch started at Frank's right eyelid. "So now you're an expert in law enforcement as well as horse manure, *Doc?*''

Undaunted, Gray snapped, "You don't have squat in evidence, including probable cause. I'll bet my license on it.''

"A lot that's worth these days. As for evidence, I'll get what I need."

"No doubt. But whether the end result is your plan for outright rape or simple intimidation, unless she's willing to let you screw her just to get out of here, I'm telling you it isn't going to happen."

Frank began to rise, only to check himself. Settling back on the desk, he crossed his arms and resumed that all-too-familiar smile. "My hunch was right. She's got your juices stirred, too."

Gray had heard enough. He motioned to Anna. "Let's go."

With more eagerness than a pup heading for the exit at his clinic, she started for the door. The next thing Gray heard was the release of the snap on Frank's holster, followed by him sliding a round into the chamber of his sidearm.

He and Anna came to an immediate halt.

Gray looked over his shoulder. "Are you nuts?"

Frank's gaze shifted to the gun as though belatedly realizing what he'd done. Redirecting it toward the ceiling, he said to Anna, "You don't leave town."

"I've done nothing wrong."

"Then you don't need to worry, do you?"

"Take my statement, let me sign it and let me go."

He tilted his head as though seriously considering the idea. "I think I'll wait until morning. Give you time to reconsider your attitude."

Gray pointed at him, intent on drawing his attention. "The next time she comes here, it'll be with an attorney. Are you prepared for that?"

"Paid for by who?" Frank taunted. "You gonna do it, Saint Gray? The way you're running down your business, it's a good thing you collected on all of those insurance policies."

A red veil of fury dropped over Gray's vision and he took a step forward. Luckily for him, Anna checked him by gripping his arm.

"I'll be paying my own way," she told Elias. "With pleasure." And this time she didn't wait for Gray to beckon her, she stormed out of the building.

Fighting his own temper, he didn't catch up with her for several yards. When he did, she didn't so much as spare him a glance as she headed for her van.

"You could say thank you," he said, no less angry than she was.

"If it wasn't for you giving me a hard time about that damn dog, I wouldn't be in this mess. You could have taken her and let me go. But no, you had to cop an attitude yourself, and now look at what you've done. As far as I'm concerned, you're no better than he is."

As that triggered a spasm of guilt, Gray found himself mesmerized by her profile. In the obscure and changing light, passion blazed in eyes as exotic as an Egyptian cat's, her lush hair lifted off her shoulders like a night raven in a graceful glide. The romantic analogies were ludicrous to someone who'd lost interest in women, in everything he'd ever cared about. But like it or not, there was no denying this woman was something else. He needed grounding fast. He *needed* to know, was he setting himself up to make the mistake of mistakes?

"Did you set the fire?" he asked.

"Sure. Then I hunted down the dog, half gutted it and came back to Shangri-la here so I could endure Dumb and Dumber."

Gray grabbed her arm and swung her around to face him. "Knock it off. I'm too tired for your games, and God knows I'm so fed up with things in general that I'm already wondering why I should care what happens to you."

"Then why did you come over?" she replied, giving as good as she got. "Because if it's for some of what he wanted, you aren't going to have any more luck than he did. I don't put out. Not on demand. Not as an I.O.U. Got it?"

"I wasn't asking."

"Let me guess—" she shrugged off his hold "—you're another one who expects the woman to offer out of gratitude."

An odd bitterness filled Gray's mouth, the ashes of old pain. "I lost my wife. I was *not* asking."

She grew quiet and slowly, reluctantly, searched his face. "So that's what's wrong with you."

Once again, he appreciated her candor. He also was relieved that she didn't mouth any meaningless condolences, and accepted his explanation without more questions.

"All right, so tell me what I owe you," she said instead. "And I'll leave you in peace."

Gray sighed because he wanted her to go. It was the strangest feeling, but he almost ached with the need. However, he also knew Elias.

"You can't."

"Pardon?"

"In the morning, I'll call someone, a friend. He's a lawyer and he'll know what can be done."

She purged the air in her lungs in a way that could have been a laugh, if he hadn't seen her expression.

"I don't believe this. Why did you bother coming over there if not to help me get away from him?"

"Think about it. I suspect you'll figure it out."

Although her gaze searched his face, her expression remained closed.

"Talk to me," Gray urged. "Or would you prefer dealing with Frank all by your lonesome?"

Her lips compressed, she shook her head. "I'm not staying, Doctor."

"You don't have a choice, because he *will* come after you. That much I can promise."

"He'll have to find me."

"Oh, he'll do that. You don't know about Frank Elias and his obsessions. Is that something you can afford...Sasha?"

6

He knew... Sasha could see the truth in Gray Slaughter's chilling gaze, and she needed only to glance toward the van, remember there had been no time to lock it, to understand how. Her next worst fear realized, she studied the man challenging her, concluding that, no matter how she weighed her chances of fleeing at the moment, they were slight. Almost worse than when she'd first been forced to make a run for it. Time, that's what she needed. It was already her enemy, but she had to figure out a way to change that and make something work in her favor.

"What do you want?" She took heart in hearing that her voice didn't sound as unsteady as it had after Elias's assault.

"The truth."

"I promise you, Doctor, you want the truth about as much as I'd be interested in a sidewalk mammography."

He nodded toward the police station. "You almost had worse back there."

It had been a bad situation, and if she let herself

dwell on it, she would probably start trembling again, so she maintained her focus on a counter-offensive. Wasn't that what her father used to tout? The Vince Lombardi quote: "The best defense is a great offense."

"All right, let me put it this way," she countered. "Why, knowing what you think you do, have you stuck your neck out to help me?"

"Forget me for the moment, it's Frank you should be worrying about. He may be small-time compared to what you're used to in Las Vegas, but whatever he lacks skillwise, he makes up for in dogged determination, *Officer* Mills."

Although it shouldn't surprise her at this point that he also knew her profession, Sasha dealt with what her paternal grandmother had likened to "Death's cold grip on the neck" in silence.

"You're not getting it," Gray continued. "It's pride with him, and I think you're someone who understands pride."

For his sake, she hoped he never learned how thoroughly. "What do you suggest I do? The man's intent on framing me."

"Forget the fire for the moment." He gestured toward the van. "It's the automatic and the money that concern me. In this part of the country that kind of paraphernalia usually means drugs or freighting illegals."

"The gun is my service weapon, my ID is authentic."

"Then how can you be relocating the way you claimed? If you'd left the LVMPD, you'd have surrendered both."

Sasha swallowed against the adrenaline charging through her veins; her heart was pumping as though she was pushing to win a mile sprint. She had to remind herself that this man had risked taking a bullet for her—after going through her things and drawing conclusions he clearly saw as incriminating, no less.

The unexpected touch of his fingers against her cheek had her jerking back.

"Come inside," he said grimly. "I'll get you some ice for that. The skin isn't broken, but it still has to burn like hell."

It did. She also needed the chance to rein in her emotions and cool off. She couldn't afford any other errors in judgment. Besides, they were too exposed out here. If she was to make her escape, she needed time…and privacy.

"All right," she murmured. "Let me lock up first."

"If you don't mind." He reached around her to lock the passenger door, then circled the van, took out her keys and rolled up the window. When he finally handed over the keys and her bag, but not her gun, she knew something else—it would be dangerous to attempt anything rash while Dr. Gray Slaughter was awake or conscious, because he was going to be even less of a pushover than Frank Elias.

The wariness compounded as Sasha entered his home. It was darker in here than in the police station, as silent as a mausoleum and not that dissimilar in looks considering the impersonal, old-fashioned furnishings. Usually, she found dimly lit, quiet places soothing, but she had to stop just inside the sparsely furnished living room because of the overwhelming sensation of negatives, what felt like a near vacuum of oxygen. How different things had looked from the outside. There was a complete absence of life. In fact, she sensed death lingering here.

"Something wrong?" he asked after securing the front door's dead bolt.

"It's dark. I don't want to step on the family cat or anything."

"There isn't one."

It probably ran away from home ages ago. "Should I keep my voice down for any sleeping babies?"

"The kitchen's this way."

Lifting her eyebrows at his touchiness over the subject, she followed him as he stepped left through a doorway to a combination kitchen and dining area. Visually, it was no improvement, the green-white-and-chrome decor reminiscent of a fifties B movie, on the sci-fi end of budgets. But it was exits Sasha paid particular attention to. She noted the aluminum storm door beyond the half-glass inner one. Double doors weren't ideal. Until she saw the rest of the place, she decided the route they'd entered remained her best option. As she tucked her keys into the right front pocket of her jeans, she positioned them to be able to grab the van key first...or to use as a weapon if that became necessary.

"Here." Working by the light over the kitchen sink, Gray took a towel from a drawer and drew a handful of ice cubes from the icemaker in the only modern appliance in the place—the side-by-side refrigerator-freezer. Then he passed the bulky mass to her. "Want something to dull the bruising on the inside?"

Before she could answer, he stooped before the cabinet next to the refrigerator and took out an unopened bottle of scotch. That had her wondering where the opened one was. Had he already emptied it?

"No, thanks," she said as he reached for a second glass. One wouldn't be enough and two would be too many. "Just a glass of water if you don't mind." She had aspirin in her bag to address the headache she was developing. But as he turned away, she amended, "On second thought, yes. Please."

If he was confused or suspicious of her change of heart, he gave no indication. "On the rocks or with water?"

"Plenty of ice, please, then just a splash of water. And if it's not too much trouble, I'd appreciate an extra glass of water on the side. I'm feeling pretty dehydrated."

The drink he handed her would put her over the legal limit for driving—probably what he intended—but what interested her more was seeing that the one he made for himself could have been mistaken for apple cider.

"Are you catching up for lost time," she asked, "or is that a sign of how upset you are with me?"

Gray took a leisurely drink before replying, "Why don't you just tell me what triggered what happened next door?"

"You're the one who has the history with the man, you explain it to me."

"There's nothing complicated about Frank. From the instant he laid eyes on you, his chronic itch wanted scratching. I'm sure that's nothing new to you."

"I can't believe you're blaming me for lucky genes, Doctor."

"I'm not referring to your looks, and you know it. But the plainest person can possess an intrinsic animal magnetism, or sexuality, call it what you'd like, that's equally if not more provocative...and can be tempered."

"So now I provoked him?"

"For all of his flaws, Frank tends to stick with

sure things, and he's got plenty of those right here in town.''

At this rate, he would have her draining her drink, after all...if she didn't throw it at him. ''Okay, Doc, I confess. Once I realized how easy it was to make the jerk act like putty in my hands, I couldn't resist. Fighting off rapists beats watching late-night TV anytime.''

''What I think is that in your eagerness to get away, you made a poor judgment call. That begs the question, what could be so important to put yourself at such risk?''

To answer that even in the most vague way would initiate a whole new series of questions, so she bought time by taking an initial sip of her scotch, then a few seconds longer by taking a deep swallow of the water to keep from choking. It didn't help much. ''Look, I'm grateful for your assistance. But if you hadn't been such a hard case to begin with, none of this would have happened.''

Gray saluted her with his glass. ''I can see Frank will have his hands full tomorrow with or without counsel.''

''Chief Elias couldn't recognize a serial killer if he stood at his door with a trick-or-treat bag full of body parts.'' Sasha hesitated a moment and then ventured, ''What will it take for you to let me go?''

''I gave my word.''

She pretended resignation and asked, ''Then where's the closest motel?''

"Sonora, east on the interstate about twenty miles. But don't insult my intelligence by asking me to believe you'd stop there, let alone be back here first thing in the morning."

"What else do you expect—"

The ringing phone had Gray scowling and then motioning for her to give him a moment. From the sound of his side of the conversation, she surmised the caller was a customer with an ill animal. It was exactly the opportunity she needed.

Signaling to him that she wanted to wash up, she snatched her purse and exited through the other passageway she assumed led to the hall and the rest of the house. It did. Directly opposite the kitchen, she found a room set up as an office. Next to it was a bedroom, and after that the bathroom. Closing and quietly locking the door, she eyed the window over the tub.

"Small gifts," she murmured.

Knowing that sound would be her enemy, she turned on the water faucet in the sink and placed the towel with ice in the base of the bowl, listening for a certain splashing sound. Satisfied with the tone, she stepped into the bathtub and eased open the window. Relieved that the window didn't squeak, she jimmied free the screen, then tossed out her purse. Hoisting herself up and through the narrow opening, however, was a feat better suited to a member of Cirque du Soleil. She was agile and small enough overall, but the window was higher due to its location, and she had to be careful not to hit the shower door while twisting like a theme-park trained dolphin to get herself out. Easy enough normally, though she wasn't feeling "normal" these days.

But escape she did. Dropping to the ground with a grunt of pain that had little to do with the distance of her fall or the dry, packed ground, she grabbed up her bag and took off to the left—immediately crashing into something that shouldn't have been there.

"I'm sincerely disappointed." Gray Slaughter gripped her arms to steady her.

Deciding that she had nothing to lose, Sasha lunged at him with the determination of a linebacker at a playoff game. Shouldering him in the belly, she sidestepped left and took off running again.

She made it around the first corner, but as she rounded the second at the front of the house, she went flying forward, hitting the ground like a safe dropping three stories onto concrete.

The next thing she was conscious of was the dirt in her mouth and something as heavy as a buffalo crushing her. Just as she was certain her lungs would explode, the weight eased off her...but then her arms were being twisted behind her back. Spitting out grass and dirt, Sasha gasped from pain as much as the need for oxygen.

"Wait..."

"That's what I asked you to do while I was on the phone."

"I can't...breathe."

To her great relief the knee trying to permanently fasten her spine to her navel lifted. With no time to adjust, she was yanked up like a stuffed toy. Slaughter kept a firm hold of her, but Sasha didn't care. She was too grateful that her lungs were working again, and for the chance to blink away the tears and dirt from her eyes.

"You're faster than you...look," she wheezed.

He picked up her bag. "And you're not as bright."

She couldn't argue with him there. "Where—where did you learn that tackle?"

"Worry about it."

Grasping her by the waist with his free hand, he started directing her back toward the kitchen door. It was the worst of all places he could have touched her.

Gasping, Sasha fought the blinding pain and would have fallen again if not for his equally fast response.

"What is it?" he demanded, steadying her with his body.

Muted by the wave of nausea that followed, she could only bend forward and struggle to get past the worst of it. "Nothing. I'll be okay in a second."

"All I did was—" Dropping her bag, he tugged at her shirt.

"What the— Hey!" She pushed away his hands, having had her fill of groping men for one night. "I said I'm okay."

"Let me see, damn it." Freeing the shirt from her jeans, he lifted it and turned her into the faint light off the back porch. "Christ. Why the hell didn't you say you'd been shot?"

Once she was fairly confident that her stomach was going to stay inside her body, she threw him a resentful look. "When would have been a good time? At the start, when you decided I was a lousy pet owner? Or later, as the tramp willing to do anything to get my way?" Feeling the day, the last week catching up with her, Sasha looked away and continued to blink hard, this time against overpowering emotions. "It's only a graze," she muttered. "And nothing compared to what will happen if you don't let me go."

7

Shortly after passing the road sign indicating Bitters 5 Miles, the woman driving the BMW Z8 stiffened with new alarm as the engine light flashed on.

"Stupid automobile!"

It wasn't a year old and outrageously expensive, how could the engine be sick? This is what she deserved for her extravagance. God was punishing her, would punish her like the angel pursuing Adam and Eve out of the Garden of Eden.

But this was no garden. She was in the middle of nowhere, a hideous, barren place not that different than where she'd come from, but without the luxuries. She'd noted all its deficits during the meandering, desperate attempt to find her way back to the interstate and here. Considering the endless darkness stretching before her, she had no hope that this "Bitters"—Americans forever perplexed her with their town names—was an improvement over the last disaster she'd exited at. There the gas pump had been malfunctioning, and the toilet— She would rather have risked the wildlife and peed behind a bush.

Now she couldn't afford disdain. She had to seek help at Bitters because the stupid car was running on fumes as well as whatever that light meant.

Clinging to the steering wheel with a grip that triggered the cramps she'd been experiencing since the first night she'd been traveling, the woman checked her rearview mirror. At least she was safe again. No one else was on the road. *Spasibo, Mama.* Now if only her sainted mother could convince the Holy Virgin to forgive her for her vanity and self-indulgence, and bring her to someone who understood overpriced sports cars. This was exactly what she'd been warned when she'd bought it, how no one outside of a metropolitan area would be able to fix it should she have trouble. The head mechanic at the dealership had insisted, *begged* her, to pull over immediately should anything ever go wrong.

Pull over? Easy for him to say, she thought with another spasm of self-pity. He wasn't the one in a strange place with a phone that refused to work, worried that when it finally did there would be no answer on the other side.

"I hate you," she cried, pounding on the dash. "Turn off!"

The light stayed on.

Blinking at tears that threatened to lead her off

the road, she eyed the odometer again, gauging how far away she now was from the exit. Two miles? It had to be less.

"I am strong," she recited, remembering the therapy and self-help books she'd read by the dozens. "I can do it."

Sniffing, she shifted into Neutral, turned off the ignition and let the Z8 cruise on its own momentum. The night was mild. Walking would be nerve-racking, but what hadn't been so far? She could manage.

As the car began to slow, she steered to the shoulder until the vehicle came to a full stop.

Would it ever start again? She had counted on this sleek, red beauty to finance her future. But, she allowed with a sigh, that was the way of life. As her *baba* used to lecture, "To live a life is not so simple as crossing a field."

Feeling tears collecting again, she pulled free the keys, climbed out of the BMW and locked up. Brushing back her shoulder-length hair, she inspected her surroundings. The other warnings flooded back into her memory, how not to venture off into the prairie if something went wrong, how there was as much danger out there as there was on the road, things that did more than bite or sting.

"All I ever wanted was to be warm again," she whispered to the night.

With no desire to find out what creatures stalked this unwelcoming terrain, she began walking briskly toward the lights. Although dim and minimal, they consoled her somewhat. She was a woman who needed her solitude, needed it desperately, but the company of people, especially strangers, would be reassuring right now. If she could also get a cup of hot coffee and use a clean rest room, she would endure. Blossom.

"I am strong...I am strong."

Her jogging shoes, still too new to be comfortable, made each step awkward. She was used to high heels, expensive leathers, not these heavy things with soles she suspected were made from military-truck tires. As ugly as they were stiff, they were no less foreign to her than her jeans and Texas T-shirt. Her style was the business suit, preferably silk and exquisite, and handcrafted shoes. These monstrosities reminded her of the old country, difficult times and too much she wanted to forget.

"The point is to blend in with the tourists, not stick out."

Remembering those cautionary words, her lips, bare of the expensive makeup she was envied for, twisted without mirth. "What tourists?"

All but lost in her dejection, she was slow to realize something was missing.

My bag.

Horrified, she began running back. But after only a few steps, the lights of another vehicle appeared.

What to do? There was no choice but to seek

shelter in the first shrubs large enough to hide her. Even as she sent up another prayer, she nevertheless veered off the road and down a craggy draw to seek cover in the deeper terrain. Stumbling over the uneven ground, she barely missed a dive into a thatch of prickly brush.

Ducking behind it, she watched as a vehicle slowed, then pulled in behind hers. Thieves? Of course! Who would ignore such a beauty standing alone for the taking? And in it all that was left of her future.

She cursed the interlopers in the large vehicle parking behind her car. Then she bit her lower lip as her eyes adjusted to the darkness and she could tell more about it. Oh, no, she thought. Please God, no.

Both driver and passenger doors opened. Two men emerged, the cab lights exposing that both dressed in dark attire. They were barely a hundred feet away, yet she couldn't make out many details about them except that they appeared large, intimidating. Then they spoke and she knew visual identification wouldn't matter.

The Russians.

An involuntary cry burst from her.

In the next instant the man on her side turned his flashlight toward where she hid. She ducked lower. The beam slid right over her hiding spot and passed. A second beam duplicated the trail of the first. It wasn't unlike the prison camp searchlights from the old days, and she knew like those, these dogs of war would not give up easily.

Her worst fears materialized as the men started down the steep incline.

Terrified, certain that she'd been spotted, she turned blindly into the darkness and began running.

8

1:07 a.m.

Once they returned inside, Gray handed Sasha her glass and directed her toward the hallway.

"What for?"

He understood her wariness, realized she wasn't convinced that, despite what he'd said earlier, he wasn't ordering her to his bedroom to take up where Frank had left off. In his opinion, he was probably the safest male in Bitters tonight, as physically spent as he was emotionally finished, and from more than wrestling and playing verbal chess with her.

It had been an altogether shitty day thanks to Dub Witherspoon's favorite cow needing help in delivering a dead bull calf. Dub hadn't taken "I don't do house calls anymore" for an answer. As a result, all Gray wanted when he got home after the nine-hour ordeal was to get quietly drunk and escape from that latest scenario and the scent of death.

But to his unwelcome and reluctant houseguest, he merely said, "You're under my roof, you don't take foolish chances with infection."

To his surprise, she went without any additional lip.

In the bathroom, he motioned for her to hop up on the vanity, then shut off the water she'd left running and squeezed out the washrag. Afterward, he locked the window. Replacing the screen would have to wait until morning. He hoped she *was* intimidated by him; he didn't think he was in good enough shape to do many more rounds with this spitfire.

With her semi-safely perched, he opened the linen closet to rummage through the offerings there. Most of his medical supplies, even those appropriate for humans, were in the clinic, so he settled on hydrogen peroxide, antibiotic ointment, cotton balls and whatever he had in the way of gauze pads and bandages.

He set everything beside her. "You'll have to lift your shirt again and open the jeans."

Hardly voiced as a request, he accepted that she first took a good swallow of her drink. The wound had to be giving her more trouble than she wanted to admit—denim tended to be abrasive even without a pair of male hands working it like sandpaper against tender skin—but he knew it wasn't pain alone feeding her reluctance. It was him. He'd proven to be not much better than Frank. She had to detest him for that.

When she finally relented, Gray grunted at the inflamed slash marring the left side of her small waist. In this brighter light, the shocking contrast against skin otherwise flawless filled him with an even deeper outrage. He understood too well the brutality behind such an assault, and how lucky she was to be sitting there shooting mental arrows into him.

All he said, though, was, "Roll the waistband down a bit more, or I'll get this crap all over everything."

"Just do the best you can."

"Suit yourself."

He opened the new package of cotton balls and the peroxide and went to work.

"You took a huge risk not bothering to get this tended to properly."

"I've been a little busy."

"How did it happen?"

She acted as though she'd suddenly gone stone deaf, which was just as well. The condition of the wound demanded his concentration. And although peroxide didn't usually sting—at least not in comparison to what he should be using—this abrasion was no simple scratch. It was also inflamed, the tissue swollen. That meant his slightest touch had to sting like a needle in the eye, and Gray thought she did pretty well to simply stiffen and suck in a sharp breath with every new dab.

"Hang on. I'll finish as fast as I can."

Like a model posing for a sculpture, or an assassin contemplating a target, she simply stared out into the dark hallway, lost in her own focus.

Hoping she wasn't plotting some new attempt to outwit or outmaneuver him, he said, "You need to know something. I may not like what you just pulled, but it doesn't change anything. You're in my home and that means something to me. Elias won't touch you again."

"And who's going to keep *you* in line, Doc?"

"I did not take you down for a free grope. That tumble left me sore, too."

"I was on the bottom."

"You betrayed my trust." Then Gray swore softly. Not due to her attitude, rather for the discoloration he noticed on the cotton. "You'd better take a bigger swallow of your drink, think up a few new expletives, something, because I've got to get a little rougher than I intended."

He held up the stained cotton for her to see and she gazed at it with eyes darker than New Orleans coffee, almost as dark as her lashes. Raising her glass to her lips, she murmured, "Do what you have to do."

The drink wasn't as potent as a shot, and before Gray reached for another cotton ball, her hand was shaking enough to bounce an ice cube out of the glass. It skidded off the counter and directly into the commode.

"Five bucks says you can't do that twice."

For such rich-colored eyes, her answering look cut like a laser.

"That's what I like about you," he countered. "You're no chatterbox."

"And you were right to stay away from plastic surgery. At least you put the dog under before starting on her."

"That was a low blow, even if you are hurting, Officer."

"You're right, I'm sorry."

"If only I believed you meant it."

"I—" Gasping, Sasha fell silent as she endured the most painful swab yet. "Believe this then...that money you found belongs to my mother's lover. I figured it was small retribution for this graze. I also took it knowing it wouldn't be smart to stop at an ATM machine."

Gray tossed the last soiled swab into the trash and washed his hands. "Is your mother okay?"

"Do you think that son of a bitch would be alive if he'd hurt her?"

God almighty, he thought. Who was this woman? "Has there been a murder?"

"Not by me."

Maybe he was a fool, but he believed her. "So who's Anna Diaz?"

"My—best friend."

"Isn't that a bit risky?"

"She died just over a year ago."

"Then she's in no way connected to whatever is going on?"

"Not in the least. But we could pass for sisters, and I loved her as though she was. I wouldn't have taken her identity if it wasn't necessary."

Gray reached for the antibiotic ointment. "You shouldn't have scratched the photo. I would only have glanced at it otherwise. The scratch made me look more closely."

"Uh-huh. You tackle like a pro, your observation skills are better than the average person's... Anything else I should watch out for?"

"As I said before, worry about it." He spread the ointment, frowning at the unexpected pleasure he took from her curiosity and reluctant admiration. As a rule, he shut down any questions about himself or his past. Knowing how unwise this breach in pattern was, he attempted to alleviate that. "So where's your mother?"

"I don't know."

He didn't miss the lower pitch in her voice, the strain that lay beneath that admission. It had him thinking of what she wasn't saying, and he didn't like the possibilities, disliked them so much he abruptly wiped his hand in a tissue and took her glass out of her hand.

"By all means," she drawled as he gulped down the rest of its contents. "Help yourself."

"I'll freshen it up when we get back to the kitchen."

Opening a pair of large gauze bandages, he secured them with several Band-Aids. "That should hold. We'll have to repeat the process in the morning, though. You were a few hours away from a serious infection."

He tossed away the wrappings and washed his hands again, almost smelling smoke from the mental brakes locking in her head. That told him she still planned to be out of here by then. So much for thinking he'd gotten his point across.

Taking up her glass again, he led the way back to the kitchen.

Once there, he refilled both of their drinks. "About your mother..."

"She's not up for discussion."

"I'll ask anyway. Are you looking for her? You said you don't know where she is. And if you're on the run because you stole her boyfriend's money—"

"Correction, he shot, then I took the money."

Gray slid her freshened drink toward her. "Then it's reasonable to assume that he's not too happy with her, either, if only because of her relationship to you."

Sasha ignored the offering and walked around the room like a caged animal. The way she slid her hand to her side told Gray that she could use the help against the pain. Guessing why she refused, he eyed his glass longingly, but slowly placed it down beside hers and tried a different angle of questioning.

"Cops get shot at every day. Generally they're seen as heroes not fugitives. Or is it just the gun-happy boyfriend you're running from?"

"How many ways do I need to tell you to butt out, Slaughter? I'm saying this for your welfare as much as my own."

"But you believe information can keep a person alive. Hasn't it allowed you to assume another person's identity?"

Sasha laughed briefly, the sound hard. "Stick to vaccinating pups and kittens. Anna was an orphan. I'm not compromising anyone's safety by using her ID."

"What about me? As far as I'm concerned, there's no more vulnerable place to be than in the dark, where you're leaving me."

She spun away from him to circle the dinette table. "I didn't invite you to snoop around in my van. And I don't—damn." She grasped her side.

"You'll want to avoid sharp turns like that one, fast moves of any kind for the next several days," Gray told her.

Holding herself rigid and then sighing with relief, Sasha said with surprising mildness, "You've been decent, and I'm grateful. As for the subtle interrogation, forget it. I'm the best judge of what is and isn't viable."

To hell with it, Gray thought, and swept up his glass. He welcomed the cold sting from the ice against his teeth as much as the bite from the alcohol. "This boyfriend has a record, doesn't he?"

Completing the turn around the kitchen table, Sasha stopped before him. "Look at me."

That was one thing he didn't want to do, at least not when he wasn't in his doctoring mode. Especially not when there was little more than his imagination between them. Because a god with a fondness for Mona Lisa–like smiles had designed Sasha Mills's lips. Only he hadn't been able to resist adding just enough fullness to trigger erotic thoughts. Perfect torment for melancholy bastards like him who thought they already knew all the tricks hell had to offer.

"Now hear me, Slaughter," she continued. "Once and for all—leave it alone."

"No can do. You ended up on my doorstep, and as you've already heard and surmised, I have too much time on my hands to weigh and analyze. Okay, so at least tell me this," he said as she began to argue. "Are you, for want of a better word, AWOL from your job? I'm assuming your precinct commander doesn't know your whereabouts?"

"Every time I tried to talk to him, it almost got me killed."

Now he understood the hunted look in her eyes, the pacing and edginess. "What do you think has happened?"

"I suspect someone I trusted sold me out. Nothing else I can think of would explain it."

"Call IA."

She lifted a finely arched eyebrow. "You know about police procedure?"

"This may be the middle of nowhere, but not everyone living here is half-baked or on the fast track to senility. Why didn't you call them?"

"Because I *am* a cop. A city cop with all the pressures. If you know about IA, you know about the Blue Wall. You don't go to Internal Affairs, not if you want to stay a part of the team. Besides, the word is that most IA people are political hatchlings eager to make their mark by feeding off carcasses. I'd prefer not to be their Thanksgiving turkey."

"You have to trust someone."

"First things first. I'll reconsider that down the road." But she shook her head as though the problem didn't bear consideration.

Gray's instinct was to press onward. "What about your mother? Where does she fit in all of this? She's got to be worried sick about you."

Sasha resumed her pacing.

Mistake, Gray thought. He didn't know if it was intuition or sudden deductive clarity, but he saw it—her predicament. "This isn't about you or being a cop at all. Not directly. Even the money is irrelevant. You got sucked in trying to save your mother."

Sasha returned to the counter and reached for her purse. "If you don't mind, I'd like to take care of my bill and—"

"Whoa." He gripped her wrist.

"Slaughter, enough," she pleaded wearily. "I really, *really* have to get out of here."

"Think so? Regardless of what you've been through tonight, you've had minimal exposure to Frank. I've known him most of my life."

"Don't tell me...he's your in-law."

"He was once my best friend."

Groaning, she closed her eyes. "I should have stopped at the next convenience store, bought the dog a box of Band-Aids, me a bigger bottle of aspirin, and taken my chances on the interstate."

"Sasha."

"Stop it." She tugged free and backed away from him. It cost her; she had to hold her side again. "Don't you dare say my name as though we're reunited soul mates."

"You can't deny I'm a part of this now. It may not be what either of us wants, but I'm guilty by association, and it's my right to decide how much deeper I want to go."

"My suggestion is to start backstroking, fast."

"Do yourself a favor and face down Elias tomorrow. Hell, I know you didn't have anything to do with the fire. As I said, this area is a freeway for illegal aliens. When Frank gets his head screwed on straight, he'll see that's more likely what happened at the church. Despite what I said earlier to calm him down, folks have been bitching about the situation for years, and we've earned our reputation for being less than hospitable to that traffic. The fire could have been a 'thanks for nothing' message sent by a courier, a mule, someone traveling in the flow trying to look like a helpless migrant worker and finding his trails increasingly compromised. But you have to let Elias learn that on his own. And since you and the dog need the rest, what's the problem?''

Sasha smoothed back her long hair. ''How about not wanting to wake finding a gun barrel pressing into my forehead?''

He considered the scenario for a moment. ''You believe someone is after you. Is that why you were on this smaller highway instead of the interstate?'' When she failed to respond, he nodded, confident that he was close. ''If this someone was hunting you, don't you think they'd have made their move by now? At any rate, how far could you hope to get tonight feeling the way you do?''

Her expression began to expose some doubt. After several more seconds, she said, ''I'll have to leave first thing in the morning.''

''Right after you give your statement.''

''You're sure this lawyer you mentioned can help?''

''He knows Frank every bit as well as I do. In the meantime, the guest room is yours.''

She looked anything but reassured by that. "How about that room over your garage? How bad is it?"

"Loaded with old crap that I haven't looked at in over a year. I suspect field mice have turned the place into a nursery school." When her expression remained dubious, he added, "If you're concerned about being manhandled again, don't be. I'm the guy who called Elias a pig, remember? In any case, I was serious about having lost my wife."

"How long has it been?"

"Fourteen months."

The softening in her eyes and around her mouth vanished. "Give me a break."

"You find that difficult to believe?"

"The last grieving widower I met was when I was providing escort to and from his wife's funeral," she drawled. "He made a pass leaving the cemetery. 'Night, *Doctor*."

9

In the master bedroom of a warehouse office, the phone on the nightstand beside the king-size bed buzzed softly. With an animal-like growl, a naked man rolled off the blonde tangled with him in the black satin sheets and snatched up the phone.

"What?" he snapped.

Melor Borodin didn't like interruptions when he was working, and as much as he enjoyed sex, this qualified as labor. The panting bleached blonde behind him didn't come close to being his idea of a lover, and it would take more than a paper bag over her head to help. Aside from the caking makeup, her body was beyond the generous description of voluptuous—in a city renowned for stabling some of the most gorgeous showgirls in the world, no less. He was having to fantasize about the long-legged hostess he'd just hired at Red Square to keep an erection—and now some asshole was making that feat impossible.

"Lev here."

Borodin sat forward, digging his toes into the plush carpet the color of the genuine elephant tusk stretching the length of the bar before him. "You have news?"

"*Da.* Half of what you wait to hear."

He gripped the phone's receiver tighter. "You disturb me for fragments?"

"You said keep you informed," came the hesitant reply. "We thought—"

"Stop immediately." Furious, Borodin pinched the bridge of his nose, struggling to harness the rage inside him. Mercurial from birth, his boiling point was dangerously low these days, thanks to this situation. But they were well into their third night of tracking the two bitches, and to his way of thinking, the delays and constant excuses would have pressed a monk's patience.

"I told you before," he continued, his voice all but dripping venom, "thinking is not your job, it's mine." What he'd actually said then was that they had smegma for brains, and saw this call as verification that he was right. "Hold."

With a sigh, he leaned back toward the blonde, who'd risen on one elbow to take a noisy sip of her melting piña colada through the straw. Stroking a hand across her dimpling rump, he kissed the shallow indentation at her waist. "Would you

mind? A small business matter needing attention.''
Lest his accent confuse the simple English, he nodded to the bathroom to make himself clear.

"Oh. Of course.''

Grabbing up the tulip glass, she launched herself
off the bed.

Borodin watched pale flesh jiggle and wiggle until the door shut behind her. Sighing over the injustice of it all, he sat up again and said into the
receiver, "All right, tell me. But, *pojalsta,* resist
names.''

He was as cautious regarding security as he was
meticulous to detail in his business, and vengeful
with anyone who cost him, whether it was profit,
embarrassment or anything else. This Lev and the
dolt with him weren't expected to blend into so-
ciety with the ease that he did with increasing success. Such ability was virtually impossible, and
counterproductive to why he'd hired them in the
first place. But he had not come this far to be un-
done by clumsy apes dropping their guard, speaking without always assuming that there were others
eavesdropping, or otherwise targeting them for the
next big sting to parade before their media. He was
the progeny of one of the most controlling of gov-
ernments. He'd been weaned on the nectar of sus-
picion, and at the virile age of thirty-five, believed
in nothing and trusted no one.

"I remember,'' Lev replied. "We only mean to
assure.''

He wouldn't be assured until they had both women. "Which did you find? *No names.*"

"The...the elder, *gospodin.*"

Borodin stared at his reflection in the bar mirror waiting for a reaction and felt none. He was disappointed, hoping for at least a twinge of something. But then, it was early yet for satisfaction.

Rising, he stepped closer to examine his right cheek, scarred by an angry hook-shaped gash. A fraction of an inch higher and he would have lost the eye. "And the other?"

"We are temporarily to lose contact."

His image in the mirror vanished in the white-hot heat of his anger. "There are only two fucking decent highways across the goddamn state!"

"*Da, du,* but the *doroga,* the way, is not easy once you get off. And she go to—to the *pole*—"

"Ground."

"*Da,* the ground like rabbit. We think she is miles in front."

"You're wrong. She isn't ahead of you." Borodin remembered the fierceness of his prey as she'd cursed him seconds before meeting fire with fire. "She may have plans, but they'll mean nothing to her without her mother. Stay put, and keep looking. And check in more often."

"But *gospodin,* sir, our phones do not work. One must drive miles, the other stand guard. You understand what I try to say?"

Borodin glanced over to make sure the bathroom

door was, indeed, shut. "It's not my job to understand you, and I don't give a shit if you have to stick a pole up your ass and hoist yourself like a flag to get a signal. Keep me informed, and if you value your life you won't be outsmarted again."

He disconnected before he went into a full rage. Actually, he enjoyed the passion triggered by his anger; it was one of the few times he felt truly alive. But soon, he thought as he caressed his wound, soon his restraint would be rewarded. In the meantime there was much to do.

For as long as Melor Borodin could remember, he had been plotting. The art of strategy was his favorite subject next to deception. Even his name was illusory of the person he truly was. As their only child, his parents had given him a patriotic Soviet name to honor the party and its national heroes—*M*arx, *E*ngles, *L*enin, *O*ctober and *Revo*-lution. It had a nice ring to it, but at a precocious nine years of age, he concluded it was complete crap for someone who would never feel the slightest alliance to a political persuasion. His devoted party-member parents could be satisfied with their little cubbyholes of power in decaying Moscow, but he always knew he was destined for better things. If he'd had any doubts early on, Gorbachev and Yeltsin had convinced him. If those two geniuses could line their pockets with American currency, he'd reasoned, why shouldn't he?

And now here he was, surpassing his own imagination, so close to being a legitimate businessman and potentially legally untouchable that he occasionally found himself laughing at the thought. But the betrayal endangered all of that. Fortunately, his absence of trust and preference to place "eyes behind eyes" justified itself. There was still vulnerability, but he would address that in the morning. Right now he needed to be sure everyone else in his circle remained loyal.

As though on cue, the bathroom door opened. Back to drudgery, he thought with a sigh. But what he saw had him frowning.

"What is this?"

Crossing to the woman who was now dressed again in her LVMPD uniform, he stilled the hands securing her belt, then began unbuttoning her dark brown shirt. "You misunderstand me, *blini.*"

"I thought—" she moaned as he reached inside her bra to lift her plump breasts and stroke his thumbs across her nipples "—you said you had business."

"I delegate," he said, falling back on his broken English to disarm her. "Is correct, yes? My business tonight, *blini,* is you. Say you will stay. I am not giving you your present yet."

She giggled, leaning into him as he thrust his cock between her khaki-clad legs. "Are you sure? That's a pretty big present I just had. But I do like when you talk to me in your language. For example, what does that word mean? You've called me it before.''

If he told her he was comparing her to a pancake, and not just *any* pancake but a Russian-size one, she would probably neuter him with those fake talons she called fingernails. Instead, he gave her the crooked smile she said made him look like a young Clint Eastwood. "Is what you Americans call... endearment, *da? Blini,* my lovely."

Her odd yellow eyes, already evidencing the two big frozen drinks she'd downed, grew dreamier. "You think I'm pretty?"

His laugh rumbled in his chest as he spun her around and pushed her none too gently onto the bed. "I will show you what you are."

10

The door to the guest bedroom stood wide open and the bed looked as if it hadn't been slept in. Stopping in midstep on his way to the kitchen, Gray's insides clenched with an increasingly familiar dread. So much for being certain when he'd said good-night to Sasha Mills that she would be here in the morning. No, she hadn't made him any promises, but he believed he'd impressed upon her the seriousness and vulnerability of her position.

"Slaughter, you are a certified dumb shit."

What ticked him off as much as her leaving was that he hadn't heard her take off, not even the damn van's crappy engine coughing to life like a chain-smoker in the last stages of emphysema. And all he had for his troubles were eyes that burned as if they'd been dipped in baked sand and a head he

could swear a six-month-old pit bull had been using as a chew toy.

But a second later, he came into the kitchen and
picked up the scent of coffee, spotted the pot of
fresh brew on the machine and momentarily forgot
his aching head and raw belly. It helped that the
kitchen door stood wide open, and beyond it she
was pacing across the yard, alternately cursing the
tiny phone in her left hand and sipping from the
mug held in her right.

Gray exhaled and took his time pouring himself
a mug of the aromatic, he hoped stabilizing, coffee.
Sasha Mills was proving altogether too capable at
getting under his skin. After almost two years of
not giving a damn what anyone said or thought
about him, not caring about anything, period, adjusting to her was as easy as waking to a muscle
cramp. He wondered if she was feeling half as
pleased with his appearance in her life.

Stepping outside just as she failed again to make
a connection, he said, ''You can always use the
one in the kitchen.''

She looked far better than she deserved to after
the night she'd been through, a vast improvement
to the face he dealt with in his bathroom mirror.
Her wet hair indicated she'd also showered—another thing he'd slept through—and had changed
into clean clothes, although the outfit was more of
the same, a denim shirt and jeans. But the shirt was
of a lighter denim than yesterday's. Trying not to

notice how damp tendrils cupped her breasts like fingers, he focused on the darker shadows under her eyes. They made her older, vulnerable...yet still nowhere near as ancient as he felt.

"What do you people do in an emergency?" Sasha asked with the sardonic drawl he'd used.

"Oh...empty a .12 gauge into the air, drive through town pounding on the horn...use the *standard* phone. Wireless service is inconsistent out here."

"I was hoping things might change with the time of day. I've had that luck elsewhere."

"You've stayed in one place that long?"

She shot him a wry look. "Nice try."

The realization that he would very much like to see her really smile caused him to misdirect the mug and it clicked against his teeth. Hoping she missed that, he nodded inside. "As I said, you're welcome to use it. The kitchen phone."

Sasha shut the lid on the tiny mechanism, slid it into the front left pocket of her jeans and reached for the wide-toothed comb on the decrepit picnic table. "You know I can't do that."

Just what he needed, he thought as she lifted her arm to run the comb through her hair. He turned away from the sight of her breasts lifting and the dawn reflecting in her glistening hair. "I don't know anything of the kind. I'm the guy left dangling out in the dark, remember?"

"Well, I can't, or won't. Take your pick."

"And you don't much care which I do." Gray took a longer, more sustaining sip of his coffee. "I'll bet men underestimate you all the time."

"It's my favorite wet dream." She nodded toward the police station. "What time does your friend show up?"

Gray shot her a droll look, but let that one pass. "When he decides to leave whomever he's bedded down with at the moment, and my bet is that's Gerri Rose Pike, considering her husband was probably tied up most of the night." At her questioning glance he explained. "Tim Pike. You might remember us mentioning him. He almost single-handedly runs the volunteer fire department."

"The one with the thing for horns and sirens."

"When he's not at the station, he's the manager at the convenience store. A hardworking, dedicated guy, but away from home a lot...and there's just no genteel way to say this, but Miss Gerri isn't a stay-at-home kind of gal."

"It sounds as though you have a regular little Peyton Place going on around here."

Gray shrugged. "What else is there to do?" He glanced around. "Sonora or El Dorado would need a major oil find, or we'd have to reinvent Microsoft to lure Fortune 500–type investors out this way. Add to that we're in a pretty bad dry spell. Ranchers tell of having to use cattle prods to get the bulls to show any interest in the cows."

"Sounds as though your old friend Elias should have that problem."

"Ex-friend, if you don't mind. I have my share of shortcomings, I don't need any of his via association."

"Fair enough. What time do you open the clinic?"

"When I feel like it."

He felt her gaze linger on him, but was relieved when she didn't verbalize the obvious questions. He'd about worn down the latest, hopefully last do-gooders on his case suggesting that he talk to ministers and doctors to get himself out of his...whatever it was he was in. He rejected calling it depression, though others did. He wasn't depressed, he was *done*. Finished. His body just hadn't gotten the message yet. Besides, she had no right to ask questions when she answered so few herself.

All she said was, "That hangover must be worse than I guessed."

Gray rubbed his several-day-old beard that increasingly had more silver than brown in it. He knew exactly how it added to his overall look of neglect. "I'll live. Your cheek looks better than I expected. How's the side? You shouldn't have gotten that wound wet."

"I didn't. I took a sponge bath. Washed my hair out here with the hose. By the way, when I changed the bandages, I noticed your ointment seems to be working."

"Watch out, that came dangerously close to sounding like gratitude."

"It was." She tilted her head as she studied him. "It rattled you to find that I was already up. Or did you think I'd left? You're a strange man, Slaughter. On the one hand, you're not happy that I'm here, on the other you insist I stay. You can't have it both ways, you know."

When had he become so transparent—and illogical? Scowling, he asked, "Why didn't you make another run for it?"

"Maybe I believed you."

Nothing was that simple, especially not with this woman, and that made him uneasy even as he experienced another of those odd little rushes. Nuts, he fumed silently.

"Well, you make good coffee, I'll give you that. Are you as talented with a skillet?"

"That sounds suspiciously like the fee for room and board."

"You have to eat, too."

"What would you do if I wasn't here?"

"Go down to the café. We can do that if you like, but I figured you wouldn't want to attract attention." The sudden consternation in those dark eyes told him he'd guessed right.

"I'm only surprised you have anything edible in there."

"Good point. Could be I don't." In all honesty, he couldn't remember the last time he had looked.

"You do. I checked."

Wondering what else she'd looked into, he murmured, "Do the best you can, and I'll track down J.M., then catch a shower."

"Who's J.M.?"

"Jules Malachi Moffett. Your legal counsel."

"You were serious about that? Why can't you walk over to the station with me when Elias does show up, and serve as my witness? Surely he's not going to cop an attitude or try anything after what he pulled last night?"

"And what if he's already run a check on Anna Diaz?"

Sasha shook her head. "Trust me, he hasn't. For some reason he put it off. Otherwise he would have been pounding on your front door hours ago. Maybe the computers were down. It happens."

"So we need somebody to keep his mind off trying again. Someone to press home the point of how much trouble he could get into over his behavior. J.M. is the best BS artist I know."

"He is?"

Her hopeful expression had an irritating effect on his conscience. "No. The truth is he's the only attorney for miles."

"What an endorsement. Any other good news you'd like to share with me?"

"Yeah." Gray figured he might as well get it all

out at once. "He may prove to be my second mistake in less than twelve hours. But there's one thing about him that should make him useful to you." Starting back toward the kitchen, he said over his shoulder, "Gerri Rose is his niece, meaning he's as fond of Frank as I am."

11

J.M. entered Gray's kitchen without knocking or any other greeting. He looked about as cheerful as a mercenary pulled away from his war for a financier's kid's bar mitzvah. Dressed as a world-weary soldier—the TV variety—his khaki shirt had enough pockets to qualify as luggage, a bushman's hat swallowed his small head and his camouflage pants were baggy enough for double occupancy. Sasha hoped against hope that he was a long-lost in-law or a lost tourist, but it was his baby-blue terry-cloth slides that left her unable to voice the guess for fear of the answer.

When J.M. noticed her staring at his feet, he made a face and said simply, "Bunions."

He went straight for the coffeemaker and poured himself a mug of the brew. Returning to the table, he stretched to eye the egg-sausage potato hash Sasha had barely touched. He flipped up cheap plastic sun shields to expose fashionable wire-framed glasses beneath.

"Are you done with that?"

"If you'd like some, I could—"

He dragged her plate to his side of the table and sat down.

"Or better yet, help yourself." Sasha wouldn't have minded making him something, but it seemed communal pot feasting didn't turn him off.

"Any more toast?" he asked just before scooping a forkful into his mouth.

Mesmerized by the odd-looking little man who didn't appear to be any fonder of shaving than Gray was, Sasha rose and popped two more slices of wheat bread into the toaster. He was even using *her* fork, she thought in disbelief.

Behind her, Gray drawled, "You'd better take off that hat, or you might end up swallowing the chin strap, too."

"Still too bright in here."

That had Gray rising and closing the door. After pulling down the miniblinds on the window, he repeated the process for the blind over the sink. It cast the room into a gloomy dusk, but J.M. did brush the hat off his head, letting it dangle off of his shoulders by its rawhide straps. The move exposed silver hair cut in a burr.

"Five minutes," J.M. mumbled between mouthfuls. "If you'd called five minutes later, I'd have been on my way down to the coast."

"Planning on driving straight in this time?"

J.M. gave Sasha a pained look. "The curse of living your whole life in one small community. Everyone's a narrator of your life. No," he added to Gray. "My ex's ex invited me to go deep-sea fishing with him on his yacht."

"Then maybe you should thank me, since it was undoubtedly a setup. Isn't he living on it now that Cleo has taken a healthy chunk out of his assets? He probably blames you for not warning him what he was in for."

J.M.'s growl sounded more like a settling house. "Who warned *me?* What the hell, though. With this hangover, I wouldn't have made it past San Antonio anyway."

Sasha shot Gray a sidelong look. "Your mentor?"

He ran his tongue inside his cheek for a moment before directing his attention to J.M. "This is—"

"Anna Diaz from Louisiana," she interjected, offering her hand to the lawyer.

She waged a staring match with Gray, until J.M. clasped the tips of her fingers.

"Charmed." The attorney then reached for his coffee. After observing the silent interplay going on, he drawled, "When somebody figures out what somebody wants from me, would somebody kindly fill me in?"

"Frank got rough last night," Gray began before she could. "You heard about the fire?"

"You know Tim and those sirens. The only thing louder was the cussing from those he woke, including my neighbor's thirty-pound theory of a kitty. Now, *there's* my idea of shark bait. Did I tell you—''

''Another time, J.M. I need you to stick with me on this.'' Gray leaned forward, resting his forearms on the table. ''*Anna* here had the misfortune of stopping to rescue an injured dog about the same time in relatively the same place as the church. Naturally, as the only stranger passing through town, she's Frank's prime arson suspect.''

J.M. stared at Sasha. Bloodshot, brown eyes, as probing as they were sad, held her gaze as his Cupid's-bow mouth made a delicate O.

''Why would he think a lovely creature like you would want to burn down our only house of worship? I myself have attended at least eight weddings there, including three of my own.''

The insanity of this whole situation had Sasha helpless to do anything but try to find her role as they went along. ''It sounds like a lovely place. I'm sorry for the loss.''

He shrugged. ''Four walls and a bunch of pews...it could sub as a courtroom for all the spiritual ambience it has. Then again, being an agnostic, what do I know? Define 'rough.' For instance, did Frank do that to your cheek?''

Sasha couldn't decide if he was the fool that he pretended to be, or if he entertained himself by taking the long route to every point. ''Yes, but you won't get him to admit it. He'll only say I resisted arrest, or worse, led him on. Dr. Slaughter was already fed that line.''

J.M. nodded, his doleful expression adding bags to a face a cartoonist would need extra pens to depict. ''Yes, that sounds like Frank's style. On behalf of my sex, I apologize.''

Sasha leaned forward to impress her need. ''I'm not out to cause trouble for him. I want to make my statement and be on my way.''

Gray stared at her. ''What are you doing?''

She understood. He didn't fathom how she could underplay what had happened. What he needed to comprehend was that, while his agenda was to put Frank in his place once and for all, it wasn't hers. She had neither the time nor the energy to take on all of the Franks in the world.

''If I hadn't intervened when I did,'' he said, enunciating each word, ''he would have raped you.''

Despite having spent many an hour with lawyers going over crimes and witness testimony, some that had left her almost physically ill, she found Gray's declaration uncomfortable and embarrassing. ''It wouldn't have gotten that far. I would have stopped him.''

He and J.M. exchanged speaking glances.

''She could be tougher than she looks,'' J.M. offered.

''Trust me, she is. But when has Frank ever played fair?''

"Don't remind me. It's bad enough that I'm aware of his liaison with Gerri Rose, do you know I saw his patrol car parked at Widow Greene's house on Tuesday morning?" He mouthed *four hours* and held up fingers spread in a W before popping the last piece of toast into his mouth. Once he swallowed, he leaned back in his chair to consider Gray, and suddenly a gleam entered his eyes. "What about you, *Dr. Slaughter?* Where do you fit into this unpleasant situation—aside from being the rescuer of the lovely Ms. Diaz? What were you doing visiting Frank at that hour anyway? The man would as soon piss on—"

"Easy," Gray warned.

"I was merely going to point out that your presence at the station was unnatural. In fact, I can't remember the last time you were there."

Although his face took on that stone-mask expression again, indicating he knew what J.M. was driving at, Gray remained cool. "Anna's dog, remember? I was done treating her and wanted to settle the bill. That's when I walked in on what I did."

"Resulting in you slugging him."

"If he's sporting any bruises this morning, they're not from me. Not that I wasn't tempted. In fact, the only way to get Anna away from Frank was to give him my word that she'd report back there this morning."

"That I can believe. And so she spent the night with you? Here?"

Ignoring the unsubtle innuendo, Gray continued. "He says he wants a written statement of everything she did, and everything she saw last night."

J.M. refocused on Sasha. "Tell me."

She did, and when she was done, he nodded agreeably.

"That sounds cut-and-dried enough. But back to you turning this mausoleum into Motel Six," he said to Gray.

"Get over it."

"Would that I could, but it's too fascinating. In fact, I'm becoming increasingly grateful that you caught me, old son. Imagine you actually noticing what's going on beyond your personal little wallow, and taking in a total stranger, no less." To Sasha he said, "No offense, my dear. It's just that Gray here happens to be our resident hermit, and—"

"Goddamn it, J.M., you see what he did to her, you heard what I said. Stick with the issue," Gray snapped.

"We could, my boy, but I promise you that Frank isn't, and won't. He's undoubtedly burned brain cells he can't spare wondering what roused you out of your self-designed coma to chivalrously come to Ms. Diaz's aid. And I guarantee you, the conclusions he's jumping to lack more than good taste. As your attorney, I'd be derelict in my duty if I didn't run them past you myself so you'll be prepared.''

Gray set his mug on the table with such force, some of the remaining liquid spilled out onto the table. Swearing, he immediately mopped up the mess with his napkin. ''If you'd been me walking into that scene last night, you couldn't have turned your back pretending nothing was happening.''

''Hopefully not, considering that my favorite fantasy is shooting the bastard myself. The indelicate point you're forcing me to make is that I'm aware *neither* of you is being totally straight with me.'' J.M. beamed at Sasha and tapped the side of his nose. ''Professional instinct.''

There was no doubt that Jules Moffett would not be her first, second or fifth choice as legal representation if she'd had other options, but since that wasn't possible, Sasha saw it was up to her to salvage things and try to make the best of an increasingly bad situation.

''I'm sorry, Mr. Moffett, I don't mean to be uncooperative, let alone rude, but the only thing you need to know is that I didn't have anything to do with what happened at the church, and that it's imperative I be allowed to leave.''

''If it's a matter of a critical appointment, jury duty or an ill relative...perhaps you'd elaborate?'' he coaxed. ''That would give us particularly strong leverage.''

''It's nothing that simple.''

"Practically everything else carries a penalty of twenty to life."

Silent, Sasha sat there and matched him stare for stare.

Finally, the attorney set his elbows on the table and rested folded hands against his lips. "Grayson, after all these years of friendship, have you put me in a position where I could lose my license to practice law?"

"I thought you can't be an accomplice to something you don't know about?" Gray replied.

"A review board is as likely to believe that as much as I believe I'll be chief counsel for the next president." J.M. turned back to Sasha. "Let me explain why I have to know what's really behind all of this. Going about things as you are, you might as well be asking a blind man to paint the Golden Gate Bridge."

"If he has a law degree send him over," Gray muttered.

Unperturbed, J.M. continued, "Surely you know that, as your attorney, anything you say to me is strictly confidential?"

Sasha could only shake her head.

"What if I say pretty please, pass Go and don't take the two hundred dollars?"

"Can I get you another coffee?"

J.M. slid his hands under his glasses and, rubbing his eyes, laughed. "My God. I don't know whether to be flattered or offended." Sighing, he tried again. "Something. Give me a clue as to my parameters, at least. What do I definitely stay away from? Anything. Otherwise—and I'm being serious here—Frank, for all of his weaknesses and incompetence, could, with a bit of luck, stumble upon yours."

Sasha understood. She'd worried half the night about much the same thing. "I can only warn you that I can't still be in Bitters when Chief Elias runs a check on the name I'll sign on that statement," she replied.

J.M. grimaced. "I was afraid you'd say something like that. All right, I'll bite. What happens if he does?"

"Then arresting me won't matter because I'll be as good as dead anyway. Unfortunately, in the process, innocent people could get hurt, some maybe even here."

Slack-jawed, J.M. followed her gaze to Gray. "Did you know that?"

Gray slowly nodded in the affirmative.

"Then why the hell didn't you put her in her vehicle and wave bye-bye? Jesus H...you really do have a death wish. Or—" His eyes narrowed in speculation. "Don't tell me you fell head over heels for the woman?"

"Will lust do?" Gray countered.

J.M. snorted. "That goes without saying."

"Do you two mind?" Having heard enough,

Sasha rose before she fed a plate to one of them and branded the other with the skillet.

"It's about Frank," Gray continued, suddenly serious again. "Keep it focused on Frank. He's screwed with enough lives. You know that, *him*, as well as I do."

J.M. grunted in agreement.

"Just get her out of there free to leave."

Despite her offer, J.M. rose with his mug and refilled it himself. Sasha wondered what was next. Of course, if he turned them down, she had only one option—to take her chances. What she needed to know is would Gray try to stop her this time?

"You're lucky," J.M. said, turning to her, "that I'm a ham at heart and a gambler in my soul. Ms. Anna Diaz of Louisiana—" he stretched out his hand again "—you have yourself an attorney."

12

It was well past eight before the trio emerged from Gray's house, having waited until Frank's patrol car pulled in at the front of the station. Although J.M. had warmed to his challenge and appeared increasingly pumped, Sasha and Gray grew quieter with each exchange, to where they now even avoided eye contact and only addressed J.M.

After a few yards, Gray angled off to the clinic. The one thing they'd unanimously agreed upon was that his presence would only add to Frank's defensiveness.

"Good luck," he said to them.

J.M. gave him a thumbs-up sign. "When the going gets tough..."

Sasha kept walking, believing silence a good balance to the cliché, cheerleader reply. Besides, she wasn't sold on her counsel. She tried to moderate her skepticism, dismiss it as fatigue on top of a strong sense of persecution, something the chatty little man's nonstop interrogation while Gray showered didn't help. But while she appreciated how critical it was for an attorney to be factual, she was, nonetheless, unconvinced how details about where Elias had touched, how hard he'd groped and if she was bruised, mattered. Their dialogue had turned into its own wrestling match. In the end, J.M. bemoaned going into battle handicapped, and she fretted over his learning it was much worse than that: the gulf between cop and attorney. What was he likely to do with *that* information? Most of all, though, she dreaded releasing the more vengeful side of Frank Elias. He wasn't a unique species and she'd met his kind before.

"Chin up. Everything will be fine." J.M. walked in full-length strides, his hands fisted and swinging at his sides, the picture of a man on a mission. "Frank's big on intimidation, but he's never been a student of the law. Hell, I'm not sure he could recite the Miranda to you without pulling out his little card."

Sasha ended up fisting her hands, as well. "The idea is not to get ourselves in the position of finding out."

"Sure. Of course. But what I mean is, I doubt he even knows what grounds he has for keeping you here. In fact, I bet as soon as he sees us walk in together and realizes Gray wasn't bluffing, he'll back down faster than my niece's snotty Chihuahua when he comes face-to-face with their neighbors' rottweiler."

Sasha doubted it. However, all she said in response was, "So it's not only cats you dislike? I'm rather surprised that you and Dr. Slaughter are such good friends."

"Ha! Show me a vet and I'll show you somebody scarred and lying if he says he loves *all* creatures great and small. That's what I like about Gray—we agree that the only good snake is tattooed on a sailor's arm, and that kids who befriend rodents need psychotherapy."

As certain as she was that he was toying with her, Sasha couldn't help glancing back at the clinic, wondering about the pup she'd brought in last night. But there was nothing she could do for her at the moment.

With energy belying his years, and his previous condition, J.M. bounded forward to reach the front door first, and with a sweeping gesture beckoned Sasha inside. The overhead lights hadn't been turned on, and it took her a moment to adjust to the dimness. When she did, she noticed that Frank was once again alone in the station.

He stood at the far side of the room by the coffee machine, and when he spotted J.M. he broke into a snickering laugh. "Who the hell are you supposed to be, Rambo in his granny's slippers?"

Straightening himself to his full height, which left him, nonetheless, at a disadvantage to Sasha, J.M. replied, "Have your fun, but you're on notice, my boy. Unlike Ms. Diaz, I happen to know your approach to law matches your approach to life, and I'm here to make sure the 'if it feels good do it' approach doesn't come into practice today. At least nowhere near my client.

"As for my attire, I happened to be on my way out of town when Ms. Diaz called me. Once I heard what she had to say, I knew it would be an insult to make her wait until I changed."

It took a conscious effort for Sasha to keep herself from shrinking back toward the door. Dear God, she thought, he was performing as though he was on "Court TV."

Frank wasn't impressed with the posturing either. "On your way out of town, my ass. Where to, Senior Citizens' Commando School?"

But he laughed a little too hard at his own joke and, although he looked presentable—freshly showered and shaved—his unsteady gait warned that he wasn't in much better shape than the two other men Sasha had been in the company of so far this morning. That left her wondering...was Bitters more aptly named than she knew, some page out of a horror novel, a last karmic port of call for lost souls and assorted losers?

"Hilarious, Frank." J.M. led the way to the chief's desk. "You're as good a comic as you are a cop."

Elias strolled to his chair and casually lowered himself into it, leaving Sasha and J.M. standing. "That's a strange remark when you're hoping for my cooperation, slick."

Seemingly unfazed by the hostile volley, J.M.

made a ceremony of holding out a chair for Sasha. He settled into the one on her left. "By all means, keep score, Frank. But that begs the question, how many demerits have you given yourself for the injury to Ms. Diaz?"

"First of all, if you're calling that an injury, I'm gonna arrest you the next time I see you behind the wheel for driving without proper corrective lenses. Second, if she says she hurt herself in any way other than slipping, she's lying."

"And I'm strongly advising my client to proceed to the hospital in Sonora after we finish here. I think it would be in her best interest to be photographed and thoroughly checked out by a doctor."

This was news to Sasha, but she kept her peace, interested in how Elias would take that blatant salvo.

He only drawled, "I'm shaking in terror."

His demeanor less cheery, J.M. leaned forward. "So much so that it caused you to forget your manners? You didn't invite us to sit down. You should at least offer Ms. Diaz a cup of coffee."

The cop slid his gaze to Sasha. "Help yourself."

It was on the tip of her tongue to ask when was the last time the place was inspected by the board of health. But after the trouble such remarks had earned her last night, she would staple her lips shut before she risked saying anything that would create additional animosity. "No. Thank you," she forced herself to add.

Casting J.M. a "You see?" look, Elias drawled, "Now that we have the pleasantries out of the way, what are you angling for?"

"What should have occurred last night instead of you detaining my client. Under the flimsiest of circumstances, I might add."

"As I told her, she was close enough to that church to have seen something. But what does she try to sell me? Some story about a white pickup truck. How lame is that?"

"If that's what she saw, then that's all she can attest to. You can't punish a witness for the information she provides just because it doesn't lead straight to a quick, clean arrest for you."

Elias stroked the inside handle of the mug as though it was a trigger. "Now who's twisting things around? By her own admission she was up there. What's more, she had time to torch the building and get back here before Pike came outside and spotted the suspicious discoloration in the sky."

"Wait one damn minute." Facade or not, J.M.'s cheer vanished faster than cash spilling from an armored security truck. "This is supposed to be about making a witness statement. Are you now saying you're set to accuse her of arson, because if you are, I demand you make the charge clearly, here and now, and declare the evidence in your possession."

"Nope."

J.M. leaped to his feet. "This is absurd. It's an outrage."

"Do you mind? You're spitting on my desk." Elias moved a single file to the opposite corner of the otherwise empty desk.

Red-faced, J.M. sat back down. "How would you like a visit with some real cops? I *do* still know people in Austin."

"Anyone who'll return your call before happy hour?"

Sasha closed her eyes. She hadn't believed things could get worse, but J.M. was managing. The mention of bringing in additional law enforcement personnel alone almost had her breaking into a sweat. Of course, he couldn't know how that move would ricochet back and hurt her, but what a bitter irony that he was creating the very situation he'd warned Elias might.

"I understand you've had a good deal of illegal alien traffic," she said, hoping to redirect J.M.'s so-called strategy. She was concerned about the excitable man's coloring as well, suspecting that he suffered from high blood pressure. All she needed was for him to have a stroke or heart attack. With her luck, Elias would try to pin that on her, too. "I was also informed that the residents of Bitters are less than welcoming."

"If your fences were repeatedly cut, your property vandalized, your animals—including pets—stolen for food or butchered out of spite or for intimidation, you wouldn't lay out any welcome mat, either." The skin across Elias's cheekbones tightened and anger obliterated the laughter in his eyes. "Of course, I don't expect someone named *Diaz* to acknowledge there even is a problem. For all I know, a load of wetbacks is why you're in town in the first place. I wonder what we'd find if we looked inside that van of yours."

The accusation made her grateful that she'd followed her instincts last night and brought her things into Gray's guest room. At the same time, she dealt with the repeated blow that Anna's name wasn't proving the safety shield she'd hoped.

J.M. bought her time by declaring his outrage. "Do you have any idea what a prejudicial statement you've just made? Such reckless outbursts from someone wearing a badge is unconscionable."

"Sue me. Better yet, save yourself the money and hold a town meeting and just see how many folks agree with me."

Drawing a slow breath, J.M. brought his hands together until the fingertips were touching. "Let's keep this focused," he said as though calming himself first and foremost. "You have, at best, a nominal witness to an alleged arson"

"The goddamn brush didn't walk to the steps on its own!"

"—who you're denying the right to make her

statement,'' J.M. concluded in the full righteousness of a Baptist preacher.

"*You* call her a witness. I'm not sure what I'd call her yet."

"Because you're trying to cover up your assault—"

"Watch it, J.M."

"Then explain what happened, Frank."

The younger man pointed into J.M.'s face. "You don't talk to me that way. I am the chief of police."

"Would that have exempted you from using a condom?"

"You son of a bitch." Elias lunged forward, sending J.M. scooting his chair back in sheer terror. Checking himself, he cursed again and flicked spilled coffee off his fingers. "Have you taken a look at the church?" he demanded.

"No." J.M. shifted back into place, but everything about him remained cautious.

"There'll be no services on Sunday or any Sunday in the near future, and the people who worshiped there deserve to know who did this to them and why."

"I couldn't agree with you more," J.M. replied, "but what does that have to do with Ms. Diaz? Her only crime is being on the wrong road at the wrong time…a fact, I might add, she made no attempt to hide."

"Clever, don't you think? Admitting to being at the scene of the crime. A perfect contradiction to the theory that the guilty never confess they've done anything wrong?''

''Brilliant. And along the way she also sees the value of running over a dog, never mind the danger that also presented to her own person, and then again risks injury to herself to rescue and carry the poor beast to the clinic. You're right, Frank. This woman isn't just clever, she's diabolical. Lock her up immediately.''

Elias chuckled. ''Can I get that in writing?''

''Oh, for...'' J.M. pushed his hat back off his forehead, now beaded with perspiration. ''What you need is some kid to steal another tractor and get it stuck in a muddy stock pond. That's about the limit to your sleuthing ability. Now, Ms. Diaz is still willing to give you that written statement you think you have to have. Let her do that, and we'll be on our way.''

''And if I say no?''

It was all Sasha could do not to get up, walk out and head straight for her van. She must have made some involuntary movement, because she glimpsed J.M.'s hand beneath the edge of Elias's desk motioning for her to be still.

''You'd better elaborate,'' J.M. said.

''How about that I haven't even done the simplest file search on her yet?'' He shifted his gaze to Sasha and his grin grew more challenging. ''You have your ID on you?''

''I'm afraid not.'' She had intentionally left her purse behind for exactly this reason.

"When you get a minute, bring it over."

The knot in her stomach was expanding by the minute and threatening to burst through her diaphragm. Afraid it showed, she let more of her revulsion show. "Now who's being clever? Are you so afraid I'll file charges against you that you want to know how to find me in case I succeed in costing you your job?"

Looking neither guilty nor worried, Elias countered, "I'm not going to lose my job. And you forget, I don't have to wait for your license. I can run a check on your van plates."

"Do it." Her bravado was risky, but chances were the data on the sale wasn't in the computer yet. At least she hoped the used-car salesman she'd dealt with was as inefficient about filing the information as some she'd known back in Vegas.

J.M. stood and balanced his weight by his fingertips on Frank's desk. "This is getting embarrassing, Frank, although it's increasingly clear you don't recognize that. Don't force me to humiliate you completely."

"Yeah, you're doing such a good job impressing your client so far, she's defending her own rights better than you are."

J.M. smiled grimly. "I'm aware you think I'm pathetic. But do you know why that amuses me? Because we're really so much alike. The only difference is that I know who I am and admit it. You, on the other hand, think you've got this town and everyone in it by the balls. But you're wrong. Harass this young woman,'' he continued, nodding to Sasha, ''and I promise you that I will have the last word.''

''That's quite a threat for a drunk headed for the financial sewer.''

''Oh, I wouldn't take hearsay as gospel,'' J.M. replied. ''My pockets are a little deeper than my niece fears. What she should be worrying about is if she's still in my will at all.''

''I can't wait to share that threat with her.''

''Maybe she needs to hear about what happened to Ms. Diaz, as well. You've been testing good Baptist tolerance long enough, Frank. We may tend to be hypocrites here in Bitters, but never doubt that we are expert at being righteous ones apt to rise up for the most self-serving reasons.''

Frank's narrow-eyed gaze drilled into him. ''What's between me and Gerri Rose is none of your business.''

''If we were drinking buddies, and you were half as good at your job as you think you are, and I didn't feel so goddamn sorry for Pike, I might agree with you,'' J.M. countered. ''As it is, I'm thinking Gerri Rose might be compelled to worry about her health, if not her reputation, if she knew where you gutter around when she's not available.''

''You know what she'll tell you?'' Elias sneered. ''Anytime she gets with me is better than whatever *Timmy* can offer.''

''Spoken like a teenager in a pissing contest. It

would serve you better to think where you'll go if you're sent packing from here. The only place that will have you will be another three-cop town. And how long will you hang on there before they realize their mistake? You won't have your family's history to fall back on as you do here. No one will cut you slack because they remember your parents with fondness.''

Red-faced, this time Frank didn't check himself. Seeing what he intended, Sasha and J.M. ducked as he sent the mug of coffee sailing across the room.

The projectile shattered against the door marked Rest Room, and as coffee streamed down the beige wall, Frank snarled, ''That's enough. You want a lesson in threatening, old man?'' Frank hitched his chin toward Sasha. ''Make your statement, and you can do what you want...in the area.'' He smirked at her disbelieving stare. ''Yes, in town, until the investigator from the insurance company does his bit. He's supposedly on his way. So you see? If you'd quit riding my ass, you could be out of here this afternoon.''

''At which time you'll think of another reason to delay me,'' she muttered.

His irreverent grin returned as he passed a pad and pen over to her. ''That's always a possibility. And remember...I still want to see your license.''

13

When Sasha left the police station less than five minutes later, she bruised the palm of her hand hitting the bar across the glass door. Whatever doubts she'd had about this morning, the results were ten times worse. Furious and more frustrated than ever, she couldn't wait to be out of earshot of the station.

"It could have gone a lot worse," J.M. said, his subdued manner suggesting otherwise.

She jerked to a stop. "Excuse me? Want to share your idea of how?"

"Legally, he has the right to hold you for forty-eight hours. I didn't want to say anything earlier so as not to worry you."

Sasha knew that, but he would have needed more substantial evidence. By the time the insurance investigator was through, he would probably have it. Damn, she thought, she'd expected the assault to work in her favor and cancel that concern. Only J.M. had let that offense vanish from the table like morning dew on summer grass.

"The man was practically doing a 'I'm the king

of the world' dance as we left. He's probably ripping up my statement this very second.''

"He won't go that far," J.M. assured her.

"Excuse my lack of gratitude, but thanks to you, I'm in more trouble than ever."

J.M. grimaced. "Maybe the banter did sound as though it got out of hand at times, but really—"

Sasha pointed toward Gray's house. "Did anything I said earlier stick with you?"

"It's the license you're worried about," J.M. replied. "I understand. But take it from me, Frank isn't a dishonest cop. He doesn't have ambition or the guts. He's lazy, Anna."

As far as Sasha was concerned, J.M. should be barred from making any further character assumptions. His liquid indulgences had corrupted his ability to read human nature on any consistent level. "If he is, that dressing-down you gave him just cured him, at least where I'm concerned. So unless the new space station decides to drop on Bitters or someone strolls down Main Street with a written confession—and I think the odds are dead even on that—he's going to press me for that ID. And you know what, J.M.? That's not the worst of it." She rubbed at her forehead. "The goal was for you to make sure I'd be *free* right now, free to get the hell out of here."

"I'm sorry. It was his indifference to Gerri Rose knowing about him that threw me," J.M. admitted, bowing his head. "As much as I disliked the idea,

I thought he cared about her. She's so much younger than the other women he's shown interest in. I thought he would protect the relationship. Her. But I can see now, it's all about his ego. She's just another score to him.''

Denial. Sasha had seen it too often in her several years as a cop, and it never got easier to witness. ''I didn't have to spend more than five minutes in Frank Elias's presence before I recognized that he's the lowest grade of alley cat. Snap out of it, J.M.''

As she turned to leave, he touched her arm, his expression sheepish. ''I'll go see Ike—the insurance agent,'' he explained. ''He should know more about this inspector who's coming, or at least some specifics on the schedule. Maybe...''

Sasha stopped listening. What she saw over his shoulder made his familial problems nothing compared to hers. In fact, all of her surroundings ceased to exist as she spotted the Chevy Suburban at the far end of town heading toward her like a big, black dust-covered scorpion.

14

"That...that sounds like a good idea," Sasha told J.M. She started backing away.

"Wait a second." J.M. began to follow her. "I'd really like to hear your other perceptions on Frank. His contract comes up soon."

She had no time to reply. Sasha spun around, heading for the clinic as fast as she could without breaking into an all-out run. Running would attract too much attention, and the Suburban was getting closer, close enough that there was no mistaking it was the one she'd hoped never to see again.

"You're right again," J.M. called after her. "Listen, I want you to know, I'm doing your case *pro bono*. Tell Gray, okay?"

His fee was the least of Sasha's worries. Grabbing at the front door, she yanked it open, rushed inside and immediately pressed herself against the cooler inside wall.

She shut her eyes, wholly transfixed on sound, but all she heard was the blood pounding in her ears. *Stop it,* she willed. She had to be able to hear.

Less than a half minute later, the Suburban was

directly in front of the clinic, and to her it sounded as loud as a tank. Were they slowing? Stopping? Her van in the back…they must have spotted it. Heaven help her, she didn't have her gun, nothing with which to defend herself.

"That cinder block withstood a small tornado. You don't have to help hold it up."

Opening her eyes, Sasha saw Gray at the opposite end of the room by the hallway. For once his imposing presence provided relief as she realized that, if he was facing the two large windows and didn't appear to be noticing anything out of the ordinary, the Suburban must have continued on by. It was only then that she also realized there was no one else in the reception area. In fact, it was so quiet there didn't seem to be anyone in the building at all.

"Tornado…" Hearing how thin her voice sounded, she cleared her throat. "That's stretching things, don't you think?"

"The National Weather Service agrees with you. Therefore, the insurance company refused to pay, much to old Manny Gutierrez's disappointment."

Sasha both envied and resented his calm, but she tried to match it hoping to keep Gray's focus off of why she'd behaved so oddly. "And he was…?"

"A handyman at one of the spreads around here. He'd hoped to use the storm as an excuse for driving through that plate-glass window on your right."

He nodded as though wanting her to take a look. She did, although she experienced a sudden kinship with a mouse being toyed with by a big cat. At least looking gave her the opportunity to see there was no vehicle out there.

"He said the wind literally picked his foot off the brake pedal and pushed it onto the accelerator, shooting him straight inside," Gray continued. "Of course, Manny was also legally blind, but too proud to wear glasses."

"Not an uncommon dilemma with the elderly."

"That's what I've heard." Without missing a beat, he added, "You okay?"

"I'd feel better if it was twenty degrees cooler."

"Actually, I'm thinking you look a little... hounded."

"I suspect that's the standard reaction for anyone who's spent time around Elias."

Grunting an affirmative, Gray's gaze shifted to the windows again, first the one on the right this time, then the one on the left. "Speaking of, where's J.M.?"

"Gone to talk to someone named Ike. The insurance guy."

"Ike Jarrett. Why?"

She wasn't sure she could explain the disaster that had happened next door. "It appears that the insurance company is sending an inspector to look at the church. J.M. is trying to appease me by finding out when."

"It didn't go well." Gray's intent study reflected more understanding. "No wonder you look like what breakfast you did eat isn't agreeing with you."

"For the record, your old friend may be a sweet guy, and a terrific drinking companion, but on a professional level, I'd have been better off if you'd missed him this morning." Taking a chance, Sasha stepped away from the wall in order to pretend to inspect her surroundings, and risked another glance outside. The empty street had her drawing a deep breath in relief.

"You're not free to go?"

She exhaled. "In no way, shape or form. I'm to stay put while Elias hopes for the insurance guy to find something to further incriminate me."

"Of all the hare-brained…" Gray butted his fist against the doorjamb. "You weren't allowed to make your statement?"

"Sure. But by the time he let me, the gesture was equivalent to a pat on the fanny."

"What about Anna Diaz's license?"

"He wants it. What he wants more is for me to *bring* it to him. What I can't believe is that he hasn't run the van plates through the system yet. Don't think I'm not appreciative, but the guy's a gift to the criminal world."

"Can't argue with you there. He graduated second from the bottom in his class. Fortunately, crime in Bitters amounts to someone writing one too many hot checks, or some kind of domestic dispute. He's been lucky that when he does botch something, it only affects one or two people, so most folks don't pay attention.''

''Well, I suspect he'll be more energetic about turning up the heat under me if only to pay me back for bringing J.M. into the picture.''

''Sorry about that. I thought he would help.''

''In that outfit?''

''Believe it or not, he used to be one of the best. Highly respected in the state.'' Crossing his arms over his chest, Gray offered a one-shoulder shrug. ''His downfall was his attraction to women who liked his status and money more than him.''

''And for that he's self-destructing through booze?''

''There's also the matter of a few cases that didn't turn out well, winning when it would have been better to lose and losing one that cost an innocent man almost ten years of his life. That's why he prefers not to take life too seriously.''

Sasha matched his stance. ''Oh, I don't think it's life he has the problem with. I think it's himself.''

''You are tough, lady.'' Gray sighed. ''I take it he brought up Gerri Rose?''

''I got the impression you wanted him to.''

This time Gray shook his head. ''His presence should have been enough to make Frank think about it. I never intended for J.M. to use up his ammunition early, let alone misfire.''

"Wish you had made that clearer. The man *is* looking at life through veils, and he didn't merely misfire, he shot the whole caisson at once, then grew reckless, hoping bravado could cover his blunder."

Remembering the worst moments of that fiasco did bad things to her blood pressure, and the negative atmosphere of Gray's clinic offered no relief. Hardly a student of feng shui, she thought, glancing around at the four mismatched chairs, each uglier or more damaged than the next. And while she thought the color gray had its place, the marble-design linoleum added to the dullness. What's more, the metal display case of pet supplies needed restocking, and the magazine rack contained a spare *three* mangled copies of who knew what. Sasha wondered if children or pets had committed the vandalism. At the same time, she found all this informative since the atmosphere exuded wasn't unlike his house—barren, neglected and unwelcoming. No, she had no reason to expect him to understand her reaction to J.M. when he was in a state of denial all his own.

"How long do you think I can hold him off?" she asked, hoping it was the one question he could answer.

"Frank? You're the cop."

"While he acts like he got his training off of TV. So since you've known him for some time, give me your best guesstimate."

Whether it was the connection or the question that displeased him, the corners of Gray's mouth drooped. "He may keep his distance for a couple of hours, let you think he's forgotten or changed his mind. But whether or not he has a clue about what he would stir up, I can't see that he'll let the matter drop. Not in this case."

"Because of you."

"Yeah. Once he fixates on getting someone..."

"That part I have memorized." Sasha shot a more desperate glance outside.

"Use the phone already. You know you want to."

So badly he couldn't begin to imagine. So badly she couldn't let him see her eyes because she knew they would give away her dread and desperation.

"Who are you looking for out there?"

If she told him, would he continue offering his property as sanctuary, or decide he'd stuck his neck out enough and shove her out the front door? It was one thing to run interference on her behalf against an overconfident good ol' boy. It was entirely another to stand between her and men probably carrying enough firearms to wipe out half this town.

The Surburban made it a moot point for the moment and she offered a self-deprecating shrug. "Caught me. The white pickup, what else? I saw one that looked about right just as I was leaving the station."

The way Gray stood there, she knew he didn't believe her. Had he noticed the Suburban, too? How long had it been driving up and down the road?

"Don't look at me like that," she said, turning back to the window. "Surely you know who around here drives one? Never mind Elias's flip remark, I mean people likely to be on the street at that hour? And don't say service trucks on an emergency call. I would have remembered a logo or name on the door."

"That still leaves plenty of options."

"It wasn't a new model."

"No matter. I told you, we're not Wall Street or 1600 Pennsylvania Avenue. Folks aren't cheering about the economy here. They're having hard times, trying to make their vehicles last."

In other words, because he knew she was lying about the Suburban, he doubted her about the white truck.

"Point taken." Exhaling, she lifted her hair off her nape and pretended to massage out the kinks in her neck. "I guess things are a little quiet for you this morning, but don't let me keep you from taking advantage and catching up with other work."

Gray glanced around the empty room. "You see something I don't?"

He seemed so blasé about it that it momentarily

threw her. "Okay...how's the dog? Does she need another shot or pill or something?"

"She's had her pain pill. You on the other hand could use one of these." He reached into the pocket of his plaid shirt and drew out a small, amber container, which he tossed to her.

"What's this?"

"Antibiotics. It'll be all right. Just let me know if the urge to chase cars grows too strong."

She tried to give them back. "Cute, Slaughter. I think I'll pass."

"You have an open wound and you've been handling a stray dog that you know nothing about. Don't ask for trouble. Take them."

Reluctantly, she pocketed the container.

"I mean ingest. Now."

"Relax, Slaughter. Do you need to watch?"

"If necessary. Does my presence bother you?"

"Reverse that. I'm trying to let you escape. Go do what vets do. You're the guy who's put out because I'm around, remember?"

"Am I?"

Whether deliberate or involuntarily, the intimate reply was as welcome as a bullet coming through the plate-glass window. He was doing this after what Elias had pulled, after denying his own sexuality?

"Did I nod off and miss something?" she asked. "What are you pulling?"

"Verbalizing my doubts about how long you can last out there on your own."

"Then you say that. Unless—" she crossed to him "—you *did* mean what you told J.M." She let her gaze drift over him, absorbing details, like the fact that his plaid shirt brought out a hint of blue in his eyes, that the white background emphasized his sun-bronzed skin and the white scar on his freshly shaved chin. She came so close, if either of them took a deep breath, her breasts would touch his chest.

"What if I did?"

"I'd be suspicious, guessing that maybe you're using me."

A shadowy something darkened his eyes. "To what end?"

"You tell me. You said you and Frank Elias used to be best friends, and now you're not."

"That has nothing to do with you."

"It does if he more than dislikes you, if his feelings are about hate and revenge. Then I think you could see me as your opportunity to drive Frank crazy by making him think about us here... together...alone." She watched the way his eyes lingered on her mouth, yet his stance grew stiffer as he tried not to let any other part of his body betray him. "He's not so hard a read that I couldn't tell he's wondering what we've been up to...and now here we are with so many long, flat surfaces around. What do you want to bet there isn't a coffee mug left intact in his office?''

"You're pretty confident of yourself," he replied, his voice gruff.

"What I am is aware of how powerful a motivator revenge is. So what *do* you want? To play doctor, Doctor?"

Gray didn't deny her accusation, and he didn't back off. On the contrary, he began lowering his head toward hers…and suddenly she knew an unexpected, odd excitement, wholly opposite to the revulsion she'd experienced with Elias. This was a gut-twisting desire to learn what it would be like to have his mouth against hers, to feel his heat merge with and intensify her own. It wasn't just because she'd been denying herself intimacy, sex, for some time; it was this man, the unique chemistry that spawned whenever they were in the same room.

"You must really be scared."

The unexpected response snapped her to attention.

While his warm breath continued to caress her lips, Sasha found his gaze speculative, even troubled. Thankfully, the sudden absence of voices must have panicked the dog back in her cage for she began an anxious whimper that quickly became an urgent barking.

Grateful for the excuse to put some space between them, Sasha murmured, "Excuse me," and brushed past him to hurry down the hall. But at the door to the kennel, she couldn't resist glancing back.

No, it wasn't good that he was standing by the window gazing up and down the street. However, the way he rubbed his mouth and neck eased her humiliation. So, she hadn't been the only one to get caught up in the moment. It wasn't her secrets alone that bothered him.

Good, she thought. Because he had secrets of his own, and he had no right to expect candor from her when he wasn't willing to return it in kind.

The problem was, the longer she stayed, the worse this combustible atmosphere between them was apt to get. And she had to stay, she understood that now, not just because of Elias, but due to that Suburban. As long as it hung around, it wasn't safe to get back on the streets.

15

Las Vegas, Nevada
9:33 a.m. PST

Sirens always made Melor Borodin move fast, and he ducked into the front door of Red Square, his humorously named answer to New York's Russian Tea Room, even though logic dictated that if the law was after him, they wouldn't be announcing themselves. Old habits died hard, though, and only upon hearing the secondary blast that fire trucks use did his insides unclench. By the time he saw Demyan Kopelev coming to greet him in long-legged strides, his pulse resumed its usual, meditation-like 58–60 tempo.

"You are even earlier than I expected. My apologies for not being at the door to meet you," the restaurant's manager said with the subtlest hint of accusation.

Blond, soft-spoken, poetically handsome and seriously homophobic as a result of the kind of attention his looks attracted, Demyan—the Russian

derivative of Damian—had more in common with
Melor than the fourth-century brother he was
named after, who chose martyrdom rather than
abandon his own blood. So much so that Borodin
continuously looked for signs of betrayal, even an
outright coup. The only thing stopping the young
cutthroat so far was his pride in running a smooth,
tightly run and *well-financed* operation. Not interested in starting at the bottom, and lacking Borodin's audacity to reach for what he wanted, to take
risks, Demyan had yet to figure out how to get the
income and devoted personnel, especially here in
a city where territory was more finely delineated
than anything on a road map.

"Success doesn't ease one's schedule, Demyan," he snapped. "It complicates it." In a
sweeping glance of his employee's attire, he took
in the Italian linen shirt, the excellent crease of the
pants, the butter-soft leather of his shoes, even the
manicure, before deciding that while the pretty
prick was spending his income on the best of everything, he wasn't spending more than he earned.
"I have much to attend to this morning," he added
with a fatalistic shrug. "But am I inconveniencing
you, perhaps?"

"Of course not."

Demyan glanced over his boss's shoulder, and
Borodin understood why. While he still used only
one bodyguard, now it was the massive Boba, as
he and Yegor affectionately called Boris.

Looking relieved that Boba lingered back at the door, Demyan added, "What was I doing but supervising the first deliveries."

"You have someone dependable taking your place?"

"Dependable enough not to let that damn laundry service screw us again."

Borodin glanced around the unlit foyer with its walls as red as the canopy outside. The mirrors were freshly cleaned, the carpet vacuumed, the arrangement of calla lilies on the marble-topped sideboard looking as though just arranged. He gestured toward the reservations desk. "Bookings doing well?"

"Very. Revenues continue to increase. Would you care to come to my office and—"

There was no time, but Borodin waved away the offer for a different reason. "That's not what I asked." He already knew what the books said. The money he flushed through here assured solvency whether they unlocked the front doors for lunch at eleven every morning or not. What was important was for their patronage to grow steadily, creating a semblance of symmetry between the cash he laundered and the actual business.

"Excuse me, I phrased myself poorly." Demyan's expression grew less confident as he accompanied Borodin into the equally dark lounge. "We're booked through the weekend. Among tonight's guests will be a state representative and a two-star general. Lunch is still a little quiet, but I've been trying a few specials.''

That gave Borodin a chance to purge some of his frustration. "What do you think I opened here, a fucking cafeteria? Next you'll be having us serve borscht. No specials. What you need to do is find a hostess for that shift as good as our alluring Michelle.''

Demyan nodded. "You're right. The men walk in with their mouths watering, and she keeps them dazed and ordering until she's ready to kick them out. I will look into the matter.''

Satisfied, Borodin stopped at the bar. "What's this?'' There were two ice buckets loaded with four bottles of cooling vodka. Four slender shot glasses were set beside them.

"The flavored vodkas I was telling you about.'' Looking increasingly uncertain, Demyan continued, "But considering the hour, we could postpone this until tonight?''

"I won't be back. I may have to go out of town.'' And the truth was, Borodin could use a good shot of vodka, but he wasn't sure about this flavored crap. "All right, let's get it over with.''

"I've narrowed the selections down to four—strawberry, chocolate, mango and pear.''

"You sound like you're selling Italian Ices at the mall.'' But Borodin accepted the slim glass the man poured for him. It was the strawberry, and resisting the urge to throw back the thickened liquor, he sipped. Although his expression remained unchanged, inside he grimaced at the syrupy sweetness. He hadn't been far off with the ice-cream reference; the stuff tasted like a kid's Popsicle. Without comment, he signaled for the next one, and put down the unfinished drink.

The next was mango, a favorite breakfast fruit of his, but he left that sample unfinished, too. The pear flavor had him uttering another curse under his breath, and he quickly reached for the chocolate. The moment the flavor touched his tongue he began laughing.

"*Da.* Women will love this shit. By the time they realize what they've been drinking, they'll need taxi service home."

"I thought so myself," Demyan said with growing enthusiasm. "Perhaps we should look into a limousine service for our best patrons? Maybe something designed with cameras and recording devices? You know, more and more of them come here with companions that are not their spouses."

A delicious idea, Borodin thought, black-market sex videos, blackmail—albeit shortsighted. But he patted the younger man's smooth cheek. "And who will fill those tables out there after we've fleeced our customers and scared them away? You must think like *spekulanty.*"

"A speculator, yes. I thought I was."

Borodin wagged his finger. "*Nyet.* You still think like we are back home running the streets like stray dogs willing to do anything to survive. No more of the cheap *vzyatka* or dealing with *defitstny*. We are men of business now. Everything is *po blat*.'' Then he slapped the man on the back and said, ''I agree with everything but the pear. Every peasant has tasted pear. As I said before, we keep the menu lean in all areas, especially the *zakuski*. Force them to order the expensive stuff, the caviar or smoked salmon. Always think *lyuks*. Remember, lean in servings, too, lean everywhere but the bill.'' He added a wink to temper his warning.

Demyan nodded again, the image of deference. ''I understand, Melor, *spasibo*. You are patient with this slow learner.''

''You're as slow as a fox, that's why I put you here.'' Borodin's phone sounded and he looked at the message. ''Walk me to the door.''

Startled, Demyan asked, ''You don't want to go over the computer printouts?''

''Another time. As I said, I have much to do today.'' As they approached the waiting Boba, Borodin added, ''I may be gone for a while. Keep a firm grip.''

''You know I will.''

''I'm not just talking about this place. Watch your ass. The Italians are not happy with our up-scale presence, and they have the authority in their pockets to cause us trouble with the city, everything from ordinances to the cops. So be a hard case with the staff, watch the deliveries for sabotage as you do cheating.''

''Understood.''

''And no hanky-panky from the valets. They fuck with anyone's property where it reflects back on us, they'll never be physically capable of parking a car again. Be generous with good performance as I am with you. But control with *knout*,'' he added, making a fist.

''You've been warned then?'' Suddenly pale, Demyan's gaze shifted to Borodin's bandaged cheek. It wasn't the first time he'd looked at it.

''Just do what I said.''

''You can count on me. *Do svidaniya*, Melor.''

Nodding, Borodin shook hands with his employee, preferring the American formality. As he exited through the opened door held by Boba, he wondered when, let alone if, he would return. Already reaching for the phone again, he had the connection by the time he settled in the passenger side of the black Cadillac. ''Well?'' he demanded upon hearing Yegor's familiar voice.

''Akim called. They think the van has been located.''

That should have been good news, but it wasn't what his right-hand man had indicated in his message. ''So what's the problem?''

''It is next to police station.''

Borodin gripped the phone tighter. ''She's been arrested?''

"*Nyet, nyet.* By animal hospital."

"What the hell is it doing there? Did they actually see her? Are they sure they have the right vehicle?"

"Akim say for sure. He look through glasses. *Górod* very small. They drive through too much and people look."

"Then tell them to back off and wait."

"What if she stay? What if she go to police?"

Then they were screwed, but Melor didn't think that was the case. "She hasn't, otherwise Akim and that other buffoon would have been arrested by now." But there was no doubt their situation had grown more tenuous. There was less and less doubt that he was going to have to leave town for longer than he intended. The question was, when?

Not before Tatiana and her troublemaker daughter had been permanently silenced, he vowed bitterly.

"I'm headed for the brokers'. I'll also give our not-so-petite blond *stukachi* a call and find out if she is sitting on information. Just in case, you start cleaning up things there. I'll call you after I'm through."

Disconnecting, he leaned forward and asked Boba, "You understand where to go?"

The big man glanced into the rearview mirror and nodded.

"Stop at a florist first."

As Boba made an efficient but illegal U-turn,

Borodin sat gazing out the window at the booming city, but seeing instead a dark-haired she-wolf with bedroom eyes and breasts to make a man salivate. He fingered the bandage over his cheek.

What have you done, my clever little cunt? Where do you hide that you don't raise curiosity? You can't be using your ID or credit cards, I'd have been informed.

But she did have his cash. What's more, it was entirely possible that she'd switched vehicles again. He doubted it, though. One good thing, if Lev and Akim had problems with the phones, so did she.

Thinking of his men, he frowned, belatedly wondering why they hadn't reported anything regarding their recent acquisition. He would have to ask them about her during the next call. He craved details, especially if she was doing a great deal of begging. Of course, she was no real challenge, showing her fear all too easily. But the other...

Are you worried, Sashitska?

He closed his eyes, willing her to hear him, feel him getting closer. It was a most soothing meditation.

16

"Pest."

Sasha stood in the doorway of the kennel losing the battle to stay deaf and blind. The dog was missing no opportunity to break free of her steel cage, and while Gray had escaped the awful racket by standing out front chatting with an apple-cheeked mustached man who'd walked over from the hardware store, she'd reached her limit for listening to the whimpers and whines.

"Do you see anyone coming at you with sharp needles or anything?"

In response, the dog pawed at the bars and bit at the latch.

"Well, you can't come out. He said you'd move around too much and rip open those stitches."

Once again the dog pawed the latch and this time threw her head back and uttered a wail worthy of a coyote.

Sasha stepped closer and peered at the recovering animal from different angles. "Are you hurting? He said he gave you something for that. Isn't it potent enough?"

Whatever Gray gave her, it sure wasn't making the pup tired. Not that Sasha blamed her for not lying down. Despite the towel that was now wadded up into a messy clump, the bulk of the dog's body had to make do with the steel bars. How comfortable could that be? And yet Sasha had put her out in the outdoor pen twice this morning and the animal hadn't been happy there, either.

Hands on hips, Sasha eyed the dog. "In case you haven't noticed, your voice carries. You know what they'd call you in the old country? Okay, not *my* old country, but my mother's? *Sabaka.* Know what that is? Well, literally, it's dog, mutt...but it also happens to be what they call nagging old women. Get the hint?"

As though understanding she was only playing, the dog offered a throaty growl and pawed the air.

"What a charmer you are. Sure, you get your way, but the Grim Reaper out there will get on my case all over again, and this time he might give you that lethal injection, no questions asked. Is that what you want?"

Sasha didn't need the responsibility of another life, but she had to admit that this sweet-eyed minx was making it somewhat easier to get through each torturous minute of waiting and wondering. That triggered her conscience anew as she remembered how tempted she'd been to cut her losses, leave the dog to her own fate.

"There are no easy answers, pal." Reaching through the bars, she stroked the dog's snout. "Oh, dear...your nose is warm again."

Gray didn't need to instruct her to watch for that. What was causing the fever, though? She had been careful to keep her water dish full.

"It's the accommodations, I know. Okay, come on. If he thinks sleeping on that is fun, let him try bare mattress springs. But behave," she said, undoing the gate and letting the animal out. "The first time you tinkle where you shouldn't, you're going back in the slammer, and from then on you'll stay no matter how loud you complain."

As soon as Sasha eased the dog to the tile floor, the pup set a paw on her sneaker. Whatever her intention, the image was precious.

"Uh-uh. No staking claim, forget it. I have to travel fast and light. Flattered by the gesture, though. It's a little late for introductions, but what do you call yourself? I wonder. How about we try Jessie? There's a kid back in Vegas I know who's a scrapper like you. Barely eleven and hell on wheels."

"What happened to her?"

At the sound of Gray's voice, the dog plopped down on Sasha's feet and hid her face between her ankles.

"What is it about you that brings out the best in everyone?" Sasha drawled to the man filling the doorway. She leaned over to pet Jessie. It was easier than looking at him and remembering what had passed between them a few hours ago.

"Cease fire, will you?"

He was right; she was acting like a too tightly wound machine. "Is it too early to claim cabin fever?"

"I understand the pressure, believe me," Gray replied. "I'm not saying I *know* yours, but I understand."

"Is that what you've been doing up front? Being social to give me space?"

"It's been a while since I paid attention to the smoke signals around town. So what happened?"

"To whom?"

"The kid. Jessie."

He'd heard more than she'd wanted him to. "Don't get excited, Slaughter. She has nothing to do with why I'm here."

"Maybe. But you care…it's in your voice."

Yes, Jessie was another thing preying on her. Missing a visitation day was bad enough. Leaving without saying goodbye was worse.

"She's in a state school," Sasha admitted reluctantly.

"Why?"

"Aren't you concerned that someone will tiptoe

into this place and steal your money while you're back here pumping me for information?''

"You said it yourself, there isn't much to worry about.''

"Drugs then.''

"Locked away. Why'd the kid get stuck there?''

In his own way, he was no less relentless than Elias. "Because she OD'd her mother's boyfriend after he raped her.'' She arched her eyebrows as though asking, "Glad you asked?''

Ignoring the sarcasm, he replied, "Doesn't sound a fair break for a crime that was basically self-defense.''

"According to the assistant D.A., shooting, stabbing or bludgeoning him during the rape would have been more acceptable. What Jessie did could only be seen as premeditated. Premeditated...her mother's an addict, for pity's sake. The kid's endured nothing but abuse and neglect in her too-short life. As far as I'm concerned, she showed remarkable restraint by not doing something more violent. She actually waited until the bastard was passed out before she finished him off.''

The incident remained too fresh in her mind. "Imagine knowing what to do at that age. Naturally, no foster home could be found for a kid labeled 'cunning and street savvy,' so she's where she is until she turns eighteen. In the meantime, her ability to trust men has probably been shot to hell. Anything else you want to know?''

She knew what she sounded like—the same thing her sergeant had called her when she'd told that fresh-from-the-bar lawyer off—and waited for Gray to do an about-face and walk away, regretting her presence more than ever. But he stayed, seeming content to watch the dog chew on her laces.

"You visit her, don't you? You try to help her hang on."

"Don't try to turn me into a Mother Teresa. That fit is no better than any of the other conclusions you've drawn about me."

"Okay, hard case, if you're ready to eat, I'll go on down to the café and pick up something. What do you want?"

She almost declined, not wanting to be obligated more than she already was. Then she remembered that the café was situated next to the convenience store—where there was a pay phone.

"I'll do it."

Gray frowned. "That might not be a good idea."

"Why, because you think I'm going to run? I have the drill down pat. 'Elias will chase me to my grave if I try.' Anything else?"

"What about your concern over being spotted?"

The question hit her like a belly shot. He'd made no further comment about her preoccupation with traffic out front, not even when she moved her van directly behind the clinic and out of sight of the street. She knew he remained curious, but assumed his annoyance with her overrode that.

"Concern needn't be anything more overt than a muscle flex," she said, focusing on the dog. "It doesn't necessitate giving up breathing."

When he didn't respond to that, she knew he didn't believe her studied calmness, and quickly asked him what he wanted to eat. "My treat. It's the least I can do to repay you for all of this...southern hospitality."

Finally relenting, he said, "Have it your way. You may end up thinking differently, though, once you realize word about you has started getting around town."

So that's what he meant before. He'd been feeling out people he trusted, or used to be friends with to see what Frank was saying about her...and possibly J.M., too, considering how they'd parted company. But none of that offset her need to use that pay phone.

"I'll cope," she told him, and nodded at Jessie. "Would you mind much just letting her be on the floor here? She really hates that cage."

After a moment he nodded, and conscious of his speculative gaze, she got out of there, pocketing his money because he insisted on paying his own way. As for her, she wasn't even hungry; the pulling at her stomach was all nerves.

Cautious, she decided to take a detour, rounding the back of the police station, café and fire department, too. Although it was the lunch hour, traffic in town was light. Even at the convenience store, there was only an eighteen-wheeler parked along the road with its diesel engine idling, and one car at the gas pumps. Despite that, she was grateful the phones were located at the back of the premises by the air pump and car wash, virtually out of view.

Sasha punched in the code on the prepaid calling card she'd bought just yesterday morning on an impulse, and then the phone number. After several rings, she heard the recording she already knew from memory. Trying to stay optimistic, she tried again.

Where are you?

For her sanity's sake, she had to believe this streak of silence was due to the continued disrupted service. She didn't want to consider anything worse, but her imagination worked overtime.

When she finally gave up, accepting that it was time to get to the café, she saw a man—she guessed him to be the driver of the rig—do a double take before climbing back into his truck and pause to stare at her. He was a pleasant-looking guy who rather looked like her father in his earliest marine photos, clean-cut and sporting a maroon and white Texas A&M cap. Mr. All-American. Probably in a hurry to be back on the road, if those two bottles of water, bag of chips and wrapped sub sandwich were anything to go by. For an instant she saw herself responding to his smile, going over and asking if he was heading east. But the pragmatic in her recalled that she carried little money, no change of clothes…and no gun.

Seeing she wasn't going to acknowledge him, the man climbed up into his cab and Sasha continued to the café, wondering if she'd just missed an important opportunity, her last chance for escape.

As with the rest of the town, the eatery was nowhere near busy. Unfortunately, one of the customers there was Chief Frank Elias.

17

The no-name café was a dusty, dismal establishment, although the poor lighting and dark-paneled walls were welcome after the blinding sunshine. The decor consisted of battered street signs lining the walls, along with framed photos of kids. Rows and rows of them, Sasha noted wryly. Kids with cows, kids with chickens and kids with pigs, goats, sheep—just about every farm animal. Considering the faded condition of some of the pictures, they had to date back decades: 4–H events, Sasha decided. Or Noah's ancestral line.

Seating consisted of a dozen mismatched and scarred tables, along with an equal number of booths, suggesting that once the town had been a more prosperous place. More than likely the proprietor had anticipated a greater windfall from the interstate. Sasha just hoped that the lack of business wasn't indicative of the cuisine served here.

Only two of the tables were occupied, and the diners were old-timers, grizzled, sun-aged men wearing overalls and straw hats decomposing on equally weathered heads. One or two wore baseball caps, and Sasha suspected none of the headgear came off until the men stepped into the shower. They appeared in no rush to go anywhere, but had undoubtedly known each other so long, there wasn't much left to talk about, either. Sasha heard more silverware and pots clanking in the kitchen than dialogue.

No one paid her any attention at first. That gave her a chance to prepare herself for Elias, who sat at the counter on the round-seated stool nearest the register. Neither he nor the waitress in the baby-blue uniform unbuttoned to her bra-enhanced cleavage noticed her, until the short-order cook in the kitchen snapped through the breezeway, *"Customer."*

The blonde with enough curls to coif a period movie tore her flirtatious gaze from the chief and, in less time than it took to flip a burger, gave her a dismissive once-over. "Put it down wherever you want," she said, returning her attention to Elias. "Ain't no maître d' here."

The snipe made it easier for Sasha to approach the checkout counter. "Thanks for the warm invitation, but I'm ordering take-out."

Clear green eyes, truly lovely but for the excessive makeup, flashed dislike before the girl sullenly shifted over and dropped her order pad onto the counter. "Go on."

"A special, and—" Sasha eyed the faded and mostly scribbled chalkboard menu over the girl's head ''—a chef salad. Please.'' Who could ruin a salad? she reasoned.

As she scribbled down the order, the waitress sucked in her cheeks, probably having read in some fashion magazine that it accented her cheekbones. She needn't have bothered with the artifice; she had adorable features, sweetly formed lips despite the frosted-pink lipstick, and the kind of nose everyone considering rhinoplasty hoped to end up with. Add the smattering of freckles the makeup couldn't hide, and you ended up with a vibrant youthfulness that Sasha suspected the girl hated.

''The chicken-fried steak comes with mashed potatoes and boiled okra with stewed tomatoes,'' the waitress recited tersely. ''No substitutions.''

''Then I take it that's what Dr. Slaughter wants.''

The blonde glanced up from her order sheet, and in that second looked no more than seventeen, although she was probably closer to twenty-one or two.

''You're ordering for Doc?''

''That's the one I was telling you about,'' Frank drawled. ''Spent last night with him, too.''

Sasha did her best to ignore Elias's unwelcome input, but couldn't avoid hearing the murmuring that told her the others in the place had heard and were game for a bit of juicy gossip. ''Dr. Slaughter would also like whatever pie is available today,'' she told the young woman.

The waitress simply gaped. "What are you talking about, Frank? She don't look like no arsonist."

"Thank you," Sasha replied. "I don't know what one looks like either, but I assure you, I'm not."

"Are you shacking up with Doc, though?"

Sasha nodded to the order pad. "He mentioned the pie twice, so I suspect it's his favorite part of the meal."

The blonde smiled mischievously as she wrote. "That's him all right. No denying his sweet tooth, regardless of his mood."

"Especially for brown sugar," Elias mused.

Sending him a sidelong look, the waitress said to Sasha, "He hates boiled okra. I'll slip him in an ear of corn. He'll like the chocolate cream pie, though. And to drink?"

Sasha hadn't thought to ask. "What do you have that goes well with scotch?"

The blonde's laughter turned her cover-model pretty face into something far more interesting. "I like you." She reached out her hand. "I'm Gerri Rose."

Why hadn't she guessed? Sasha recovered, but not fast enough. By the time she shook hands, she could see the doubt return to shadow J.M.'s niece's green eyes. "Anna Diaz."

"Doc usually gets iced tea, unsweetened."

"Make it two then."

"You two know each other long?"

Sasha merely shook her head and kept her gaze lowered as she dug in her pocket to get out the money, hoping that would be enough of a hint that she wasn't willing to elaborate.

"Ms. Diaz was just passing through," Elias informed Gerri Rose. "Until she met old Gray."

Sasha ignored him, and after a brief giggle, Gerri Rose delivered the order to the cook, who was already working on it.

Elias swiveled to face Sasha. "Glad to see you took me seriously."

"If you don't mind, I'd like to get through this with the minimum of conversation with you."

There was no missing that Frank misread her attitude and took pleasure in it. "You do work at making things tougher on yourself."

It was all she could do not to shudder in revulsion as she felt his gaze moving over her. She knew he was reliving what he'd done last night and urging her to remember the crude things he'd said. The temptation to tell him exactly what kind of lowlife she considered him forced her to reach into her pocket to close her fingers around the square of embroidered linen, a keepsake that helped her stay focused.

"I don't see your wallet," he said when he realized she wouldn't rise to his baiting. "Did you bring your license with you?"

"Sorry."

"I bet you are. You're the first woman I've met

who went anywhere without her bag. Most of you females can't leave the house without carrying half of it with you.''

She drew out the bill Gray had given her for his meal, and a five of her own. Gerri Rose brought the teas and made change, which Sasha waved away. ''Doctor Slaughter said that was yours.''

''Thanks.'' She pocketed the cash. ''Gotta admit, he's one of my best tippers.''

''That's our Saint Gray,'' Frank drawled. ''Always caring and considerate of the so-called gentler sex.''

''You could do with a lesson or two,'' Gerri Rose murmured as she sacked the tea.

''Complaining, baby? I'm the one with the scratch marks on my back.''

Gerri Rose's cheeks blazed hot pink. ''Will you shut *up*.'' She glanced over at the table of old men, and then back at the cook.

''Just telling it like it is,'' he replied, turning to grin at Sasha. ''You should try it yourself, sugar. Gerri Rose here sees Gray like some tragic hero. Tell her how the sneaky rat was the one who suggested you hire J.M. to try to humiliate me.''

Gerri Rose was as unassuming as she looked. ''He's the only lawyer in these parts. If you say she needs one, I reckon it would have to be J.M.''

''That's not why I asked for your uncle to accompany me,'' Sasha said, fed up with the cop. She made sure her gaze held Gerri Rose's. ''I found out last night how safe it is to be alone with your…friend. And I'd prefer not to be put in that predicament again.''

Someone behind her choked then coughed, and the chief cast them a glowering look before replying, ''You don't seem to have learned much from the experience. That mouth is still too loose for its own good.''

Gerri Rose glanced from Sasha to Frank, her young face showing too much of what she was thinking. Sasha lowered her gaze, unwilling to worry for the innocent who was, sad to say, in for a great deal of grief if she didn't wise up.

''What're y'all talking about? Frank, I don't like this.''

''Police business, baby. That's all.''

Sasha leaned closer to Gerri Rose. ''You look like a nice person—and smarter than he wants to believe.''

''She's twenty-one,'' Elias declared. ''Leave her alone.''

''To what end, wasting her best years in this fabulous hub of civilization where she thinks you're as good as it gets?''

''Want to take her place?''

The outrageous question had Gerri Rose snatching up a wet wash rag and throwing it at him. ''Frank!''

''You're wasting your breath, Mrs. Pike,'' Sasha said with sincere compassion for the woman. ''If you're looking for sensitivity or discretion, you'd better take a second look at what's at home. People like the chief here aren't big on faithfulness. It's all about quantity, not quality, eh, *Frank?*"

Gerri Rose's bosom heaved, her trembling chin jutted. "You son of a bitch, Frank. What have you done now? What's she talking about?"

Elias behaved as though he hadn't heard her. He only had eyes for Sasha. "What I want to know is what's made you stay with him?"

It was the strangest question, and yet Sasha understood. Frank saw nothing, knew nothing but his resentment and jealousy of Gray Slaughter. "I'm not going to bother trying to explain it to you," she replied, "because you wouldn't understand."

"That's bullshit."

"I rest my case."

Once again there was a whisper of reaction suggesting approval from their meager audience. Incensed, Frank swept his dishes off the counter and rose. "You think you've got him? He'll never get over Mo. Try being smug while dealing with that, bitch!"

The glass in the ancient wood-frame door should have fallen out as Frank slammed it behind him. In the aftermath, everyone behaved with self-consciousness, as though realizing something unhealthy had occurred that they wanted no part of. A couple of the old men rose and shuffled out. The others sighed and bowed their heads even lower over their empty plates and coffee mugs.

Gerri Rose wanted to say something, but clearly had difficulty summoning the nerve. Finally, she stepped close to the counter and glared at Sasha. "You take your trash mouth and your inflated boobs and go make trouble for someone else. I feel sorry for Doc if he thinks you're anywhere *close* to a replacement for Mo."

As she spun away, Sasha bowed her own head. What on earth did she say to such a child?

"Order!" the chef called.

Gerri Rose recklessly bagged the food and shoved it at her.

Sasha reached out and gripped the girl's slender wrist. "Listen to me. I am no problem for you. But *he* is your nightmare. Do yourself a favor and—"

Jerking free, Gerri Rose backed away until she came up against the back counter. "You've got nothing to say that I want to hear."

It wasn't the worst experience in her life to walk out of there with every pair of eyes staring after her. She'd dealt with drunks puking at her feet, angry men urinating on her patrol car, *in* her patrol car, mothers spitting at her because they wouldn't accept that their sons could commit murder. No, this was nothing worth her peace of mind…and yet it added to her depression.

Outside Sasha drew in a deep breath, wanting to rid herself of the deep-fried hostility behind her.

Although he'd exploded, maybe Elias would back off some, now that more people in town were on to him. But what would help more is if J.M. called about that insurance inspector.

About to head back toward the clinic, Sasha's gaze was drawn to the unusually loud bird chatter across the street in a huge old cedar. She'd missed the building last night because of the cinder-block wall covered with vines that hid half the property. "Public Library," she whispered, reading the polished steel sign.

Right now one thing about libraries drew her interest—they were all beneficiaries of grants, and had computers.

18

Sasha crossed the sun-baked road, wondering what would melt first before she reached the other side, the soles of her shoes or her brain. As for the library, she wondered whether it was a grant or bequeathal from some late rancher that had created such an artistic structure in such a tiny and otherwise haphazardly designed community. The whitewashed cinder-block building resembled a mini–Guggenheim Museum. It suggested that once the residents of this town weren't as apathetic and lost as they seemed to be now.

Inside she discovered the library was even darker and more deserted than the café but carefully attended. An unsmiling, all-business woman stood in the octagonal workstation in the center of the main room. Sasha suspected her gray suit and white blouse hadn't been chosen to match her permed and coiffed hair, but rather out of pride for her position. It would have been reassuring if the woman had been wearing a quilted vest with a clunky dough pin featuring her grandchildren's smiling faces. Nevertheless, Sasha summoned a pleasant smile and walked up to the counter.

The woman immediately stopped studying her printout and slipped off her reading glasses, letting them rest by their rope around her neck. She offered no welcoming smile in return.

"Hello," Sasha began. "Do you have a computer I could use for a few minutes to look up some information?" She already knew they did, she'd done a quick scan of the place as she entered, spotting one to her left.

The woman glanced down at the bag Sasha held. "Is that what I think it is? Food is prohibited in the library."

"Oh, I wouldn't think of eating in here. I'm about to deliver this, but I need to research something online for a second, and then I'll be on my way."

"And you are...?"

"Anna Diaz."

Still attractive in a strong-boned way, the woman lifted her head as though to study Sasha through the glasses she'd removed. "I don't know you."

"No, you wouldn't. I'm not from around here."

With the dignified stature of a justice, the woman nodded as though that information resolved everything. "The computer is for the use of our residents. It's supplied on a grant, specifically for that purpose."

Trying not to look amused because they were

whispering in the empty chamber, Sasha scanned the quiet room, finally settling her gaze on the object of discussion. "But no one is using it." As far as she could tell, no one else was in the building besides them.

"At the moment. However, that's not to say someone won't walk in any minute."

"Fair enough. If that happens, I'll give up my place without a complaint. And I'll happily pay you for the use regardless." She hoped the woman would be softened by the offer of a fee, if not swayed by her politeness.

The librarian's gaze drifted over Sasha. "We can't let just anyone come and use the equipment. It's very sensitive."

"I do appreciate that." Sasha understood that she'd been sized up, and because of her casual attire been classified as trailer trash or worse. "Would it reassure you to know that I've used computers for years, and I'm quite familiar with them?"

Looking unconvinced, the librarian gave Sasha another once-over, but her cool demeanor remained unchanged. "There's no way I can be sure of that, is there? Do you have references?"

"Do you know Dr. Slaughter? Gray Slaughter?"

The woman drew herself erect. "I'm afraid I do."

Sasha hesitated, admittedly curious. "What's

that supposed to mean?'' Had she heard from Elias, or was it old gossip?

"Let's just say he's not the gentleman his father was,'' the woman replied.

If so, he apparently wasn't the only one, Sasha thought. "Well, Dr. Slaughter is treating my dog, who was injured on the road.'' As soon as she spoke she realized her error.

"Is that supposed to reassure me? Not only are you confirming that you're careless with your pet, you're dealing with a man not even fractionally committed to his profession.''

Before Sasha could attempt to explain, the door opened. She glanced over her shoulder and saw an eager-faced boy of no more than ten enter. He waved at the librarian, adding a "Hi, Grandma,'' and went straight to the computer.

Sasha couldn't help but laugh. "Well done,'' she told the librarian who had the grace to blush. "I'll pass on your best wishes to Doc Slaughter.''

Once outside, she stood on the sidewalk, her appreciation for being outmaneuvered evaporating the way a single raindrop would on this sun-baked concrete. Defeat and heat beat at her in alternating waves. There was no question that it was time to get back to the clinic before the food she was carrying became a modern-art project of its own, but disappointment stayed her. She'd so needed a chance to see what was happening in Vegas before Elias did take her license.

As she began down the curving sidewalk, she heard a vehicle on the road behind the library. The sound affected her like a commercial jingle you didn't really like, but was imbedded in your memory anyway.

Pausing to glance back, she saw a truck emerge from behind the far privacy wall. As it made a right at the corner, she heard a familiar miss in the engine.

That was it!

As the truck disappeared around an empty building with another For Rent sign, she took off after it. The bag and her wound cut her speed, but she hoped that with the road being in terrible condition, the truck couldn't go too fast. A face-off wasn't what she was after anyway; she just wanted to get close enough to read the license plate.

As she charged across the street, she heard the deafening blast of a horn…and out of the corner of her eye saw a vehicle bearing down on her.

19

Brakes squealed as Sasha made a desperate attempt to avoid collision, but it was too late. Barely achieving a matador-like twist, she bounced off the side of the patrol car and went flying. She learned again that there was something to the "slow motion" description by people involved in accidents; it did seem to take forever for her to hit the ground. When she did, it was with a brain-jarring finality that played havoc with her vision, so much so that at first she didn't believe she wasn't looking into Frank Elias's car.

"Jeez, are you all right?"

Everything else in her body chose that instant to resume functioning...and register shock and pain. But the voice bled through the chaos and her eyes were working, as well. It wasn't Elias, thank heaven.

"Lady...miss, are you okay?"

The officer downshifted and bolted from the patrol car; however, it was the icy liquid seeping through the bag and her shirt that snapped Sasha back to full awareness. Despite a sharp, burning pain that told her the bandages on her side had ripped loose, or maybe worse, she rolled to her knees to try to save what was left of the drinks in the sack. One plastic lid was only partially loosened, but the other was badly cracked and the foam cup crushed. The food containers weren't in much better shape.

She could only gasp and wheeze as she tried to avoid the awful sensations as the patrolman helped her to her feet.

"Ma'am? Are you hearing impaired?" he asked, ducking to look into her face.

"What? No, I'm fine. Just wet, sore and humiliated." Or rather, she would be if she could stop the ocean sounds in her ears and decide whether it was her right thigh, butt, elbow or side that hurt more. As she brushed dirt and gravel off herself, she glanced back at where she'd fallen and knew she should count her blessings for not having hit her head on the curb.

"I know this is a quiet street and all," the youthful cop continued. His voice was high and unsteady, exposing his own state. "But you can't be zipping around without looking where you're going."

Good Lord, Sasha thought, blinking as she really looked at him for the first time. He was Opie all grown up. Of course, within seconds, her memory corrected itself and she recalled the movie director who'd played that famous TV character. She would have laughed at herself if it wasn't for the pain. "You're right, Officer. I apologize."

"Who are you? I don't believe I've seen you around before."

That's all she needed, for him to tell Frank what had happened and where she'd been. With her luck, Elias would think she was trying to run away, the same way Gray would if she didn't get back.

"No, I'm just passing through." As she shifted her hold to keep the contents from breaking through the disintegrating bottom of the sack, she took a step backward. "I'll be more careful. Thank you, Officer."

"Kenny. Uh, Ken Plummer. Can I drive you somewhere, Miss—?"

God, he was young, Sasha thought, shaking her head and continuing her retreat. The reddish-blond hair and freckles, far more pronounced than Gerri Rose's, accentuated that. And he couldn't weigh more than her, he was so slightly built. "I appreciate it, but I'm only up this way."

Looking understandably perplexed, he pointed over his shoulder with his thumb. "But you were headed that way. Ma'am," he called after her as she made an ungraceful turn and hobbled across the library's property, "your elbow's bleeding. I really should—"

"Gotta deliver this," she called back. "Thanks again!"

Sasha broke into a painful trot, wanting to duck

around the Main Street wall as fast as possible, then she made another reckless dash across the road. Thankfully, this time there was no traffic.

Afraid that young Plummer might insist on being gallant and follow to make sure she made it okay, she ducked behind the café to return to the clinic the back way like before. She couldn't help but notice that the old-timers who'd been in the café were still there and watching her. Even though there was no sign of Gerri Rose, the condition of her clothes and her odd behavior would no doubt offer plenty of speculation guaranteeing that the girl would hear sooner rather than later. And tell Elias?

"Just one break, that's all I'm asking for," she muttered under her breath.

By the time she entered the back door of the clinic, she couldn't deny that the tackle last night, combined with this fall, were taking their toll on her.

Gray came backing out of the kennel. "Let me guess, they were out of chicken-fried steak and you helped them shoot and process a cow?"

He hadn't looked up because he was rolling the wheeled bucket to the washroom. That gave Sasha time to peek into the kennel, now reeking from the smell of pine cleaner. Jessie was locked up again, but in a different cage. Her ears lifted as the dog spotted her and gave a happy-sounding "woof."

"Uh-oh, what happened?" she asked.

"You don't want to know, not if you plan to eat," Gray replied from the bathroom across the hall. "Suffice it to say, your friend is either having a reaction to the medication or else she isn't house-broken."

"She was fine when I left."

"Maybe that's the point. Could be she got stressed thinking the one person who'd been nice to her had abandoned her. I'm a vet not a psychic or analyst."

And she was in pain, and she needed his bad humor about as much as the mongrel's fixation. "All I'm saying is that I wasn't gone that long." She continued down the hall and into the kitchen area.

"Long enough for her. Long enough for Frank to stop by and spread more of his own personal brand of goodwill."

Sasha heard him dumping the contents of the pail down the commode, then run fresh water into the bucket from the deep industrial-size sink.

"He said you'd left the café at least ten minutes before he did," Gray called. "And the way I see it, that was a good twenty minutes ago."

She grimaced. Leave it to Elias to stir up trouble. Easing her armload onto the counter, she called back, "Did he stop by to report on that insurance guy?"

"Don't play dumb and don't fish, neither works for you."

Hearing that he was coming down the hall, Sasha turned toward the entryway. "Then be honest yourself. You're not upset because of the dog."

"Okay." He stepped into the room wiping his hands in a paper towel. "He said you came on to him just to taunt Gerri Rose."

She rolled her eyes. "You believed him? For your information, I couldn't get out of there fast enough."

"Right. And you couldn't get back here fast enough."

"You should have told me that Gerri Rose worked at the café."

"I thought J.M.—" As he joined her at the counter, Gray stared at the mess. "What the hell happened?"

"I had a bit of a confrontation myself."

"You can say that again."

He opened the lid on the first foam container, and even Sasha had to admit it was a pitiful sight. There was almost no way to distinguish what the meal was supposed to be except that white gravy and mashed potatoes were featured.

"What did you do, sit on it?"

She wished she had, then maybe her tailbone wouldn't be smarting so. "Do you have a microwave? Give me a second to wash up and I'll separate things and put yours in there to warm."

"You can't repair that mess, it's practically pureed. Besides, I hate microwaved beef."

So did she. "Then take my order." She pushed the other container toward him. "It's only a chef salad, but—" She grimaced as she opened it and grimaced again. The odd-colored house dressing was the same color as the water had been in the pail.

"That's perfect." Gray took his meal to the large plastic-lined trash bin and dumped it in. "So? Are you going to explain this?"

"I spotted the truck."

For the first time he looked at her and noticed the shape she was in. "Why didn't you say you're hurt?"

"I'm okay."

"You're bleeding through your shirt...and where else?"

Just as he did, she gave herself a quick once-over. Sure enough, her tea-saturated shirt now showed blood smears on both sides.

"Let's take a look." Gray nodded across the hall. "Damn it, you're limping, too. Why the hell didn't you say something? Do you need me to carry you?"

"Don't be ridiculous, I'm sore not maimed."

He followed her to the room across the hall, which was much like the one they'd used last night. "I'll help you up on the table."

Sasha swatted away his hands as he reached for her. "I'm not getting up on any doggy table."

"Last time I cleaned that wound, the whites of

your eyes looked tanned compared to your face. But you want to fall flat on your face? Fine. Ease off the shirt and drop the pants.''

That's the last thing she needed to do. She felt vulnerable enough around the man. ''Go play dictator with someone else. All I need to do is wash off my elbow and get a new bandage for my side.''

''How do you know a bandage will be sufficient this time?'' With that, he swept her off her feet and up onto the table. ''Now, are you going to take off the shirt or am I?''

It took Sasha a moment to answer because her bottom was smarting from the contact with the table. ''Next time ask me where else it hurts, would you?'' she said, shifting to rub the offended spot.

Seeing by his expression that he was serious about the shirt, she started unbuttoning it. With a satisfied nod, Gray moved on to collect what he needed. Sasha was relieved, since the mere thought of his hands on her was having an effect on her body. Thankfully, when he returned, he stayed at the back of the table, focusing on her elbow first.

''So what condition is the truck in?'' he asked grimly.

''It was a car, a patrol car to be exact.''

He paused in his ministrations. ''You collided with Frank? When? He didn't say anything about that.''

''With Kenny Plummer.'' As he resumed working on her, she explained what had happened. ''I guess there's not much hope that Elias won't hear about this," she added at the end.

Pressing a regular bandage to her elbow, Gray moved to the front of the table. When he saw that she hadn't unfastened her jeans, he did so, while staring straight into her eyes. "Count on it."

She didn't know what was worse, his face close enough for a kiss or his fingers doing what a lover would do. "Could you try and look at it from my perspective? You would have wanted to be sure about the truck the same way I did. Don't look at me like that, it *was* the truck. I remembered how it sounded, and I thought if I could get the plate number—"

"You think Frank's going to believe you?"

Good point, she thought as he tossed the soiled gauze pads away. Subdued, she replied, "Whether he does or doesn't is irrelevant. I needed to know for me."

A heavy silence settled in the room. Sasha didn't mind at first. It took all her concentration not to humiliate herself as he attended to her side. She suspected he wasn't being quite as gentle about it as he'd been last night, but when he dropped the box of gauze pads twice, she knew something else was going on.

"Go ahead and vent," she said. "I'm sure it'll be for my own good."

"You deserve to hurt. Maybe if you hurt enough, you'll start being more careful."

"At least I know the truck exists and that it's here."

"It's not *here,* it got away."

"The driver was male."

"Odds were fifty-fifty that it would be."

She closed her eyes against the sarcasm as much to relish the cool ointment against her skin.

"And the library? What was that about?"

Sasha had hoped he would forget about that. Now she understood by his tone that it was what bothered him most. She suspected Elias was questioning the librarian at this moment, and then he would rub that in Gray's face as well.

"A computer."

At first he simply stood there, then he demanded, "Look at me."

She kept her eyes downcast. "I function better without laser burns in the back of my skull."

"Look at me." When she did, he continued, "Were you going to mention that at any point?"

"Not if I could help it, no."

"Thanks for the vote of confidence."

"You don't understand..."

With a surprising show of temper, he spun around and threw the roll of adhesive tape. It went flying out into the hall, bouncing against the wall before disappearing from view. "There's a computer!" he roared, pointing toward the reception area. "There's another in my office at the house."

"I'd have to know your password. Also, I'd leave a history of what I'd done, where I'd been."

"How would I know that? I'm not a computer geek."

"Others might."

He leaned so close their noses almost touched. "That's all that you would have had to say to me. Me…the guy who saved your ass and took you into my home."

She didn't reply because there was nothing to say. He was right. But being careful was more important.

When he realized that not only wasn't she going to apologize, but she wasn't going to respond at all, Gray pulled a jacket off the hanger on the back of the door and tossed it at her. "You're done," he muttered. "And so am I."

20

Las Vegas, Nevada
10:55 a.m. PST

The glass doors to the offices of Joseph, Bains and Sorenson had been open for almost two hours when Melor Borodin entered the twenty-story complex's expansive atrium. The greenhouse-like lobby was humming with people, but as he wove his way between them and passed the flower-adorned fountain in the center, he only had eyes for what was occurring inside the brokerage firm.

He slowed his pace as he spotted two men in the office of his broker. Detectives, he concluded from their cheap, over-dry-cleaned suits, maybe FBI already? He had no doubt they would eventually be called in, but he'd been hoping not yet, not before he was through. Having no desire for even the most innocent contact, he cut a sharp left and bequeathed an admiring smile for the brunette at the reception desk.

"Renee, how stunning you look this morning,"

he said to the young woman with the cover-girl smile and vacant eyes. "*Pojalsta,* you know my English. Describe this superb color for me."

She tucked her neck into her shoulders in a little girl–like shrug. "Violet, I guess. How are you, Mr. Borodin?"

She pronounced his name "Borden," but he pretended not to notice. He could overlook a great deal, since she was like a number of other receptionists he'd come across—a complete blabbermouth who could be trusted to also spread whatever misinformation he wanted circulated.

"You're probably here looking for Tatiana, aren't you? Oh, dear." Her tongue peeked out of the corner of her perfectly painted mouth as she slid a glance toward the office where the three men stood in close conference. "I shouldn't be saying anything, but this is so spooky. And you're one of Mr. S.'s most valued customers, so you have to know sometime. *She's gone,*" Renee whispered.

Borodin wondered if the pretty dimwit knew how holding her left hand against her face as though hiding herself from lip-readers fooled anyone. He affected confusion and dismay.

"Excuse me, I am not understanding…who?" He looked across the room again at the men, then the empty desk outside the office. "Tatiana? This is impossible."

"Tell me about it."

"She has quit her job? But she is the only one to translate and explain to me."

Renee responded with another of her irritating pantomimes. "You don't get it, and I've been put under stricter orders than usual not to discuss the matter." Nevertheless, she leaned farther across her desk, the neckline of her surplice bodice gaping invitingly. "It's totally bizarre if you ask me. She and her daughter are missing. You haven't seen the reports on TV? Oh, the authorities are trying to keep it hush-hush, but pictures are on the news night and day."

"I have been, how do you say...out to business." Placing the long, white florist's box on the edge of her desk, Borodin pretended not to notice her covetous glance and added with proper concern, "You speak *podushum, da?*" At her clueless look he pretended to struggle. "Is heart-to-heart, you understand?"

"Well, the thing is, there's not that much to tell yet. We're all as confused as we are shocked. We knew something was wrong Tuesday when Tatiana didn't come in or call, she had such an impeccable reputation—oh, gosh. Did you hear that? I'm talking about her in the past tense. But she did. She's never taken a sick day, let alone been tardy. So there we were, expecting her to walk in at any moment to explain how she'd been caught in some big traffic accident. When it got later and later, Personnel tried calling her house, then her daughter's place...but all they got at either residence was the machines. Finally Mr. Sorenson phoned the police, and that's when we learned Sasha didn't report for work Monday night." Renee dropped her voice an octave. "You did know Tatiana's daughter is a police officer?"

Across the room, Arne Sorenson and the two men stepped out of his office. Borodin turned his back to them. To make himself look less noteworthy, he slid his hands into his pockets and rounded his shoulders, giving himself a less commanding presence. "Tatiana has beautiful photograph on her desk," he said quietly. "I am always admiring. She has tremendous pride in only child."

"True, but it's increasingly likely that pride was unwarranted."

"This I cannot accept."

"You're not the only one." As the girl scooted her chair closer to the desk, an overgenerous waft of Obsession followed. "Like it or not, I understand they've found oodles of cash at Tatiana's house, and drugs at Sasha's apartment."

Not exactly "oodles," Borodin thought; however, he again appreciated and was entertained by how willing people were to expand and embellish for the sake of drama and self-importance. Taking a step back from the cloying fragrance, his expression reflected consistent dismay. "Tatiana is fine woman, a most excellent mother. Tell me who speaks these lies of her? I will fight on her behalf."

As he made a move as though to leave her, Renee reached out to stay him. "Wait! You can't go over there now. They'll know I told you." As the phone buzzed, she signaled him to stand by for a moment.

After relaying the call, she leaned forward again. "None of us can believe it, Mr. Borodin, but do you see those men with Mr. Sorenson? This is their third time here. As far as I'm concerned, that's proof positive something's fishy. Look at Mr. S., too. He's hardly protesting as he did the first day."

And Borodin couldn't be more delighted that his initial read of the senior partner had been on target. Arne Sorenson was a man who was always swayed by the bottom line regardless of whether it was investments or personnel. If a dedicated and reliable employee like Tatiana had to be sacrificed for the good of his 401K and bonus, so be it. But Borodin didn't forget that this was the same broker who had lavished great praise on her less than two years ago once he realized that having an assistant with a similar heritage as his affluent client would help secure the account. Could be he even gave his unsolicited blessing should Tatiana be interested in an affair.

"Do you mind me asking something?" For the first time, Renee appeared sincerely uncertain. "I don't mean to be rude, but have you been injured?"

Although his back was almost to her, Borodin

lifted his fingers to the bandage. By the time he met her inquisitive gaze, he could deliver a convincing, sheepish shrug. "I am embarrassed to confess. A business acquaintance tried to teach me of fishing underwater." He pantomimed.

"Spearfishing. Omigosh!"

He nodded. "Is not for me, I think."

"You poor man. Did you need stitches? Oh, don't worry, doctors can do wonders with scars these days."

"Nurse at hospital says no operation. She says girls think it is sexy. What you suggest, Renee?"

The young Audrey Hepburn look-alike nodded, her eyebrows vanishing under her thick dark bangs. "You'd look dignified and handsome no matter what."

Long bored with the prattle and more so with her flirting, Borodin was relieved to see the two cops leaving. He kept his back to them as they passed, but as soon as Arne Sorenson spotted him and motioned him over, Borodin grabbed at the opportunity to escape.

"Excuse me, sweet Renee. I will pay my respects to Arne now. *Spasibo.* Thank you for your kindness." He picked up the box and took a step toward Sorenson's office, then hesitated. Back tracking, he extended the box to her. "Tell me please if I offend, but would you accept these in gratitude for…?"

An octopus had never latched on to a meal

faster. "Don't be silly. I'm thrilled. Thank you so much."

"It was small gesture to Tatiana for good care she takes of my business while I am out of town."

"Oh, I know. We girls were always remarking on the presents you sent her. She thought you were the most considerate of all Mr. Sorenson's clients."

"So, now you accept, for you are kind to me to explain."

Her lips shimmered and her eyes invited. "Anytime. If there's anything else I can do...I mean on behalf of Joseph, Bains and Sorenson, please don't hesitate."

Borodin responded with a formal bow. It was, he discovered, what Americans expected of Russians, as though they believed the whole country was descended from the Romanovs. Equally entertaining as he crossed to Arne Sorenson's office was noticing that the senior partner responsible for the financial health of the firm was drawing a handkerchief from his inside pocket and dabbing at his brow. No need to guess what he was going through, the gastric anxiety building as he speculated how Melor was to be handled, and what should be acknowledged. If all had gone according to plan, Sorenson did not know of Borodin's relationship with Tatiana. Their fifteen-year age difference would be incomprehensible to a man whose own predilections targeted girls young enough to be his granddaughter.

"Arne." Borodin made sure his expression transmitted bewilderment and grief as he extended his hand to the dignified broker. "I cannot believe what I hear."

"Yes, yes, it's a terrible thing. I saw you were out of town thanks to a note on Tatiana's calendar, and I must say I was relieved, because of all the people I was dreading having to inform, it's you. But come in, please. Sit down. Can I get you something? Coffee, water…despite the hour, dare I say a drink? I could almost use one myself."

And would indulge very shortly, Borodin mused with wicked confidence. But to the older man he said, "Do not trouble yourself. This is no time to intrude, and I will only stay a moment."

Consummately precise and elegant, the businessman gripped his hand again. "That's exactly why I dreaded this moment. You understand better than most. Just give me a moment to collect myself." He smoothed a hand over his tie and drew a slow, deep breath. Tall, sinewy and with the charisma of a film star, he drew himself erect as though awaiting a royal mantle to be draped over his shoulders. "She was the best, you know. In all my years in the business, I've never worked with anyone so dedicated or with more natural talent as Tatiana."

"Was." Borodin drew back in dismay. "Arne, you, too? You speak of her as of a soul lost?"

Silver eyebrows trimmed and brushed drew together as Arne steepled his hands in a gesture that could be both plea and prayer. "I must be pragmatic—she is to us regardless of what evolves. The police just left. They told me there's little hope of her returning, at least willingly. The evidence against her is too strong."

"Bah! Is big mistake. Surely there is hope?"

"I wish. But it appears she and her daughter— a cop for crying out loud—were running a side business. Drugs! Can you believe it? Tatiana wouldn't even order a glass of wine when I sent her out for lunch on me for National Secretary's Day. Why? Why narcotics when she made fantastic money here? It's incomprehensible. I remember her reaction to her first bonus. She wept with gratitude. It must have been her daughter who influenced her, nothing else makes sense. Unfortunately, the authorities are asking for permission to interview the other employees *and* clients Tatiana had contact with, just in case. My hunch is they're really at a loss as to where to take this investigation and trying to latch on to any clue, any names she might have dropped in conversation. It's too much, an outrage, and I told them so. We can't be subjecting people like yourself to these intrusions on time and privacy."

"It is, of course, my honor to help if I can. But to be honest, what could I say of use to them?"

"Exactly. Ach, this is all very embarrassing."

"Do not upset yourself. The police only do their job."

"Yes, it's all about them, isn't it? Their job, their time...they don't care about *my* dilemma. And the way they talk...I tell you, there's little finesse among them. They leave you feeling like you're the criminal."

"Ah, this I understand. In the old country that was fact of life." Borodin also thought linking Sorenson to the others could be a useful option should the need arise. But for the moment, he nodded, all compassion and concern.

So the cops had found what he had planted at both residences. Good. The bitches were costing him a tidy sum, yet nothing compared to what he stood to lose if he didn't silence them both. Nevertheless, hearing how easy it was to make the police believe in Tatiana and Sasha's guilt was gratifying and restored his faith in human nature. He relied on people believing that where there was smoke, there was fire.

Now was the time to award himself another small pleasure as he set in motion the next precaution.

"You can count on my support. Whatever I can do," he said placing his hand over his black pearl tiepin. "Please, do not hesitate." Then he sighed. "But could I inconvenience you with my business for one moment?"

"Of course. It means more than you can know

to see that you aren't letting this unfortunate situation taint your opinion of our firm. And life must go on, eh?'' Sighing again, Sorenson gestured invitingly, his smile as brave. "Now, exactly what can I do for you?''

"I am in need of liquidating my portfolio.''

Arne Sorenson's jaw went slack. "W-why? I mean...Melor, I'm not sure I understand.''

Borodin let the anxious reply hang between them for several seconds, enjoying the man's plunge into total mental disintegration. It did, after all, take a considerable investment to get the attention of the senior partner of a firm. Losing an account of that size would raise questions from the other partners.

Finally, pretending to comprehend, he gushed, "Oh, you think...no, my friend. No, no.''

The broker's relieved laugh almost sounded giddy. "You mean you don't intend to close your account after all?''

"Absolutely not. Let's leave, say, ten thousand.''

Sorenson's smile faded yet again. "This is most sudden. I mean...forgive me, Melor, but do you mind explaining yourself?''

"An opportunity.'' Borodin spread his hands. He left it at that, knowing it would drive the other man nuts. From his pocket he drew a business card, on the back of which was printed two series of numbers. "The top series is the bank's telephone number. If you would be so good, wire the balance less the amount specified, and your fee, of course, to the account identified by the bottom series of numbers. I don't need to tell you that timing is crucial."

"As you wish. Of course, it's no problem. But Melor, as your broker, it's my obligation to caution you against impulse and to protect you from—"

"I appreciate the concern, Arne. All is well, I assure you. By the way, this is a Cayman bank."

"I...see. I suppose I should have expected that."

Melor's smile widened. "Come, Arne, that is beneath you. I realize this is a temporary drain, but hardly, how do you say...?"

"Injurious." The broker swallowed. "You're right. Think nothing of it."

"And as soon as my business is completed there, I will replace the funds."

"Will you?"

"How can you doubt it?"

The news reassured Arne somewhat, though he was by no means close to being his confident self again. "So this isn't about something we've done? It's not about the scandal? Trust me, your name is one I'd fight to keep from the police regardless."

Borodin didn't believe him any more than he had hesitated in his decision to transfer his money out of reach of the feds. Tatiana had known him better than anyone. As a result, he could leave no room for closer examination, uncovered trails...anything that might sabotage him. But what he was doing was also in its own way revenge. He had a taste for it, liked to play with it, abstract it, to see how far he could stretch the concept and still derive a degree of satisfaction.

He smiled now.

"Don't be ridiculous, Arne." He extended his hand. "You can count on me."

21

Gray told himself that he had no business feeling betrayed, let alone any of the other emotions boiling around inside him. He was forty, damn it, and as the kids said, should be "way over" such nonsense.

It was a relief when Jimmy Lester drove in with a trailer of cattle that his mother needed to have vaccinated and checked. However, young Lester, quiet under normal circumstances but undoubtedly recollecting Gray's surly behavior during his last visit, didn't offer Gray any escape from himself, and the minute Gray finished, the boy hopped into the cab of his white pickup truck and hauled ass.

A white pickup truck... Gray swore at how willing his imagination was to go anywhere Sasha led it. Yeah, he thought, he needed to get a grip or he was primed to make a major fool of himself.

Oblivious to the scorching heat and depressing view, Gray lingered outside, too aware that there was nowhere to go in the clinic without seeing, hearing or sensing the woman. Hindsight being what it was, he accepted that he should have let her stay in the house this morning after that business at the station. She would have found something to eat in there, and none of the rest would have happened. Didn't the little fool realize that, instead of having a head-on collision with Kenny, she could have run into whoever the hell she was running from? He was about fed up with wondering who that was, as well, and strongly tempted to go inside and get online himself. To hell with leaving a cyber fingerprint.

And where was J.M.?

Lost in his own thoughts, he didn't think much about the slam of a vehicle door until he glanced left and saw the edge of a car at the front of the building. Parked that way, the driver was using up several parking spots, not that it mattered. Curious, Gray took a few steps toward the vehicle, and saw it was a patrol car.

"Now what?" he muttered.

He strode toward the back door. Halfway down the hall, he heard Frank's laconic drawl.

"How's it going, sweetmeat? I hear you've been taking in the sites around town."

"Chief Elias."

"Kinda surprised to hear you visited our library, though. You don't strike me as the bookworm type. Oh, wait a sec...it wasn't books you were interested in, was it? Sorry to hear that their one computer was being used. But will you look at that— there's a computer right in front of you. Don't tell me Slaughter wouldn't let you look up whatever you needed? Know what, I've got one next door, too, and it's all yours. All you need to do is ask nicely.''

"Thanks, but no thanks. If you'll excuse me, I'll get—"

"I'm here," Gray told Sasha. He joined her inside the reception cubicle and posted himself on the corner of the desk.

Frank smiled. "So you are. Funny, I passed a minute ago and thought you were out in the yard, kinda looking like an old bloodhound who can't pick up the scent of home."

"What do you want, Frank?"

"Not you, that's for sure." The cop redirected his gaze to Sasha seated behind the desk. "So what was the idea behind the computer? What were you planning to *research?*"

"Incidents of arson in Texas, maybe?"

Frank's smile waned and he extended his hand. "I think you've jerked my chain long enough. Hand it over."

While her set expression told Gray that she knew what he was talking about, Sasha didn't budge.

"And what would *it* be?" she asked.

"Your license."

"I thought you were supposed to be up the road. What about the insurance investigator coming to inspect the church?"

"Come and gone."

Gray met her questioning look. She was containing herself well, but he knew she sensed bad news coming. "We haven't heard from J.M." he said, to buy her time. "He was going to monitor that."

"Oh, yeah..." Frank leaned his elbows on the counter. "I seem to recall him being there."

"And...?"

"He left."

Gray knew better than to let Frank's smug smile get to him, but it did. If he wasn't certain it would bode worse for Sasha, he would have liked to forget an old promise and wipe it off his face once and for all. Weary of the game playing, he muttered, "It's apparent that you're dying to poke a stick into some wound, so get it over with."

"But there are so many to choose from."

"What did the investigator say?" Sasha demanded.

"He won't file his report until next week."

Gray narrowed his eyes, trying to read the nuances in Frank's expression. If the prick was here to arrest Sasha, he wouldn't merely be smug, he would be ecstatic. And if the news was good for her, he wouldn't have bothered coming at all. "But he's made some early observations, drawn some conclusions."

"Maybe that's privileged information," Frank replied. "In any case, it's none of your business, is it?"

"Well, since I'm the one being accused, it is my business," Sasha said.

"I don't have to tell you squat...yet. All you need to know is that the investigator confirms we have a case of arson on our hands."

Gray uttered a disparaging sound. "There go more consumer dollars down the sewer after the wasted tax money that's your salary. You don't have a damn thing and you know it. Cut her loose, Frank."

"I have the right and obligation to run a check on her." Frank's too-bright eyes held more than challenge. "And I plan to do my job if that's okay with you, Slaughter." Without waiting for a reply, he once again extended his hand to Sasha.

"You can't be serious," she said, pushing her chair away from the desk. "You're only doing this to taunt him and harass me."

Frank grinned. "Is it working?"

Rising, Sasha paced around the tiny room. "Before I surrender any property to you, I'd like to confer with my attorney."

"That sounds like a no to me." Frank smacked his lips together and made a hungry sound. "Great, because I am so ready to have you back at the station. I never did give you a full tour of the premises. It'll give us a chance to get really acquainted."

"Like I said before, you're a pig." Gray had to grip the edge of the desk to keep from reaching for him. "You lay one hand on her and I'll break it, then call the DPS in Sonora. There's nothing wrong with her talking to J.M. She's not a flight risk. If she were, she'd have been long gone by now."

Frank released the snap on his holster. "I do get tired of you trying to tell me my job. But you know what? I'm in such a generous mood, go ahead and call the old fart. Good luck getting him, though. He got a call a while ago and left the church looking like he'd swallowed a dose of salts. What do you suppose that means?"

Nothing reassuring, Gray suspected, but he reached for the phone anyway and punched J.M.'s number. He got the answering machine and waited for the message to end. "J.M.," he began after the tone. "Pick up...come on, I need you. Pick up the damn phone."

He waited another ten or fifteen seconds before reluctantly hanging up. When he saw the resignation in Sasha's eyes, he felt as if someone was peeling a strip of hide off his back.

Silently, she returned to the desk and reached for her purse. "I'd like to know when I can expect this back," she asked, handing over the laminated card.

"When I'm done with it." Frank didn't pretend to hide his pleasure as he took the license, making sure his fingers caressed hers in the process. "You want to come with me and wait?"

Sasha wiped her hand against her jeans. "Believe it or not, that offer is entirely resistible."

"Suit yourself. Of course, I may not get to this right away," he added, slapping the license against his other palm. "Being tied up with the fire, I've let other work pile up, so it might be tonight or even tomorrow morning before I can return it."

Sasha pressed her lips together and, shaking her head, turned her back to him.

Chuckling, Frank pushed away from the counter and sauntered toward the door. "Now, if you change your mind," he said in a singsong voice, "you let me know, hear?"

He was still laughing as he exited. Gray watched him pocket the license and climb into his vehicle. Expecting him to head straight for the station, he was surprised and relieved to see him cut a sharp U-turn and drive east.

"The bastard's going to let you dangle, all right."

"Not that I disagree with you regarding his character," Sasha replied, "but you may be wrong about the rest. If his car isn't set up with its own computer, and there's no one at the station to operate the one there, he can still radio in the number to the sheriff's office."

Gray shook his head. "It isn't, there isn't and the latter isn't likely, either." He met her curious look. "They're not too fond of old Frank since he got caught messing around with a popular deputy's wife."

With a groan, Sasha put away her wallet. "Well,

thank you for small favors, I guess. Is there any female around here who he hasn't hit on?''

''As far as I can tell, he's resisted visiting the nursing homes so far.''

She burst out laughing.

The transformation hit Gray like a man stepping out of solitary confinement into blinding sunlight. ''My God,'' he said without thinking, ''you're lovely.''

She hesitated, then grew inordinately involved with adjusting the rolled-up sleeves on the clean shirt she'd changed into.

''I'm sorry,'' Gray continued, willing her to look at him again. ''Not for that, but for the rest. I should never have forced you to stay. Maybe I was wrong and he wouldn't have gone after you. Or maybe I was just kidding myself about what I was doing.''

''Don't.''

''It's okay. I'm not expecting—''

''Slaughter, if you don't mind, I'd really prefer not to hear any more.''

Her sharp interjection worked as effectively as a razor across the throat. Retreating to his office, Gray quietly shut the door behind him.

22

Spiritualists could have blamed what was going on in Bitters on a bad moon, and psychologists on the relentless weather pattern, but Sasha knew she alone bore responsibility for driving Gray back to the kind of reclusiveness she understood had been the norm before her arrival. As the second hand on both her watch and the wall clock proved that a minute could feel like a week, she was given ample time and then some to regret her behavior, worry over what had happened to J.M. and dread Frank Elias's return.

The only thing that could have made the situation worse would have been the sudden reappearance of that Suburban. The way her luck was running, she thought that was a distinct possibility.

But it was Gray who set her to pacing. She wished he hadn't blurted out what he had. He couldn't possibly believe it helped having the chemistry between them out in the open, not when it was something neither of them wanted or could afford to do anything about. Now there was one more thing preying on her mind, on her conscience...

And she had to gauge Frank's next move. Unfortunately, with things the way they were between her and Gray, she couldn't ask him what time Gerri Rose got off at the café and if she dared hope that they were together. Then again, from what both J.M. and Gray said, Frank had other options. At this point, she didn't care what it took, so long as he was entertaining himself and leaving her and her business alone. One thing she was already grateful for—he'd given up questioning her about the computer faster than he should have. But was Elias that poor a cop, or was he giving her a false sense of security?

She was still brooding over the matter when a champagne-colored Lexus pulled up front. A well-coiffed but frazzled woman emerged, dragging behind her a reluctant motley-colored dog.

"My college-student son's," she explained as she wrestled the animal inside. "He won't stop scratching my car door." When the dog settled right over her leather pumps the way Jessie did to Sasha, the woman cast the creature a glowering look. "It's not like I'm gone for long stretches of time—an hour at the grocery, ten minutes to the bank—but he acts as though I've been away on the space shuttle."

Sasha wasn't following. "And you think Dr.

Slaughter can do...what exactly?'' She glanced over her shoulder, hoping Gray would appear. Surely he could hear them speaking?

''Well, give me a prescription, of course.''

Beginning to rise from her seat where she'd just settled to attempt to reach J.M. again, she dropped back onto the chair. ''You want him to drug your dog?''

The woman drew a lint roller from a side compartment of her shoulder bag and brushed at the hair on her pink skirt. ''Only tone him down a bit. They give whatdoyoucallit to hyper kids and Prozac and whatnot to adults, I figured—will you look at this? He's turning a Dry Clean Only skirt into mohair.''

Sasha stretched to see over the counter, but not to inspect the skirt. She wanted another peek at the poor creature who'd struck out in the foster-care department. The content critter was doing his best to lick the panty hose off his mistress.

''Stop fussing,'' the woman scolded, giving the leash a tug. ''I swear, Stony, I'd pack you off to Austin in a heartbeat if Jeffrey could keep you in his dorm.''

''Since you can't, maybe you should consider going home, changing into shorts and going outside to play ball or stick with him.''

The woman stared as though Sasha had spoken in tongues. ''I beg your pardon?''

"Or find him a home with an owner who can give him the time and attention he deserves. Don't you realize that Stony is missing Jeffrey as much or more than you are? And as you're all that's left, he's obviously looking to you to give him some attention." She gave the dog a look that basically said, "Lots of luck, fella."

The woman was anything but appreciative. "Who do you think you are? Where's Gray? Dr. Slaughter!"

When he didn't show, she started pulling the dog to the door. "I'll come back another time when he's not tied up—and has *qualified* help. Better yet, I'll find another clinic. The only reason I came here was because it was close. Stony, damn it, *come.*"

A moment later, when Gray did appear, wiping his hands on a paper towel, all that remained outside was a cloud of red dust. "What happened?"

"Uh...nothing."

"Did Frank come back?"

"No." There was no way she could avoid telling him. "Some woman wanted you to drug her dog."

Gray frowned and glanced outside again. "You mean put down an old, sick dog?"

"And here I thought the government had the edge on euphemisms," Sasha replied, wrinkling her nose. "Not put down. *Drug,* as in behavior altering. But she decided not to wait. No, that's not true, I'm afraid I wasn't as diplomatic as I could have been.''

He only let his gaze linger on her for an instant. ''No, pragmatic and sharply to the point is more your style. Why didn't you come find me?''

She accepted the jab as her due. ''Stony isn't sick.''

''Stony…Jeff Harvey's Stony? There's nothing wrong with him.''

''That's what I told Mrs. Harvey. So…'' She shrugged because the lingering dust cloud spoke for itself.

Gray was surprisingly accepting. He only wandered from window to window, generally looking as though he wanted to be anywhere but there talking to her.

''I was out back picking up trash that raccoons had tugged out of the garbage,'' he told her. ''If you had called, I probably wouldn't have heard you anyway.''

With that he retreated down the hallway. As relieved as she was that he hadn't said something more cutting, she was equally surprised at how noncommittal he sounded. If she didn't know better, she could have guessed he'd taken a pill himself.

Things fell back into a monotonous lull again. Sasha tried to kill more time by paging through the mutilated magazines in the reception room between periodic visits with J.M.'s answering machine. Gray remained out of sight, and it was so quiet in the building she felt as though she was alone.

Right at four Jessie woke. Her soft mewing had Sasha thinking of Stony and his desperate attempts to be close to his mistress. Not at all liking the parallel she saw, she took the dog outside for a quick potty break and brought her up front.

Back at the desk, she found a pair of scissors in the top drawer and a brush under the sink in the kitchen, and went to work grooming the dog. Jessie seemed of a mixed mind about the makeover, but she made it clear that she liked being talked to by nudging Sasha with her nose every time Sasha fell silent. Just as Sasha was cleaning the brush for the last time, the phone rang. She resisted her first impulse to snatch up the receiver, aware Gray was back in his office this time; when she'd passed there, the door was closed again.

But after the third ring she wondered if she could be wrong and picked up.

"Clinic."

"Yes, I need some information," a woman replied. "My regular vet in Sonora is on vacation, and I'm looking for a place to board my cat while my husband and I take a six-week cruise to…"

Sasha stopped listening, her mind stuck on the idea that someone would consciously stick a family pet in a cage with strangers for a month and a half while they partied. What was wrong with people? No wonder Gray acted fed up and burned out.

"I'm sorry," she said the moment the woman stopped talking. "We're totally booked through New Year's Day."

As she turned to replace the handset on the cradle, she saw a pair of worn boots beyond the phone. Running her gaze up along the redwood-length legs, she met Gray's unsmiling gaze.

"When you didn't pick up, I thought you were outside again," she began. "Okay, you're right. I'm all wrong for this job. But, Slaughter, not even you would think much of a person who would abandon a so-called beloved pet for *six weeks* in order to go on a cruise."

He didn't reply at first and his face remained a blank mask. He simply crossed to the front door and locked up. Then he flipped off the light switch. "Put her back in her cage," was all he said as he disappeared down the hallway.

Sasha sat in the vacuumlike silence until she heard the thud of the back door. With a whimper, Jessie set both paws on Sasha's knees.

She leaned over to scratch under the sad-eyed dog's chin. "It's not about you, Miss Mess. I've hurt him…and I'm going to end up hurting you. But no way am I locking you away again. Not at this hour. If you're game, c'mon."

The idea of closing early appealed to her greatly,

since she'd been feeling like some carnival game target all day. At least the house would offer a modicum of privacy and protection—as much privacy as she could find with Elias breathing down her neck, and as much protection as her gun offered. All she needed was for Gray to continue playing Invisible Man the way he had this afternoon.

23

Las Vegas, Nevada
2:26 p.m. PST

"**I** have to speak with you."

The childish voice had Melor Borodin passing back the new shipping manifest for the stolen air conditioners he was moving on behalf of an associate in California. Motioning to the waiting driver that he should get going immediately after switching the product from one truck to another, he retreated deeper into the warehouse where it was less noisy.

"What did I tell you about phoning here?" he demanded.

"Please don't be angry with me. I was careful. I'm at a pay phone away from the station."

At least the bubble brain retained something of his directives, Borodin thought, scanning the activity in the rest of the warehouse. The situation here didn't make him any happier. He had too few men to move too much inventory. If someone didn't give him good news soon, the feds were going to make a killing after taking possession of the inventory he couldn't dump in time.

"All right, all right." He struggled to find patience for her. "I am like a bear with bad mood because no sleep, *da?* Your fault." He rolled his eyes at the bullshit, but heard her sigh with either relief or pleasure. Who knew? Who cared?

"My news may help," she replied. "I think she's surfaced."

"How do you know this?"

"I believe she's using an alias. As you asked, I've been working as many hours overtime as they'll let me to see if something turns up. Luckily, we have people out with summer colds, and we're also short due to vacations."

Borodin pinched the bridge of his nose. Damn, the woman could go on. Into the phone, he said, "And I am forever grateful. What is news you have to tell me?"

"I've come across a search from that funny-named town you said to watch for in Texas. Bitters? It's shown up. The police there just ran a background check on an Anna Diaz. Now, it's a Louisiana license, but the last address for her on the computer was—are you ready? Sasha's. On top of that, by the looks of her MVD photo she could be Sasha's twin."

So that's the name she was using. Borodin wondered what the connection was between the two

women, but was more interested in knowing why
the cops out there were checking on her. "Who is
this Anna Diaz?"

"Ah, this is the fascinating part—you mean *was*.
Talk about weird. She's dead."

Borodin had culled Officer Gloria Carney from
the flock to create his very own spy. Eager to see
conspiracy and threat everywhere, she was also the
least likely female on the LVMPD to have a love
life. So he had inveigled himself into her good
graces, convincing her that he was being hustled,
virtually stalked by Sasha in revenge for the brief
relationship he'd had with her mother. He'd explained how Tatiana Mills had been attractive for
her age, but soon proved obsessively jealous and
demanding of his time. Borodin had played to Gloria's sympathies and her moral outrage, asking her
to gauge whether Tatiana's daughter, Sasha, was a
serious stalker he needed to fear. The queen of the
Lonelyhearts Club, who could never compete and
secretly resented the effortlessly sensual Sasha, had
been more than ready to oblige.

But what interested him now *was* Tatiana's
daughter. How had she come across a dead
woman's ID, and one who looked so much like her,
no less?

"For what reason do they ask of her?" he que-
ried.

"Would you believe she's an arson suspect?"

It was too delightful. Strictly by-the-book Sasha

accused of arson. At least it explained why she was still in that ridiculous-sounding place.

"Have they arrested her?" he asked. His people hadn't given any indication of that, and if this news proved accurate, he would eunuchize them himself.

"If they haven't yet, it sounds as though they might."

Under no circumstances could that be permitted. To free herself, Sasha would talk. He didn't know how much she knew about all his interests, but she'd alluded to enough the last time they were face-to-face. Add to that her devotion to her mother and he didn't have to question that she would ruin him in this country if he didn't destroy her first.

Once again he glanced around the warehouse still too full of merchandise. He needed time, otherwise it wouldn't be just the feds after his ass; his customers expected him to be an efficient and reliable conduit. Their vengeance would have no statute of limitations, and they didn't recognize state, let alone international, boundaries.

As his man Yegor stuck his head out of the main office door to hand off another manifest, he said into the phone, "Hold a moment." Then to the shaven-headed man he called, "Have we heard from Lev or Akim yet?"

"*Nyet.* But it has been two hours. The call comes at any moment."

"Let me know the instant you hear." Then into

the phone he said, "Darling, I must meet with you."

"So you're pleased?"

"There are no words."

"Tonight?"

She sounded so hopeful, he smiled. "You think I can wait that long?"

She laughed, a little giddy, a little self-conscious. "I'm still on duty, you know."

"What was I thinking, forgive me. It is this ID you mentioned. It would be so helpful to see a copy of it. Perhaps I can recognize this woman, maybe she worked for me as former employee. Perhaps Tatiana and Sasha used her to watch me. I think I remember someone at the restaurant..." He let the idea dangle and waited for Gloria to take the bait.

"Then of course, I'll manage. When and where?"

He mentioned the parking garage of the abandoned building soon to be torn down to make way for a new casino. He knew she would like it because it was where they'd first sojourned. "Say...one hour? Unless you can take an early dinner? We could dine on each other, my *stukachi.*"

"Oh, I'd love to so much...but I'd better not risk it. I wasn't kidding about being shorthanded here."

Borodin accepted the news with a heavy sigh and ended the call, murmuring, "Don't make me wait too long.'' Disconnecting, he then headed for his office.

Arson. This would not do at all. But he had an idea of how to get Sasha out into the open again, even if she had to take on the devil himself to get free.

When he returned to the front office, he found Yegor on the phone. ''Akim,'' the man said, passing it over.

Borodin said into the mouthpiece, ''I have new orders for you.''

24

Gray yanked open the kitchen storm door and punched the inner one so hard, it hit the stop and bounced back at him. He didn't care, just as it didn't matter that he'd closed the clinic almost two hours earlier than usual.

He went straight to the refrigerator and got himself a beer. It wasn't what he wanted on an empty stomach, but he was thirsty enough to drink a keg. Maybe it would help take a bit of the edge off; hopefully the shower would, too. Then he intended to drive over to J.M.'s.

It had been several years since the attorney had been able to manage a full-time practice responsibly. Gray wasn't about to criticize him for that. However, J.M. could pull himself together for occasional representation when he knew it was important. Well, this was important, and if J.M. had allowed himself to get dragged off course by one of his exes again, Gray wanted to know.

Drought conservation restricted his time in the shower, and it was a spare ten minutes later that Gray pulled on clean jeans and a T-shirt, and returned to the kitchen. Temporarily refreshed, he stepped into the room and saw Sasha's mutt on a king-size bed pillow. One with a pillowcase no less. At the opposite side of the room, his houseguest's curvaceous southern half was visible as she rummaged through the pantry.

"How do you feel about Spam and scrambled eggs?"

Gray picked up a glass out of the drainer and headed for the ice machine. "You're not feeding that animal my survival food."

Once the dispenser turned off, Sasha poked her head around the corner of the louvered door. "We'll share. I admit, I'm getting hungry, but I'm not up to another trip to the café, or Bitters's idea of a grocery. I doubt you are, either."

"I'm not hungry."

"You have to be, and so is she. And for more than the prison food you were serving next door."

She was right; nevertheless some demon inside him resisted the sense of her words. "It's called *dog* food, which is what she is, regardless of how you want to treat her. And speaking of... What's she doing on my pillow? That mutt's only had a sponge bath so far, and in case you've forgotten, she's given every indication that she's not house-broken.''

"She's been doing great this afternoon," Sasha assured him. "And technically the pillow is yours, sure. But it's not off of your bed. I'll want you to add it to what I owe you."

"The point is you should have asked first. You've got a real talent for not asking."

"No, the *point* is that she has stitches...and you weren't here. Again,'' she added with a challenging look.

Gray had a flashback to a time and place of false environments, of being tested and pushed and graded on his reactionary skills. It wasn't so dissimilar to what she was subjecting him to. Only this time he didn't have to respond with, "Yes, sir!"

"Keep playing fast and free with that money," he said, "and you'll have to find yourself another rich sucker to roll."

Sasha set the canned meat on the counter with a sharp thud. "I didn't *roll* anyone."

This time his reply came easily. "You say. That's all we have, though, isn't it? Your word."

Even as she turned away, he felt the nasty kick from his conscience, but his darker side egged him on to go for a full twelve rounds or for a KO. Under siege, he yanked open the freezer and grabbed a frozen dinner.

While Sasha eyed the package, she didn't comment, but lined up ingredients beside the stove like pieces on a chessboard. As she reached for a skillet, he went to the microwave he claimed to loathe and shoved in the beef enchilada dinner.

"Want a drink?" It grated, too, that he was no longer content with the silence that had suited him for almost two years.

"No thanks."

"A glass of ice water?"

She shook her head. "And you wouldn't drink it, either, if you left out the scotch. There's something wrong with your town's water."

He had planned to leave out the scotch, but was fast changing his mind. "Just another thing for you to be relieved about when you leave here."

She turned away from him and concentrated on chopping, frying and scrambling. He nuked then carried his meal to the table. The tantalizing aroma that wafted up from her pan made him accept that his dinner tasted like the mud pie it resembled.

When Sasha sat, it wasn't beside him as before, but at the opposite end of the table, and she kept her eyes on her plate as he did his. What's more, she didn't stay there long, rising after only a few bites. Gray knew it was because of him, but his mouth watered as she passed, almost reaching for her plate. Stiff-necked pride saved him. Setting her plate on the counter, she checked the sheet of aluminum foil she'd set out for the dog in lieu of a bowl. While Jessie had done better, she hadn't fin-

ished either. Dumping the dog's remainders down
the garbage disposal, Sasha was about to reach for
her plate when Jessie whimpered.

"Looks like her problem isn't only about prison
food," Gray drawled.

Ignoring him, Sasha shut off everything. "My
fault, Jess. C'mon, baby," she cooed, leading the
animal outside.

She wasn't gone long. By then Gray had not
only finished his dinner, he'd inhaled her leftovers
and almost finished washing up after her.

"I intended on doing that." She patted Jessie,
who settled back on the pillow. "But maybe I'm
not to be trusted with soap and water, either."

"You're exaggerating."

"And you're welcome to live with a ghost."

As she started to walk away, Gray grabbed her
wrist, sending a splatter of soapsuds and water
across the room. Before she could react, he had her
so close they had to share the same breath.

While her eyes kept their secrets and sorrow,
they openly searched his. "Gray, this is a mistake."

"That's the first time you've used my name as
though you really see me."

"I see you... I also know you don't want this."

No, because it cost to feel, to want...to need.
Until her, he believed he'd escaped the tax that life
demands. He'd developed himself into an emotional pauper, finding a degree of comfort in what

he'd escaped, only to realize the people he'd cheated didn't really care in the first place.

And what did he have to offer her even for one brief night? Thankfully, a greater force was driving him.

"Now who's clueless?" he asked. Because heaven help him, he could already taste her. She was a lost memory that shook him to his core.

Sasha slipped her hand to the back of his head, drawing him down to her. While everything until now had been fast and edgy, this was something else, an honoring of the truth and a savoring of sensation.

Their lips brushed together as though acutely aware that, like a matchstick being brought closer and closer to a score, things were about to change entirely.

He initiated that change, urging her lips apart and deepening the kiss. As his tongue sought hers, a desire he didn't believe existed exploded. Propelled by its power, he angled his head and wrapped his arms fully around her.

At the same time old lessons died hard. Letting go wasn't easy. He knew on some level he shouldn't yield to the hunger that caused every joint and muscle to ache, and yet desire played dirty.

As he slid his hands to her hips and perfected their fit, pleasure arced again, pushing him closer to a heady edge. In that instant he knew if he lifted her legs around his waist, he would come even before he could turn toward the bedroom. But before he could think of an alternative spot, he heard a low keening.

The dog...?

Torn between laughing or groaning, he felt Sasha step back.

"Gray...?"

That's when he heard the real reason for Jessie's cry. It was that terrible sound again. A siren.

25

Gray thought he reacted quickly, but Sasha beat him out the door. He followed. Despite his longer strides and her injuries, he didn't catch up with her until they were nearly at the street, in time to see the fire truck disappear west over the slight rise in the road. Following it was Frank's patrol car. Considering the hour, Gray assumed bringing up the rear was Murphy Cox.

They weren't the only ones to react to the commotion. A number of people were pouring from stores and offices to have a look. The reason was debatable. Gray heard someone to his right make the observation, "Two fires in one week. We'll make the AP wires yet if we're not careful."

In fact, they already had, although it didn't surprise him that people were so out of touch. Last month six illegal aliens were found asphyxiated a few miles south of the interstate in a broken-down delivery truck that was later discovered to have been sabotaged. That in itself was nothing new—cunning *coyotes* were always bilking those who were desperate to get over the border—but this time two of the victims were kids.

As Gray eyed the plume of black smoke rising against the early-evening sky, he speculated that it was a highway wreck. The black clouds soon turned to charcoal gray, suggesting that the blaze was pretty close, and that Tim Pike and whoever else on the truck were putting it out.

"What if it is arson again?" Sasha asked, echoing the speculation voiced across the street.

"You have to have something to burn," he replied, "and there's nothing out there. One good thing, though. It'll help your situation." At her dubious look, he added, "You're here."

Maybe so, but several people were eyeing Sasha as though they hadn't figured that out yet. Or maybe they were staring because the gossip mill had also passed on the fact that she'd spent the night at his place.

"I'm gonna drive down there and see what's up," Billy Emmett declared from in front of the grocery store.

"That's why the chief and them went," Don Sargent replied. "You get back to loading Mrs. Christy's groceries. Fire looks to be about out anyway."

As the disgruntled clerk obeyed his boss, there were a few off-color remarks regarding Frank's abilities—another sign of the fragile ties of friendship.

Just as the smoke was reduced to a negligible marring of the cloudless sky, a patrol car raced back toward town. Gray recognized Murph behind the wheel. The hefty part-time officer honked a warning to the people stepping farther into the street, but folks were slow to take him seriously, and he came close to clipping a few of them as he pulled in at the police station.

"It's a car," he announced, gripping both sides of the door frame to lift himself from his vehicle.

He might as well have announced the discovery of a crashed UFO. The news created a new excited buzz in the small crowd collecting around him, and it took Murph a minute to quiet the group again so he could hear specific questions.

"Too early to say whose. None of us has recognized it as local yet. But mind you, Tim and Hal were still pouring water on it as I left. I gotta get inside and get the chief's camera." Officer Cox could barely contain his pride that this important task had been issued to him.

"Well, was it a wreck, Murph?" Don asked, looking confused.

"I don't guess so. Only one vehicle involved."

"Fat fool has never heard of people running off the road," Wyatt Carter muttered under his breath only yards from Gray. The barber called to Murphy, "How's the driver?"

The patrolman shook his head as he made his

way to the station door. "Ain't one. Guess that's the good news."

"Then how'd the car get there, let alone catch fire?"

Murph looked as though the question hadn't yet entered his mind. He quickly assumed a studious frown. "I don't know. Shame to waste such a prime vehicle, though. Looks like one of those pricey sports jobs."

Sasha sucked in a sharp breath. Thankfully everyone but Gray was hanging on to every word. As she began retreating toward the house, he followed.

"What is it?" he asked.

She didn't reply, and from the way she was holding her side, he assumed that was the problem. "Did you reopen the wound while running?"

"No."

Her unwillingness to articulate what was wrong, especially after what had just occurred between them, stung. Taking hold of her arm, he forced her to stop. "Damn it, Sasha, isn't it clear to you by now that I'm on your side. What's going on?"

What he saw on her face had him instantly regretting his sharp tone, and he eased his hold. "Something Murph said makes you think you know what this is about."

"I have to find out," she said, glancing back to make sure they weren't overheard. "Can we get up there?"

"No problem. But you'll run headlong into Frank's wrath doing it, so I need to know why."

"What he said...a feeling. I can't describe it."

"For your sake, I hope there's no connection. Haven't you noticed people's reactions out there? Thanks to Frank, and probably me, they're one rumor away from blaming you for it not raining. You go over to the fire and everything they've heard about you will be gospel."

Sasha laid her hand against his chest. "Gray, I *have* to get over there...and I need to take my gun. Will you get whatever you have? Will you help me?"

He didn't see that he had a choice. It was a no-brainer that she was intent on going with or without him. Since he didn't trust her behind a wheel in her current state, let alone within reach of Frank, Gray dug into his pocket and pulled out his keys. Gesturing for her to lead the way, they got the guns, locked up and climbed into his aging blue pickup truck.

"You might want to lay low," he told her as he started the engine.

"Who do you think we'll fool?"

"I'm not just talking about the people here. Your instinct to go armed tells me that you could be a target. Now get down."

She did. People did call out to them, and a few begged a ride. Gray hoped he wasn't starting a parade, but a glance in the rearview mirror indicated that Murphy Cox was being delayed because he was trying to control that.

As they crested the small hill, Gray yielded to the urge to touch Sasha's hair that was spilling over the bench seat and his thigh. "You can't hide that cannon of yours in your waistband, and my shotgun won't go unnoticed by Frank. Once we get up there, we'll have to leave everything in here."

"I know. But that's better than nothing."

"You're beginning to scare me."

"Don't add to my guilt, Slaughter. As it is, I'll do penance for asking this of you."

"You're Catholic?"

"Actually, I was christened Russian Orthodox. Catholic friends like to tell me that makes me a black-sheep cousin."

"So your name wasn't just a dramatic impulse on your parents' part?"

"No more questions for the moment. I need to think."

"At least give me a clue as to what to watch for."

"If it's a BMW Z8, a red one, watch your back."

Although that mysterious statement spawned a dozen other questions, Gray had reached the site and had to concentrate on making a U-turn while avoiding the other vehicles slowing to watch the scene.

"Any of these look suspicious?" he asked.

Sasha eased up and studied the gawkers, the two cars and the gray truck with a gooseneck trailer parked on the shoulder. "No."

Gray's attention next switched to the fire scene. The fire truck and Frank's vehicle were farther off the road and at first blocked their view of the burned car. Tim Pike was still hosing down the vehicle, and although it would be impossible to avoid getting wet from the subsequent backwash of spray, Sasha jumped out and started running, dodging around the sparse but prickly vegetation. By the time Gray caught up with her, they were both practically soaked—and in Elias's line of vision.

"Get away from—hell, Slaughter, you, too? What do you two think you're doing?"

"Where's the driver?" Sasha yelled back at him.

"Damned if I know. We've looked around, but as far as we can tell, the vehicle was abandoned."

"No one abandons a six-figure car." Finally getting out of the line of fire from the spray, Sasha wiped her face with the sleeve of her shirt and scanned the area herself.

"And just how would you know what this wreck cost?"

Instead of answering, she circled the vehicle, and as soon as Tim shut off the water, moved in for a closer look.

"Now what are you— Hey! Get away. There could still be enough heat or a lingering spark to blow that thing all over the place."

Gray had to agree with Frank, but Sasha wasn't paying attention to either of them. He turned to Tim Pike, the well-liked fireman whose full dark beard did little to age his pleasant, round face. "Any clue as to what this is about? You got here the same time the chief did."

"If you ask me, it's another gift from the person who triggered the fire last night. Makes about as little sense, too."

Less, considering that Sasha appeared right about the value of the vehicle. Cars didn't interest Gray much, but he had a general idea what expensive was. "You're sure it couldn't have been an accident?"

"Wouldn't stake my life on it, but I do know cars like that stay on the interstate, they don't travel the back roads where gravel and oil trucks kick up rocks and damage their windshield or paint job."

"Maybe they needed gas and were backtracking."

Tim made a face. "You don't risk contaminating a high-dollar engine like that one with the crap from a small town's underused tank."

Impressed, Gray was about to ask more when Sasha called to him.

"There's something in there." She tried to reach in, but immediately pulled back and rubbed her arm. "Anybody have a pole with a hook or something?"

"For the love of—" This time Gray wasn't gentle as he yanked her away from the vehicle "Aren't you scarred enough?"

"Help me, Gray. It's in bad shape, but is it a purse or briefcase? Damn, it's a purse, I just know it is."

He looked inside and spotted the flat charred mass on the passenger floorboard. If she could recognize that mound of wet muck as a purse, he wanted to use her eyes to x-ray his next patient. His taking too long to respond cost him, though. She pulled away and began casing the area, paying particular attention to the ground. It was just as well, because Frank moved in to chew ass again.

"Slaughter, I'm through with this bullshit. Now, what is her story?"

"Give me a second." Gray went after her. Realizing that she was looking for tracks, he said, "Footprints or blood?"

"Please, God, not blood. Damn, Elias tromped through here as though he was at the White House Easter-egg hunt."

"What size shoe?" Gray was starting to put things together.

She met his gaze briefly.

"I have a little experience with tracking," he told her.

"Rubber soles just like mine, only one size larger. But if you really want to help, I'd feel better if you kept an eye out for any movement behind all that brush out there. This situation reeks of a setup."

Hearing that, Gray wanted to haul her to the safety of his truck. But doing as she asked, he replied, "We'd better work fast. Frank knows you're hiding something now, and it's making him totally nuts. The surprise will be if he doesn't lock up both of us."

"He'll have to shoot me to make me leave."

"This would not be a good time to tempt him."

"Instead of worrying about me, he should be questioning those people parked at the road, asking them if they passed any vehicles heading west."

Murph returned and Frank put him to work on the license plate. "Pike cooled the back end before it got too damaged," he said. "Clean off that crud and tell me what you make out. Then radio in for an immediate check on it."

From her crouched position where she'd paused to examine a smeared print, Sasha pivoted. She'd obviously heard, too, and her expression reflected sheer dread. "Not yet," she whispered.

"Maybe he won't have any better luck than you do with your phone," Gray replied.

"It'll work. And where he's calling, they're tied in with the new updated NCIC 2000."

"And what's that?"

"National Crime Information Center, the enhanced law enforcement system. Now it ties in the forty-eight contiguous states with the FBI." Rising, she did a slow three-hundred-sixty-degree turn, her whole demeanor increasingly dejected. "There's nothing here. They have her."

"Who?"

"Maybe you don't need to radio for ID," Tim suggested to the others. "There may be a suitcase in the trunk that's in better shape. I'll get a crowbar."

It wasn't a difficult task for someone his size, but the instant he popped the trunk, he reared back, then began choking and gagging.

His reaction had Sasha charging back faster than Gray could think to stay her. Even the "Don't!" he wanted to yell stayed locked in his throat.

As bad as Tim's reaction was, Gray knew hers would stay with him for the rest of his life. When she reached the car, she became like a photo, trapped forever in one freeze-frame. He found himself thinking "Move," knowing the longer she hovered there absorbing whatever she was looking at, the deeper the wound to her mind.

Then slowly she did move, but only to reach out, her arm moving awkwardly like a broken wing. From past experience Gray understood that, in self-defense, her mind was already shutting down to where the limb couldn't remember what to do on its own.

By the time Gray got to her, she was bent over at the waist and hyperventilating. He didn't want to look inside the trunk. He'd seen death before, knew what fire did to bodies, knew the smell… He had no desire to relive such violence. But as with everything else this woman was able to draw from him, he made himself deal with it. And then, almost gagging as Tim had, he drew her back, away from the nightmare and its stench.

Frank was next. Gray had his back to him and heard rather than saw him. Frank didn't venture as close, but even so the repulsion came fast and succinctly.

"Shit." Seconds later he was beside them, ashen-faced and swallowing hard. "Poor fucker. Sure hope he was dead before he was put in there."

"So help me," Gray ground out, "if you don't shut up, I'll make you."

The damage was done. The hands that had been gripping his shirt as though he was her lifeline pushed him away. Freed, Sasha approached the trunk again. In amazement, Gray saw her lean as close as she could to inspect the corpse. His stomach roiled against his imagination of what she was seeing, as much as it had against the remembered odor.

After what seemed a small eternity, she walked to a thicket of brush and became violently ill.

"That is one strange broad," Frank muttered.

Shooting him a killing look, Gray accepted a handful of paper towels Tim was pulling off a roll he'd taken from the fire truck, and went to offer

Sasha what comfort he could. "You know, don't
you?" he asked grimly.

She managed a weak nod.

"Who is it?"

"My mother," she whispered.

26

His eyes burning, Gray drew her head against his chest. While she didn't resist, she didn't cling to him, either. She simply stood in that terrible limbo of incomprehension and acute knowledge.

"Maybe you're mistaken." He garbled the words, and as he cleared his throat he realized the impulse to offer hope was a cruelty, too. But his intention had been to encourage her to hang on because she was the only one with answers...and Frank was about to demand them.

"She's wearing her wedding ring."

"It could have been taken from her."

"Never."

Gray glanced down at his bare left hand that gently stroked her hair. "I'm so sorry."

"They shot her in the face," she continued, her voice flat, devoid of emotion. "Her beautiful face."

"Don't. Sasha, you can't know for certain. The fire—"

"Didn't you see? It didn't burn long enough to

hide the truth. A single bullet. Large caliber. I saw the exit wound at the b—oh God. Oh God.''

"What's she saying?" As Sasha buried her face against Gray's chest, Frank moved in again. Already recovered, he was eager to take advantage of weakness wherever he saw it. "What's going on?"

Knowing it was still up to him to reason and think defensively, Gray urged Sasha toward his truck. "I'm taking her back to my place."

"The hell you are. This is a murder scene now and—"

At the touch of his hand on his back, Gray spun so fast Frank backed hard into the fire truck. "That's her mother," he growled, pointing to the carnage. "And after you've wrapped your self-absorbed mind around that, consider that, at this moment, your murderer or murderers could be hiding in any number of these gullies or thicker brush drawing a bead on Sasha or on any of us."

Tim Pike glanced around and stepped closer to the fire truck.

Frank looked as if he wanted to leave himself. "All the more reason for you to stay. You've got training, you can't leave us out here."

"You've always claimed you were cut out for life on the edge. Well, have at it, pal."

Dazed, Frank scanned the area, his gaze lingering on the lengthening shadows, and as he swallowed yet again, his right hand edged up the side of his holster. Then a dawning transformed his face. "What did you call her? Slaughter? Slaughter!"

As Gray ushered Sasha to his truck, he heard the growing commotion behind them.

"Damn it all to hell. Cox, get that carload of gawkers out of here...and get hold of Kenny. Tell him we need him. Move! Pike, where do you think you're going?"

"My job is done here."

"Your ass stays until I get EMS personnel over from Sonora."

Frank was still threatening, cursing and ordering as Gray got Sasha inside the truck. In her shell-shocked state, she didn't need much urging to lie flat on the seat again for the drive back to town.

As he feared, too many people lingered there, and from the way a few tried to flag him down, he suspected that somehow someone had already heard about a death. One pounded on the side of the truck, but he shook his head and continued in to his place.

He helped a dry-eyed, too quiet Sasha inside. Jessie lifted her head and wagged her tail, inviting a pat, but they went straight to the kitchen sink where he washed Sasha's face and then gave her a cup of water to rinse out her mouth.

He had her seated at the kitchen table and was pouring her a stiff drink when he heard another vehicle tearing into the yard. Moments later, emerging from the cloud of dust, Frank stormed in.

Her hair rising, Jessie curled her upper lip back and growled.

"Shut up," Frank snapped as he passed her. His real anger he directed at Gray and Sasha. "I should arrest both of you. Who do you think you are? Nobody walks away from me. Do you know what that looked like back there? I've got a town to control, and I don't need Pike blabbing his mouth about how you tried to make me look bad."

"Believe it or not, Frank, you managed that all by yourself. And I told you why I was getting Sasha away from there." Having failed initially, Gray tried to ease the drink into her hands. "Take a swallow. Do it."

This time she did...but then she shuddered.

"Another."

"I'll throw up again."

"Only if you were a scientific phenomenon. Take a deep breath. Another. Now try that swallow."

She did, but her hands began to tremble and she set the glass down. Gray saw that she understood what was happening, what he was trying to do. He watched with growing admiration as she retreated from her psychological abyss, and thought with no small satisfaction that Frank was about to witness what the word *professional* meant.

"If we're finished stalling," Frank chided, "could we get to it? Who are you and what's going on?"

Accepting that he needed to stand back now, Gray positioned himself where he could control Frank if needed. He saw by her brief glance that Sasha understood and was grateful.

"My name is Sasha Mills," she began, her voice hollow. "My mother was Tatiana Ivanova Mills."

"Say what?"

At Frank's startled reaction, she nodded. "Yes, she was Russian. She met my father, Sean Mills, when he was a marine assigned to the American consul in Moscow. I won't bore you with the details of their courtship. Suffice it to say it was difficult, and as dangerous as their relationship was special."

"Are you kidding me? I'm not interested in hearing about your personal fairy tales or your family tree."

"You'd better be," Sasha replied. "Because without understanding that, you can't possibly comprehend the rest."

"In that case I need some staying power, too," Frank said, snatching up her glass.

"You're on duty." Gray focused on Sasha's clenched hands, seeing how she hated the thought of his mouth touching where her lips had rested. For his part, so did Gray.

A spiteful Frank swallowed the rest of the contents in one long gulp, then set the glass in front of her. "Now get to the point."

She complied, but refused to look at him, instead staring at the center of the table. "When my mother became pregnant with me, my father knew he had to get her to America."

"That had to have been difficult," Gray said, intrigued because he remembered the times. Such liaisons would have been frowned upon, considering the cold war going on between the U.S. and the U.S.S.R.

"I'm sure. My mother wouldn't talk about it much. That's no big surprise, considering the government pressures and social patterns she grew up under. My father only admitted that he broke one rule short of being arrested and court-martialed. I suspect, though, that he managed to sneak her out much the same way that Svetlana Stalin escaped. As it was, once the furor died down, his military career was quietly but completely over, and even though they didn't deny him his honorable discharge, he lost the fourteen years he'd already invested in his career. By then my mother was settled in Minnesota at my father's family home, and he believed that was a fair tradeoff."

"How romantic," Frank drawled.

Sasha lifted her chin. "I agree. It was a rare relationship, and they were devoted to each other.

She always felt she owed him more, and so she worked hard to become an American citizen.'' She turned to Gray. ''Those were good years…until we lost my father shortly before I graduated from college. There was a situation at the bank where he was the executive vice president. It's almost a common incident these days, however back then hostage-taking was terrifyingly new, and was triggered by the estranged husband of a woman who worked there. My father tried to intervene. Unfortunately, the chief of police was the man accused of being the woman's lover and he had his own ideas about resolving things, one of which I suspect was to make her an instant widow. The plan backfired and all three of them were killed.''

Sasha paused to draw and purge a deep breath. ''I'd intended to enter law school later that year, but I put that off in order to spend more time with my mother. She couldn't seem to get over what happened, and since there was just the two of us left at that point, I convinced her that we should move, try a whole new change of scenery.''

''Las Vegas is a helluva change,'' Gray said.

Frank glared at him. ''You knew about that, too?''

''Heat,'' Sasha told Gray with a sad smile. ''Imagine a Russian who couldn't take the cold anymore. And yet how understandable.''

''To you maybe,'' Frank muttered.

"Her soul was frozen," Sasha explained. "She couldn't get warm no matter how warmly she dressed."

"Horseshit."

"Yes," she murmured. "I'm sure for you it is." She shifted her gaze back to Gray. "And so when I asked her to choose somewhere, she chose Vegas. She threw herself into our new life, going to school by day and working as a cocktail waitress by night, while I went back to school and became a member of the LVMPD."

Frank burst into laughter and pulled at his hair. "Oh, no. No, no, no. You're a cop?" But upon noting Gray's calm demeanor, he gave up the theatrics. "You bastard! What don't you know?"

"More than you think."

"I *think* you're full of it. Are you going to tell me that little bomb didn't bother you, or did you see her as a replacement for Mo from the start?"

Gray had always hated that nickname, almost as much as he resented the question. "You're drawing the wrong conclusions, as usual."

"Sure. And you haven't been jumping her bones the whole time she's been here, either."

Gray straightened from the counter. "Watch your mouth. That's the last time I'm going to warn you."

As if to show he wasn't intimidated, Frank said

to Sasha, "Are you anywhere near the part about how your personal soap opera brought you here?"

"My mother's choice of employers," she replied, "inevitably earned her the attention of the man who's responsible for her death. Once she graduated, she went to work at a brokerage firm called Joseph, Bains and Sorenson, where she worked her way up to being the assistant and office manager to Arne Sorenson, the senior partner. That's when she was targeted."

"By whom?" Gray asked.

"Melor Borodin."

"Great. Another Commie," Frank muttered.

Sasha shook her head. "He may be Russian by birth, but he's never been Soviet anything."

"And that means?"

"He's nothing like what his name stands for." She recited the etymology of Borodin's first name.

"Who the hell does something like that to their kid?"

"People trying to make the system work for them. But Borodin himself didn't begin really thriving until glasnost, and like so many other opportunists and scavengers, he became a dangerous player in the Russian mafia."

As she spoke, Gray heard more and more of her ancestry emerging in her choice of words as much as in her careful enunciation. She understood her mother's heritage as well as she knew the Ten Code.

"Your mother got involved with the guy knowing what he was?" Frank scoffed.

"Of course not. By the time he appeared in the U.S., Borodin had gained considerable polish, as he had power and wealth. To the average observer, he appeared one of so many international businessmen taking advantage of NAFTA and the new world market. To the public, his presence in Las Vegas was to open a restaurant, not unlike New York's Russian Tea Room."

"Never heard of it."

"I'm not surprised," she replied coolly.

His coloring deepened, but he plodded onward. "So I don't pay a week's salary for finger food. I also never illegally assumed someone's identity or got my mama turned into a well-done fajita."

"That's it."

Fed up, Gray pushed away from the counter. However, before he could get at Frank, Sasha stepped into his path. She laid her palms against his chest, and rested her forehead there, too. There was no missing the exhaustion behind the gesture.

"He didn't say anything that isn't true, even if he did say it crudely," she said.

Crude didn't begin to describe the insensitive jerk, but what bothered Gray more was her assuming guilt for this. However, he wasn't about to say anything in front of Frank that could be used against them later. "Don't do this to yourself," was all he told her, adding a discreet pressure of his fingers as he clasped her shoulders. And to Frank he added, "Any more cracks and you're going to answer to me for them, with or without you wearing that badge."

Before Frank could respond, Sasha interceded again. "As best I could determine in the little time I had to look into his past, Melor Borodin is a man of flexibility. He's involved in a number of illegal activities partly of his own design, and partly on behalf of associates. I think a good deal of his success is due to his willingness to be a conduit to others, and though the restaurant on the surface is legal, I was given to understand that it allows him to launder money for drug trafficking and other illegal operations. But being that he's more ambitious than many, he was also venturing into the insider trading business. That's where my mother became useful to him."

Gray couldn't figure how. "Isn't the definition of insider trading using confidential information provided by a corporate officer or other employee for financial profit? You said she worked for a brokerage house?"

"Her location, her knowledge of the market and privileged position in the firm...he used that and her to cull information on companies and people, then he or others went after them, initiating relationships to get what they wanted. By the time she saw a pattern between his stock purchases and what was happening in the news, she knew she was culpable, as well."

"Didn't anyone else at her firm notice?" Gray asked.

"Brokerage firms operate like NASCAR workshops, everything is deadline orientated. If someone suspected something, they undoubtedly thought it was just another good business decision. You have to remember, they weren't privy to seeing him outside of the office as my mother was. If you're not looking for or expecting deception, you rarely notice it until well after the fact."

"Why'd she continue the relationship after she knew what he was?" Frank demanded.

Sasha bowed her head. "The most common and least respected of reasons. You see, she was flattered by his attention. Grateful for it, she wanted to help him succeed with his business—not that she understood at that point all that he was involved in."

"Love." Frank said the word as though it left a bad taste in his mouth.

"I refuse to believe it went that deep, but agree there was no excuse." She shrugged. "At the same time, you'd need to meet your subject to understand. Melor Borodin is like the most pampered of thoroughbreds—polished, disciplined and formidable at his sport. He made my fifty-year-old mother not even care that he was fifteen years her junior."

Frank erupted in a shout of laughter. "Fifteen, dang. Mama must've been a looker...but I'll bet he liked you better."

"You'd lose," Sasha replied coldly. "We despised each other on sight. But I did try to be happy for my mother's sake. And she...I can't deny that she blossomed, and appeared happy for the first time since losing my father. Then things began to change. She seemed more and more preoccupied and nervous. When she started losing weight and I saw a bruise where there shouldn't be one, I couldn't hold back any longer. When she confessed, I knew I should go to the FBI right away. Understandably that made her all but hysterical. He'd succeeded in totally intimidating her."

"So you decided running like a pair of scared bunnies was the best solution," Frank taunted.

"The situation evolved to where we didn't have any choice. As luck would have it, the moment I tried to get help, we found ourselves targets."

"What did you do?" Gray asked.

"I believed in the system I represent. I tried to contact the deputy chief at my division. He wasn't in, so I told his aide, a desk officer, that it was imperative that I speak with him. We weren't friends, nevertheless, I knew her well enough to feel comfortable around her, and confided I was concerned for my mother's safety. She...well, I don't think my DC got the message."

"Are you suggesting this Borodin got another cop to turn on you?" Frank's expression suggested that he would believe in psychics first.

For his part, Gray could imagine several reasons for the critical omission, anything from innocent though costly forgetfulness, to professional or personal jealousy, to outright revenge for some real or imagined past incident. But from the way Sasha had described this Borodin character, he knew her hunch was that the snake had gotten to more than Tatiana Mills.

"Let's put it this way," she replied, "when my DC didn't return the call, I phoned him again, and this time I got through to him. He didn't know what I was talking about...or pretended he didn't. That's when I knew I had to get my mother out of there."

"Yeah, leave room to finger the DC in case your other theory falls flat on you," Frank drawled.

"No. Understanding Borodin's charisma, particularly his influence with women, I do think it was Gloria Carney's doing, but until I know for sure, I'm assuming nothing."

"Okay, so when you got hold of your chief, did you tell him?" Frank asked.

Sasha shook her head. "There wasn't time. What I'd said to Gloria was enough for Borodin to know my mother had talked, and it was more important to get her out of danger. I went to her place and convinced her to grab what she could and run. I planned to do the same and join her out of town. As luck would have it, by the time I got to my place, Borodin was waiting for me. The only thing that saved me was his arrogance—he only brought one bodyguard with him."

"Show him your side," Gray told her.

"I'm not interested in show-and-tell."

"Sasha, he needs to understand what this guy was willing to do to you."

"Isn't what happened to my mother proof enough?"

Her voice shook, and Gray squeezed her shoulders reassuringly. "Please."

She slowly lifted the left edge of her shirt, exposing the bandaged area.

Frank pursed his lips. "Why didn't I hit that spot yesterday?"

"You did. Why do you think I punched you?"

"And here I thought you were just playing hard to get. So what shape are the Russians in?"

"The bodyguard needs to learn to shoot with a new hand, if he isn't varmint chow in the desert somewhere, and Borodin isn't quite as photogenic as he used to be."

"Okay." Frank shifted and walked around the room, thinking out loud. "So you got away. Why didn't you call the FBI then? You were safe."

"I don't think you grasp what I've been telling you, Chief. Borodin has assets. He flies in and out of the country regularly in his own jet. How did I know who else he owned, how deep his contacts went? No, first and foremost I had to get my mother out of reach—and that included obtaining a new identity for her, for both of us."

"Which brings us to Anna Diaz. I haven't had time to check on what's come up on that search I ran. What am I going to find?"

"She was a friend who died."

"Convenient. Well, why weren't you and—" Frank nodded in the direction of the carnage "—traveling together?"

Sasha bowed her head and sighed shakily. "It was my one concession to her. She blamed herself for what was happening. At first the idea had merit—Borodin was looking for two women traveling together—but I traded in my vehicle, while she...she couldn't give up hers. It was too much of a symbol of the new life she'd created for herself. She also reasoned that we needed it to buy her new identity. Most of all she wanted to be sure that if we were followed and spotted, she would be the one who risked identification. On the upside, I figured that it might better allow me to protect her.

"Needless to say, we traveled as much as possible by night, stayed a few miles apart and didn't even sleep in the same places. We also arranged a schedule for checking in by phone. Then on Thursday morning I thought we were far enough away from Vegas that I could try to talk to my DC with relative safety. What I didn't take into consideration was how busy Borodin had been since we'd left. The chief wanted to give orders, not listen to what I had to say."

"Busy how?" Frank asked.

"He set us up, left incriminating evidence that made us look like we were in a little side business of our own. Understanding that I'd said too much and that they might be tracing the call, I hung up, though apparently not in time—at least not for Gloria. She must have passed on the information, because in a frighteningly short period of time Borodin had men on our tails again. I lost them, but got stuck here...and they...they found my mother," she ended on a raw whisper.

As Gray discreetly stroked her back, Frank scowled at her. After a long silence he said, "I guess it never crossed your mind that you were bringing your trouble to us?"

"Damn it, Frank," Gray began.

"On the contrary," Sasha replied. "I was extremely concerned. But you're the one who put the roadblock in my way, Chief."

"I'm about to again because you're under arrest."

"For what?"

"I'll let you know after I confirm or disprove your story."

Gray couldn't stand it. "You have a murdered woman on the edge of town, what's to confirm? You put Sasha in that joke of a cell you have over there and she's a sitting duck. Besides, you don't have the manpower to keep an eye on the station *and* deal with what's down the road."

"So help me, Slaughter, if she runs—"

"It'll never happen." Didn't he comprehend Sasha's dedication to her mother yet? "If she does," he replied, "you can draw on me again—and this time use the damn thing."

27

Telling Boba to stop the car yards away from the Toyota, Melor Borodin leaped out like the eager lover he wanted Gloria Carney to believe he was. But as he loped to her personal car, he was scanning the empty garage wishing that it was three in the morning rather than an hour before the evening rush. He should at least have come in a different vehicle; however, there was no time. That was his theme song these days—*No Time.*

"Have you been waiting long?"

He asked the question as he folded himself into the passenger seat of the Toyota. There wasn't enough room for his long legs, but he didn't reach down and adjust the seat. His cramped legs were the least of his concerns. For her part, Gloria hyperventilated from either excitement or heat. She had the engine off, and the windows were up, so although they were surrounded on three sides by thick, cool concrete, it was like an oven in the vehicle.

"No, I only just arrived myself. It's so good to see you."

She was lying and it both amused and dumbfounded Borodin that she not only tried but also thought he couldn't tell. It made it easy to forgo the Clint Eastwood smile that she so admired and catch her by the wrists as she reached for him.

Gloria looked instantly bewildered, then hurt...then worried. "What's wrong?"

"I cannot risk it, *blini*. I think of excitement to see you and..." With a reluctant sigh, he took her hand and brought it to his crotch.

She not only relaxed, she giggled like a schoolgirl. She looked like one, too, with her damp curls sticking to her shiny, flushed face. "You are so good for my ego. I can take care of that, um, problem for you."

He let her stroke him so he wouldn't lose what he'd achieved himself driving over here to fool her. But when she began to reach for his belt, he again stayed her hands. "My Glory, it is impossible and you make me to weep thinking of what I must resist. You see, after I speak with you, I get news of water leak in restaurant kitchen. Five pounds of caviar is looking like sturgeon pissing in Volga River. I must go make serious discussion with system contractor to fix before customers come."

Gloria tsked in sympathy. "You have too much

on your plate. I hate that this mess with Sasha and that mother of hers is dragging on, too. To think she always pretended to be so nice to me. Of course, unlike the rest, I knew she wasn't what she pretended to be. And stuck up...well, you should hear them now about the drugs. Suddenly everybody saw it coming, her mother having that expensive car and all. Champagne tastes and beer budget, it'll get you every time, my daddy always said. Hopefully it'll be over soon, though. It sure sounds like it is. Here's the printout of the ID on that Diaz woman.''

Borodin accepted the paper but barely gave it a glance. He was more interested in what else was being said at the station. ''What is news on arrest? And what of Tatiana? They say nothing since you and I speak?''

''It's been oddly quiet. But unless the files in Louisiana incriminate this Diaz person, it will be our warrants for Sasha and her mother's arrest that they've been trying to keep out of the media that will allow Bitters to keep her. And I have to relay him this ID and let him know they have her as soon as I get back.''

Borodin could not allow that to happen. Time, he thought again, reaching into his jacket. Drawing out Boba's borrowed Glock, he pressed it against Gloria's forehead and replied, ''Alas, I think not.''

The noise of the blast was deafening as the .9mm bullet, as well as the force of her head slamming backward, shattered the driver's window. Cursing the roaring in his ears as much as the stupid cops in Bitters, he reached into his other pocket and drew out the handkerchief containing a small plastic bag of cocaine.

Careful not to touch it with his bare hands, he shoved it into her gaping mouth. Then he used the cloth to wipe down the door handle and hurried back to the idling Cadillac.

28

The silence in the wake of Frank's departure was welcome, although Gray doubted it would last long. Sasha needed time—far more than he suspected she would be allowed.

"I haven't thanked you," she said, breaking into his thoughts.

Incredulous, it took him a moment to reply. "What for? You were right from the start. If it wasn't for me, none of this would have happened." In fact, when he looked at how well his behavior had helped the people hunting her, he didn't know why she wasn't aiming her Smith & Wesson on him right now.

But Sasha shook her head and her unfocused expression indicated she was fixating on an internal chronicle. "If I hadn't been consumed with making Anna's final months as full and easy as possible, I would have paid closer attention to what was happening to my mother. When I did see, I should have gotten her out of there first and asked questions later." With a groan, she covered her face with her hands. "She backtracked. *Oh, Mama, why?*"

Gray understood the emotions she'd been holding in check weren't going to stay contained for much longer, but he was willing to listen and help for as long as she needed him to. "Your mother was supposed to be ahead of you?" he asked gently.

"Always. This way, if she had trouble, I would be there as backup. Then Borodin's men spotted me as I was leaving a service station, and I had to get off the interstate. I hid for over an hour. Believing I'd lost them, I started off again, keeping to this smaller highway. I planned to get back on the interstate after Bitters, except...they weren't fooled." She shot him a brief look. "You saw the black Suburban, didn't you?"

"Yeah, but when it didn't show up again, I tried to convince myself I was making something out of nothing." Seeing the misery in her eyes, Gray had to do something to keep from putting his arms around her, and picked up the glass that Frank had tainted, bringing it to the sink. "It's not your fault that your mother came back looking for you."

"She drove right into their grasp."

"You expected her to do less for you than you were doing for her?"

"What could she do? She was no good with guns, and worse with directions. She knew that, except for the destination we agreed on each day, she should simply drive. She wouldn't have gotten off except to use the service road to make a U-turn for refueling." But the fact that something else happened had Sasha raking her hands into her hair and gripping her scalp. "They brought her car here for me to find because they know where I am." She met Gray's grim gaze. "I don't want to bring any more trouble to you."

Everything that could be done at the moment was. Before Frank left, Sasha had described the Suburban to him and what she'd seen of the two men inside. Frank hadn't gone through any metamorphosis after his inadequacies at the fire scene, even so, Gray hoped the police chief understood what he had to do now. To Sasha he simply said, "You're here and you need rest. More important, you need privacy. Go lie down."

"I can't do that."

"You can't afford not to." Then more tentative, because she had no reason to put what little faith she had left in him, he added, "I know how to use a gun...and you can trust me to let you know the moment anything happens."

Her eyes filled, and for a second she reached out her hand as though she was imprinting on a frosted windowpane. But she said nothing as she turned around and disappeared along the hallway. Gray took the quiet closing of the guest-room door as an answer, though.

"'And miles to go before I sleep,'" he quoted softly. With a sigh, he picked up the bottle of scotch and put it away without pouring himself a drink.

29

Las Vegas, Nevada
6:11 p.m. PST

"Sons of bitches." Melor Borodin slammed down the phone in his office. Would nothing go his way and stop the landslide of all his hard work? In a burst of rage, he picked up the elegant boxed unit and flung it across the room. It struck the crystal cobra on the teak coffee table in the center of the room, sending it crashing to the floor.

Seconds after the eruption, the connecting door to the warehouse opened and Yegor stuck in his slick head with a less certain Boba behind him.

"Stop acting like timid women. Get in here."

Slim Yegor, dressed in black and always looking one meal away from being malnourished, had been with him some seventeen years—since they'd tried stealing the same car back in Moscow. The Great Boris had been found shortly thereafter. Borodin wished it had been Boba with him instead of Yuri when he'd first gone to silence Sasha. Boba would have taken the bullet *and* kept after her. In any case, it was only fitting that, as he faced the disintegration of his small kingdom, he should keep these two close.

They entered, but after shutting the door behind them, stayed put. Veterans of more than one Borodin tempest, they'd learned by experience to stay out of the line of fire.

"Tatiana is dead," he announced to them.

Only Yegor reacted, and that was with the slightest lift of his left eyebrow.

"Yes, yes, I know that was the point," Borodin snapped. "But what did I tell those two? Did I not say first to use her to draw Sasha out of hiding? Sasha…not the entire fucking town." He swept the rest of the items off the top of his desk, but fortunately for Yegor and Boba the direction was toward the opposite side of the room. "They say she provoked them, and then have the balls to confess Sasha has been whisked into some kind of protective custody. They had her in the open—" he sliced the air with his hand visualizing the scene "—and they acted like they were out of bullets. Why? *Because she was not alone,* they tell me. Can you believe it? They were so concerned about making it to their vehicle, neither considered the alternative. Now what am I supposed to do, level the whole goddamn town? Boba, where did you find these two again?"

"They were with Perstev."

"Perstev blew up over Lake Michigan. They're probably the reason."

While the big man tried to recede into the wall, Yegor did what Borodin always expected of him when his boss's passions stirred toward the extreme—he got the focus back on the main issue.

"We are finished here," he murmured.

"*Da*. Perhaps we can keep the restaurant running, but even if the feds don't steal it from me, that pretty boy Kopelev will rob me blind. How do things look outside?" he added, nodding to the warehouse.

"Most profitable inventory is gone."

It was a hedge, but Borodin didn't blame him. "Who's likely to get shortchanged?"

"Volodya in Seattle."

"Finally, some decent news. He'll be willing to work it out with us. All right, Boba, get back out there and do whatever else you can. Yegor, get hold of our pilot and tell him to prepare the jet. Then start cleaning up everything you can here. Leave no compromising paperwork."

"Where do I tell Travis we're going?"

"The Caymans." For now anyway, Borodin thought.

Yegor accepted that with a pragmatic nod. "We've been working too hard anyway. So now, what about the daughter? She will talk. That could still hurt us."

True, Borodin thought. He had been explicit in

his instructions to Lev and Akim: the women were to be dealt with and disposed of so that their graves would never give up their secrets. The incompetents had achieved the barest fraction of that.

There was no point in denying he would miss Tatiana for a while. She had been like a flaming peony in a gulag, reminding Borodin that there were things he would miss of Russia, or at least should respect for their impact on his life. He would always be grateful to her for that. They used to converse for hours of their homeland...never politics, rather their profound sense of the land, books...those endless, gray winters in Moscow. That was what he would regret in losing the elegant, romantically melancholy Tatiana. That and an acute sexual passion he'd never known before. What a shame that her conscience got the better of her.

What a pity that she'd spit in Lev's face.

This was all on Sasha's shoulders, and Borodin intended for her to pay. She could not be left behind to gloat over his failure.

"Tell Travis to find the nearest landing field near this Bitters that's long enough to handle the jet," he said in answer to Yegor's comment. "I will deal with Sasha myself."

Yegor studied him for a long moment. "We don't leave for some time yet. She'll have time to prepare."

"Don't give her more credit than she deserves."

Hesitating yet again, Yegor added, "And of Lev and Akim?"

Borodin picked up the cobra that had broken into two pieces, its head cleanly severed. "I prefer not to duplicate Perstev's fate. If we're fortunate, their future won't be an issue. If they are...well, see that they aren't."

30

Bitters, Texas
Saturday, August 26, 2000
1:22 a.m. CST

The calm night didn't deceive Gray as he kept watch by the picture window in the living room. He appreciated the quiet, all right, he just didn't trust it, which is why there was no light in the house, not even the picture light he usually left on. He'd turned off the outside lights, too. Sitting in his recliner hidden by the sheer draperies, he relied on what illumination came in from the streetlights, and that created a landscape of ghostly shadows rarely interrupted by traffic. News had apparently spread fast, and it appeared few remained ignorant of what had occurred here only hours ago.

Beside him, Jessie whimpered in her sleep. She, too, seemed to be having problems dealing with the heightened tension, or else her stitches were bothering her. Gray reached down to stroke her silky length, and after a slight start, she relaxed with a prolonged sigh.

Gray felt like sighing himself. It had been hours since Sasha had retreated to the guest room, and although he'd paid close attention, things had remained eerily quiet on that side of the house. He had continuously checked to make sure her van was visible, but it remained where she'd last put it, and his truck was here by the house, leaving him fairly confident that she hadn't tried anything reckless again. Even so, he was concerned. It would have been more natural to hear something, at the least the muffled sounds of grief.

A strong woman, he thought. He knew he'd never met anyone more self-contained and resilient. He doubted all her fellow officers in the LVMPD admired her for that. One for sure didn't. Had Sasha's been a lonely life? She had to be feeling alone now, and it wasn't just the orphan thing.

Something out on the street caught his attention. Leaning forward he made a slight part in the sheers and recognized Frank. There was a first—Frank at the station at this hour. It was odd that, except for the EMS personnel, no one else had arrived from Sonora. Surely he'd called for help. Then again, Frank being Frank, it was entirely possible that he'd concluded if Sasha could evade those men in Vegas, he could handle them here.

As though reading his thoughts, Jessie growled.

She sat up and pushed her nose between the sheers to look outside, too. This time she growled louder.

"Easy," Gray murmured. "I don't blame you for resenting his treatment earlier, but we have to be quiet for your lady."

As though understanding, Jessie came to him and nudged his hand with her cool, moist nose and then settled her chin on his knee. Gray considered the quiet caramel-brown eyes gazing up at him.

"You're a flirt, aren't you?" He stroked her head and then rubbed her ears with lazy, soothing caresses.

Pulling away, Jessie grew alert again, but this time looked toward the hallway. That's when Gray heard the barefoot step he realized he'd been listening for since Sasha had retreated.

She came to stand beside his chair.

"Your biggest fan missed you," he said as a greeting.

Crouching, she set her gun aside and used her entire body to caress the dog. Gray understood her need to feel another pulse right now besides the one hammering in her head, he just wished he was the one she was reaching for.

"Thanks for giving me the time," she murmured at last.

Her voice held a huskiness and congestion that suggested she was coming down with a head cold. Gray knew it was the result of the tears that hadn't been audible through the closed door, or else still not shed.

"You should take some more. You might have eventually managed some sleep."

"Not when all I see when I close my eyes is her."

"Sasha, chances are she was gone when they put her in that trunk."

"I wish I could believe that. And before...how long did they have her? Those last moments...she had to have seen that gun in her face, felt so alone." Sighing, she retrieved the gun and tucked it behind her into the waistband of her jeans. "I should have been there with her."

Her steadiness sent a chill through him. Anguish, even hysteria, would be preferable to this. "Then you'd be dead, too. Maybe you'd have been first. Maybe she found some comfort in knowing they didn't have you."

"More likely, they tormented her by saying they did, that I was gone and how they'd done it. The same as my father."

"I don't understand."

"My father was trying to negotiate with the husband even as the chief and his men burst in. He was executed, not hit by accident. One of the officers told me so when I came to identify the body."

Once again Gray dealt with a jolt. "*You* did, not your mother?"

"She couldn't have survived that."

Dear heaven, Gray thought, she'd barely been more than a kid. And to lose both of them the same way… He pushed himself up from his chair. "I'm going to get us something to drink."

"No alcohol for me."

"I meant coffee."

While in the kitchen, he checked the door and windows before readjusting the miniblinds, then got a dog biscuit and carried the mugs back to the living room. Sasha rose from where she'd been petting Jessie, murmured her thanks as she accepted her coffee and parted the sheers to look outside.

Gray gave the dog the biscuit and settled in his recliner. "It's not a good idea for you to be standing there."

"Has Elias been back since?"

"No." Despite having questions, Gray couldn't say he was sorry, either.

"And it's been this quiet?"

"Except for the EMS ambulance that came and went."

"When was that?"

"About an hour after you went to lie down."

"And how often has he gone out there like that to the road?"

"This is the fourth time."

Sasha checked the mug halfway to her lips. "I'm going out to talk to him."

Setting down his own mug, Gray reached for his

.9mm set on the floor on his right side. "What's wrong?"

"That's what I need to find out."

Following her to the door, he laid his hand flat against it. "It's too risky. We don't know what's out there."

"The dark is my territory, Slaughter. I worked nights."

And once upon a time he had occasion to as well. "Okay, but I'll be right behind you."

31

One thing Gray did insist upon and Sasha was grateful for it—shoes. She berated herself as they emerged from the house, though, taking her forgetfulness as a blunder. Errors killed. She couldn't afford any more.

The night air was almost tolerable except for the heat that rose from the baked earth. But dust from the day's traffic hung in the air and stirred with the slightest movement. Before they'd taken a dozen steps Sasha felt it begin to line her mouth and throat. And with every step came the crunch and bite of gravel beneath their soles serving as sharp reminder that nothing was perfect, for while speed would have been hampered in bare feet, their shoes threatened to expose their presence.

Out of precaution, Sasha angled toward the deeper shadows hugging the station, her gaze on Elias still out in the middle of the street. "Look at him." She kept her voice low instead of whispering. "What do you want to bet in a past life he was at Little Big Horn?"

"You believe in reincarnation?"

Ten years ago, she could have said maybe...sometimes. But after tonight...? "I don't know what I believe in anymore."

She eased between the wall and parked patrol car. The vehicle spawned her hushed query, "What's this doing here?" At his shrug, she paused at the edge of the protective shadow and peered around the front of the building and down the street. Everything was as deserted as when she'd driven through here last night. Leaning her back against the cooling brick, she called a low, "Elias. *Chief.*"

He spun around, fear fleeting but real on his angular face. However, the instant he recognized them, the cocky mask slipped back in place. Swearing, he strolled over to them.

"You two are determined to push your luck. I could have drawn on you."

Since his hand hadn't begun to move toward his holster, Sasha let the bravado pass, instead stepping back to make room for him in the protective darkness, whether or not he had the sense to take advantage of it. She stopped when she felt Gray's solid body behind her, and welcomed the hand that came to rest lightly on her right hip.

"Where's your backup?" she asked, tilting her head to the other patrol car.

"Kenny's mother started having chest pains." Elias rested a hip against the vehicle as though it was high noon and they had nothing but time to shoot the breeze. "Probably faking it, but he's all she has, so I told him to get her over to Sonora. As for Cox—" he shook his head "—after he looked in that trunk, he turned in his badge and the keys to this honey." He patted the hood. "He'll miss it, and the free fuel."

His insensitivity aside, the news was worse than Sasha expected, but Gray was the one to voice her thoughts.

"Why didn't you say something?" he snapped.

Elias pretended as though he'd just noticed him. "Look who's feeling left dangling in the dark now."

"Hey." Since a white flag wasn't available, Sasha put her hands together signaling a time-out. Nobody would be served by an outright brawl, and it definitely wouldn't get her the information she needed. "What about the county?" she continued. "They should have sent someone out here by now. Did their crime scene investigator arrive?"

Once again Elias effected a posture of self-importance. "Can't yet. He's tied up back at their jail. Some dumb shit hung himself, only there are prisoners yelling that it wasn't suicide. Sounds like quite the commotion over there, so Sheriff Gleason doesn't have the manpower to spare. But he said he was calling in his off-duty people and would send out a couple guys as soon as he could spare them. That was over two hours ago." He glanced around the building. "Guess they were delayed."

Yes, the most coincidental things happened and often more bizarre than in fiction, but Sasha didn't like the feel of what Elias reported. "What about the DPS?"

"We can do without them."

Sasha must have made an involuntary move because she felt Gray's fingers tighten on her hip. It was all that kept her from breaching professional boundaries. "May I ask how you figure that?" she asked icily.

"Not how, *why*. I bring them in, and I lose my case like that." He snapped his fingers. "No way am I taking back seat to those glory hounds. Bad enough I have to bring in the county's deputies, but at least when they get here, I'll be better staffed than I was before—unless Gleason's a smart-ass and sends me two the size of Cox and with about the same thimbleful of brains.

"One thing worked out smoothly enough, though. The EMS team came and left without incident. By the way, since I was already short one man and that chickenshit Pike refused to stand guard over the site—like he needed to worry anyone was hanging around waiting to be arrested—I collected what evidence I could from the vehicle for the crime scene investigator. Give him a head start."

Sasha could only imagine how grateful the detective was going to be. But that wasn't what upset her the most. "You're making a mistake if you think the men who killed my mother are gone."

"So where are they?"

"Keep strolling out in the middle of the street and you may find out for us."

"Listen, you—"

"I told you who you were dealing with," she snapped. "You saw a sample of his brutality. Borodin isn't going to be satisfied with a half-finished job." She nodded into the night. "They may not be here in town this minute, but don't for a second make the mistake of thinking they're far away."

Not wanting to spend one more minute in Elias's company than she had to, Sasha turned and, touching Gray's arm to signal she'd had enough, they started back for the house.

At least sweet-faced Kenny Plummer was out of harm's way, she thought. She would have been concerned for his safety, his ability to cope. But there was no denying that losing him and Cox put Gray in increasing danger.

"Hey, hotshot," Elias drawled after her. "I phoned Vegas."

Sasha and Gray paused. While she knew she'd lucked out timewise with that side of things, and that if it was bad news, Elias would have rushed over and taken her into custody, her heart battered at her ribs anyway. She glanced over her shoulder and asked, "And?"

"Your DC's gonna have to get back to me. You

think things are busy here, they've got an officer found dead at your precinct. Now this one definitely sounds like an execution."

Needing to hear more, Sasha retraced the few steps she'd taken. "Who? Did they say?"

"Nope, and I didn't ask, but the guy I spoke with did use the pronoun 'her.' That should narrow things down some, huh? You didn't by chance phone in some IOU and have that aide bumped off, did you?"

His snicker followed Sasha back to the house. She was grateful for Gray's hand at her nape, and conscious of his concerned gaze, but she wasn't prepared to talk yet. He gave her until he had the front door locked behind them. He returned from the kitchen with a refill of coffee.

She used the time to reassure a relieved Jessie, who'd been whimpering at the window. She tried to get the dog to go outside for a nature call. The stray refused, going so far as to hide behind the couch.

"She's still running a temperature now and then," Gray said, passing over her mug. "Probably burning up whatever liquid she takes in. I think she'll be safe for a while yet. What about you?"

"It's a little late for you to ask, but I'm housebroken."

Gray didn't smile. "I know Frank tried to push every button he could."

"I can live with that. It's his tendency to bite

off his nose to spite his face that worries me. He needs help, only he's either too dumb or too proud to ask for it.''

"Well, he's no great fan of the *Times'* crossword puzzle, and he's never pretended to subscribe to *Playboy* for the articles. I told you, he was what Bitters could afford.'' In a gentler voice he asked, "You think it's her?''

"Gloria Carney?'' Just saying her name left a bitter taste in Sasha's mouth. "Must be.'' She returned to the far side of the picture window, leaned her left shoulder against the wall and gazed through the sheer draperies toward the street. But all she could envision was what Melor's idea of "execution" had been this time. "Poor fool. What was she thinking? Once Borodin silenced us, did she really believe he would need her anymore?''

Gray didn't return to the recliner, settling instead on the edge of the coffee table, which actually put him closer to Sasha. "Where do you suppose his men are?''

"I don't know. I can't even be sure there are only two at this point. There's been plenty of time and opportunity to have called in help by now.''

"That's what I was afraid you'd say. Any other good news?''

"I'm not saying I believe they have, but I'm guessing they're maintaining tight communications back and forth to Vegas. How do they manage that when our wireless phones couldn't keep a signal?

It's a bit more problematic than driving in to use the pay phone by the convenience store." The mention of that reminded Sasha of her attempts to contact her mother earlier. Had her mother been dead at that point? They'd been so close it seemed impossible that she hadn't felt...something.

"Stay in the present, honey," Gray said, clearly picking up on her train of thought. "What's to stop Borodin's henchmen from breaking into somebody's house or business, virtually anyplace that affords a view of Main Street, and using the phone there?" He scowled into his mug. "Break in, hell. Too many people here still don't bother locking their doors."

Sasha nodded, having guessed as much herself. "Elias may be right this time. They could have cut their losses and left. There's been no sign of the Suburban, and these guys tend to be hit-and-run strategists. The last thing they want is any confrontation with the law."

"You think it's possible Borodin could cut his losses and let you go?"

Sasha recalled the look on his face the last time she'd seen him, blood streaking down his cheek from the key she'd raked across it, those hazel eyes for once not laughing or mocking.

"Sasha."

She could only shake her head in the negative.

"Then let's call the FBI ourselves. We don't know if Sheriff Gleason did send anyone out here.

I told you there's no love lost between his office and Frank. Unless the EMS technicians spoke to Gleason or a deputy and confirmed the seriousness of our situation, he's probably more preoccupied with the potential scandal going on at his home turf.''

"Call the FBI with what?" Sasha asked. "I have a wild story that's technically my word against Borodin's.''

"You're a cop.''

"Who Borodin has set up to look like a junkie.'' Sasha gestured outside. "All of my proof is in ashes, if not mangled or at least contaminated by Elias.''

"You had some evidence?''

"When my mother first confessed what was going on, I told her to document as much as she could. It was all in that bag charbroiled on the floorboard of the car.''

"Let's go back and ask Frank to see what he retrieved.''

"No way. I saw the condition it was in. A lot in there was handwritten notes, so what the fire didn't get, the water— Look, the fewer people who touch the bag the better. Besides, if I told Elias there was important data in there, he would finish turning it into garden compost wanting to see for himself.''

Gray's look held increased respect and concern. "You've been hit with a lot this evening. Maybe you should try to rest a bit more. I'll keep watch.''

"I appreciate that, but I don't have the luxury of just mourning my mother, Slaughter. The cold fact is that my one witness is dead, and if Borodin's men don't get me—and God forbid anyone else in the process—there's a good chance I could be looking at hard time, while he moves on to his next scheme. And how long do you suppose I'd last in prison with or without the threat of him? You know cops are always vulnerable there."

Gray set down his mug, and resting his forearms on his knees, rubbed hard at his face. "Damn it. How could your mother fall for such a snake?"

"I told you. He's whatever he needs to be to seduce."

"But after your father..."

Sasha sent him a sidelong look. "You of all people should understand that desire has nothing to do with what's in the heart. She never pretended Borodin was a replacement. In fact, just the opposite. She was haunted by guilt believing she was betraying my father somehow, even though by then he'd been gone almost eight years. From there she swung to embarrassment because Melor was considerably younger. But...she had needs, emotional as well as sexual, only amplified because my father had spoiled her so."

The past and its wounds were still too close and raw for her, and she had to clear her throat and take another sip of coffee to fight back the paralyzing tightness in her throat and the burning in her eyes.

"I shouldn't probe," Gray said. "And I have no right to judge. I'm sorry."

"It's okay." Despite the heat wave outside, the searing sting of the hot coffee helped. She might as well be back in Minnesota, she felt so cold inside. Regaining her control, she tried to explain who her mother had been. "Did you ever read Tolstoy's *Anna Karenina?*"

He offered a crooked smile. "Sorry. I'm more the Tom Clancy, Michael Crichton type."

"I meant maybe back in school. No matter. The thing is that I saw parallels between Tolstoy's Anna and my mother. Both were prone to melancholia and neurosis. Both had been adored and pampered, which undoubtedly fed rather than addressed their neediness. Not that my father ever minded. He'd seen some of the struggles she'd endured in her home country, recognized the culture shock as she settled with him in the States and felt guilt himself for having taken her away from her only blood relations. He always felt a strong responsibility to compensate for that.

"After we lost him, she said his death had created a permanent open wound in her. Illogical as it may seem, I know that's why she bought that outrageously expensive car. It was too much car for her. But all that insurance money she'd been left with did nothing to ease her grief. She was desperate to feel something again, something other than pain. Does any of that make sense?"

Gray didn't look happy at what she was saying. "It sounds like they were close all right, but in those kind of relationships...well, it doesn't seem there would have been a lot of room for you."

"If I gave that impression, I'm sorry. Are you kidding? I was an only child, a *love child*." The memories did as much to warm Sasha as the coffee. "I was so lucky. I got the best of both of them."

"If you say so."

She sent him a reproving glance. "You're determined to see my mother as selfish, but she wasn't. She was giving and compassionate and... You went through my things, you saw her photo. That wasn't superficial beauty, she was that way through and through. It's just that she had her demons. But she was aware of them and tried not to let them touch us. When she felt them closing in on her, she would just...withdraw."

"What do you mean? Stay in bed, like with a migraine?"

"In a way, although I never heard her complain of pain. Later, she seemed to find greater comfort from closing herself in my father's study. I remember I was about four the first time I noticed the soulful music coming out of there. When I asked my father what she was doing, he said, 'She's visiting with her ancestors. Let's go catch some trout for dinner, Junior.'"

Gray choked on a mouthful of coffee. "He called you Junior?"

The unlikely nickname drew a small smile from her. "Never in front of my mother. It was our secret after I once confided to him that I really thought it would have been better if I'd have been born a boy, so he could stay home and keep Mama smiling, while I worked to support us."

"Thank God you didn't have a say in that chromosome mix," Gray drawled. Then he added, "It sounds like your father was a solid guy."

"Yeah."

"So whose idea was it to name you Sasha?"

"Dad. That's another reason I think he might have been hoping for a boy. Sasha is a derivative of Alexander, which breaks down to basically mean defending warrior." She shrugged, sorry she'd brought that up; it only reminded her of what a bad job she'd done defending her mother.

"It suits you, even more so than Anna did."

She remembered his initial comments about her alias and the sexual energy she'd felt exuding from him as he'd spoken. That energy was all the stronger now. "Thanks," she murmured.

"What's it like growing up with two cultures pulling at you?"

She stopped worrying the mug. "That's an interesting way to put it. I guess they do in a way. I grew up hearing so many stories about life in Russia that sometimes I feel it's my experience, too.

There was one tradition my mother taught me, what they called a 'poor man's fortune-telling' over there. Every New Year's Eve you put three slips of paper under your pillow, on one you write *better,* on the second *the same* and on the third *worse.* On New Year's Day, you pick one, and that's supposed to tell you what kind of year you're going to have. She would never do it. She might as well have been a Gypsy for being so superstitious. But children being fearless, I thought it great fun, and I always got the paper with *the same,* which made us laugh because that meant perfect for us. Except the last year," Sasha murmured, glancing out the window again. "The last year I pulled *worse.*"

"What did you do?"

"Lied. It was the first time I ever did. I told her it was *the same* as usual. That summer my father died."

A number of New Years had come and gone since, but Sasha never played the game again, nor did her mother ever ask. These days she always volunteered to work on New Year's to keep from thinking about such things.

"Do you speak the language?" Gray asked quietly.

She welcomed the change of focus and offered a look of mild chagrin. "Not as much as I used to. Not as well as I should. I'm your typical lazy American in that sense. Not my mother's daughter at all."

Gray shook his head. "You don't have to do that, you know, put yourself down in order to build her up. I hope you realize you're every bit as beautiful as her."

The words were a gruff caress, and not entirely deserved as far as Sasha was concerned. "I'm not as kind, definitely not as fragile. Sometimes it's difficult for me to turn the other cheek, let alone trust."

"Probably a smart thing, considering your line of work. Is that why you became a cop? To settle the score for your father?"

"That would have been an irrational outlook, since the man who shot him died, too. But in a way, I guess you're on to something. I was furious with how the police handled that episode, and I never wanted to feel that helpless again, or that useless. Yeah, being at the right place at the right time in a crisis to make sure things turn out better for more people—that's been important to me." Once again Sasha stroked the ribbed exterior of the mug like a worry stone. "Was that disapproval I heard in your voice?"

"It's not disapproval. Yours is a better answer than some I've heard, not that it's any of my business."

"Cop-out answer, Slaughter. As the man I was about to go to bed with this afternoon, I'd like to think I was attracted to an honest one."

He remained silent as he gazed at her.

"What? Did I misjudge that kiss?"

"No. I'm just adjusting."

"To?"

"Liking you. A lot."

Sasha appreciated his stilted reply. He'd been repressing his feelings for so long, any exposure had to be uncomfortable. That made the awkward phrasing more seductive than some of the come-on lines she'd heard from men who could buy this entire town several times over.

"You mean more than you *want,* don't you? Relax. I understood it would only have been a one-night fling. I'm not the type to compete with a ghost."

Gray frowned. "There's no ghost." When she failed to look convinced, he sighed. "All right, but not the kind you think. The truth is, the day of my wife's accident I was planning to tell her that I thought we should divorce. She was a police officer, too."

32

Over the southwest Texas skies
2:00 a.m. CST

The Citation Bravo banked, and immediately Borodin opened his eyes. He had shut them moments after the business jet had left McCarran International Airport in Las Vegas, and climbed to its cruising altitude, letting Yegor do the planning and worrying. For the last five minutes or so, he'd been aware of their descent, as conscious of it as the busy scratching of Yegor's pencil, and in the back the soft snoring from young Kolya, as Yegor called his protégé Nikolai.

Alert and refreshed, he asked, "So where did you decide we should put down?"

In the seat to his left, hunched forward and wearing reading glasses as he studied one of the maps spread on the table before them, Yegor touched his pencil to the circled spot on the map. "Sonora. Is maybe fifteen minutes from this place Bitters," he said in his far less polished English. "Not best news, but best airport. Worst news is this is county seat."

Borodin understood that meant city, county and state police were situated there. "Why not land us inside Huntsville Prison already?"

"*Nichevo*. We luck out maybe. Akim reports big problem at jail. All attention is there." He tapped the pencil to the map. "Landing strip is key. This one 4,037 feet. Perfect municipal airport."

"How so?"

"This airport nobody attend at night. Pilot use radio to turn on landing-strip lights. We make ourselves gift of fuel. We leave, we have maybe sixteen-hundred-mile range." Slipping off his glasses, Yegor used them to point to the back of the jet. "Maybe not so far—Boba has been eating for whole flight."

Borodin allowed a brief chuckle. "It's a good thing there's no ocean from Nevada to Texas or we would never have gotten him on board in the first place."

Yegor nodded at their mutual appreciation of Boba's fear of flying. "With full tank we make Florida, maybe Orlando. We fuel again and—" He made a sweeping climb with his hand.

After that they would be safely out of reach of the U.S. authorities. Borodin wondered how things were going back in Vegas. By now the commotion over Gloria had to be in full gear. Were the cops buying the drug angle and tying it to Sasha and

Tatiana? The story wouldn't hold together for too long, but he didn't need forever, a few hours would suffice. The fire about to start at his warehouse would also buy some time for his former employees scattering throughout the country to look for new employment with associates in other cities. Only Demyan, having closed Red Square—Borodin checked his watch—a mere half hour ago, had been kept out of the loop for his own good as well as theirs.

"Here is map from description Akim gives of Bitters." Yegor offered the hand-drawn layout of the community he'd been working on.

The sketch almost had Borodin laughing again once he saw how ridiculously small the town was. Sasha had to be going absolutely nuts there. But her loss was their gain, he thought as the business jet touched down.

He and Yegor were pulled forward as the pilot down-throttled, and glancing out of his cabin window, he checked for buildings in the area and traffic. "It looks quiet enough."

"*Da,* is small place. Only three thousand peoples. In whole of county maybe six thousand." Yegor glanced out the window, too, and pointed when, downfield, vehicle lights flashed on and off. "There. Our ride waits."

Less than a minute later, four of them exited the six-passenger-capacity jet. All except Kolya carried a metallic case. Boba carried two. It was Kolya's job to look unobtrusive. He would stay behind and supervise the refueling and handle any problems that arose—diplomatically if possible. If not, then with the Glock he wore under the sports jacket he was slipping on.

As they reached the tarmac, Yegor lingered behind to give his protégé final instructions. Borodin approached the man standing several yards away in the dark.

"You have the other vehicle we need?" he asked Akim.

The lack of greeting and Borodin's icy tone had the burly man swallowing. "*Da.* All is prepared."

They climbed into the Suburban, both Borodin and Boba claiming back seats. Yegor ran to join them and slid into the front passenger seat. Then the Suburban rolled out of the airport and headed toward the interstate.

33

"Mo was a cop?" Sasha asked.

Gray could see by her expression that she had been one hundred eighty degrees off on a few conclusions, and he'd helped her get there letting her think what she did, as he had let so many here do. It wasn't that he'd deceived by playing the tormented widower—well, except after his initial, unexpected reaction to Sasha, he amended drolly. He'd been plenty miserable without having to do that. But, God knows he'd been far from honest.

"Mo was Frank's nickname for her. I preferred Maureen." The distinction sounded petty even to him now.

"I saw the photo of her on your desk. She was very pretty. She must have been fun to be around."

It was the only picture he hadn't boxed away. At first he'd kept it to feed his guilt, and finally his disappointment—disappointment in himself as well as them as a couple. The picture was taken just after a volleyball game with fellow officers. Her spiky, short blond hair and lanky body had been gleaming from exertion, her blue eyes and wide grin adding to her sparkle. She exhibited the personification of athleticism, and her smile always dared you not to grin back—an entirely different person than who she became around him.

"She was that. Like you, she enjoyed the outdoors," he continued. "Not much of a fisherman, not enough action, but anything competitive, she was ready, willing and able to take on."

"Sounds as though she'd have been a perfect candidate for our Search and Rescue Unit. They tackle everything from lost campers and backpackers, to injured mountain bikers and cavers. I was encouraged to try out, but I'm not wild about heights and snakes."

"Maureen wasn't thrilled with snakes, either, though spiders scared her more. As for heights, she'd already championed bungee jumping and parachuting, and she was trying to talk me into trying hang gliding."

"Would you have?"

"No way. I did what I had to do while in the service. That was enough excitement for me."

"I guess it was tough for you having to deal with her working under Elias."

"You think she could find what she was looking for here? She was with the Sonora PD because it's the county seat, but that was fast proving an inadequate challenge. She'd begun talking about us moving to San Antonio or Houston, or else trying to get on with the state police."

"I didn't realize. I assumed, since Elias seemed to know her as well as you did..." She shrugged.

"For good reason. He was once her fiancé."

Sasha shifted to stand with her back against the wall and slowly slid to the floor. The expressive reaction said more than words could about how the admission stunned her.

Gray watched her settle the mug between her bent knees and stroke the thing. It might as well have been Aladdin's lamp, since she was undoubtedly thinking, "Beam me up, Genie," as she processed the crystal-clear image of the Bermuda Triangle he, Maureen and Frank had created.

To give them both time, Gray went to the window and checked for activity. There was none and the desolation and deceiving peace brought to mind McCarthy's line: "All quiet along the Potomac."

"That certainly clarifies a few things," Sasha finally remarked. "But I'm surprised you and Elias are able to continue living and working in the proximity that you do. I know size and strength-wise you outmatch him, but Elias strikes me as the kind to play dirty if the opportunity strikes."

Gray ran his thumb across the old scar on his chin. "He got away with it once. Caught me the day I was leaving the cemetery and slugged me with the barrel of his gun. At first I was almost sorry the damn thing didn't go off. I don't suppose I have to tell you about what those moments are like."

"You'd guess wrong. I'm in no hurry to die, Slaughter."

He was relieved to hear that, especially with this latest threat hanging over her head on the heels of her horrific loss. As for continuing with the explanations, he didn't know how. He'd never discussed his private life with anyone, not even during the drinking binges with J.M., and he didn't have a clue where to begin. Standing over her like a sequoia didn't help, so he tried to balance things somewhat by lowering himself into his recliner. When he felt her gaze as he started rocking, he abruptly stopped.

"How long were you married?" Sasha asked gently.

"Nine years."

"Did you know each other long beforehand?"

"Since we were kids. Well, teens. By the time my family settled here, Frank and Maureen were already a pair. Me, I was more interested in fixing up my first truck and getting it fit for the road. Thing was, any time you spent around Frank meant girls were a front-burner issue. *That,* as you've found out, hasn't changed."

"Girls coming second to a wreck on wheels... please."

He appreciated her effort to lighten the moment. "Put it in context—an only, adopted child of elderly parents, months away from turning fifteen..."

She became immediately contrite. "Adopted? Slaughter, you should have said something."

"Why? Not all orphans suffer a childhood out of a Dickens novel. It was great. My father was a neat guy. He established the clinic. Took a lot of pressure off of puberty, too. Procreation was simple math around here, but to get the timing right on a small block Chevy V–8 engine, now *that* was an accomplishment."

Not only didn't Sasha smile at his joke, her facial expression didn't change at all as she studied him. Like a terrier with a bone, she asked, "Do you know anything about your birth parents?"

"What's to know about someone who abandons you in a rest room at the Lubbock bus station? I figure my mother was unmarried, and my father might never have known she was pregnant. There are worse scenarios as far as I'm concerned. Since the Slaughters got me within weeks, I never knew anything about being adopted until I joined the service. The only reason they told me then was in case of medical emergencies. Truth is, afterward, I loved them more for what they'd done."

"I don't doubt that you did, I'm just not buying that it didn't rattle a few brain cells."

No, he'd been fine until he became a full-time nurse to Maureen, with nothing but time to think.

"Anyway," he replied, "Maureen was a long-time pal, one I was worried about. She was a year younger than us, and Frank was...Frank."

"Even back then?"

"For as long as I've known him, he's had a knack for testing people. Maybe it had something to do with his rocky relationship with his father, a decent enough guy, but no-nonsense."

"You said something about the family farm failing."

"That's right. His mother tried to take up the slack there, but she had a bad heart, and there were four other kids to worry about besides. No, don't ask what happened to them. They all left as soon as they could and haven't been back. I don't think he's kept in touch with any of them. The lack of attention had to have done something to him, too. Maybe that's why he needs to prove himself as being top dog in everything with everybody. As far as I'm concerned, it gets old when each day is medal day at the Olympics."

Sasha moistened her lips. "At the risk of offending you, it sounds as though he and Maureen were more compatible than you two were."

"No doubt about it."

"What went— *Oh.* He didn't? He cheated on her?"

Gray nodded. "We'd enlisted in the service, and he proposed. At their engagement party I caught him going at it hot and heavy with a girl out in the parking lot. The girl he fixed me up with, no less. I only went out there to save Maureen embarrassment. She knew something was wrong and was willing to handle things herself. Anyway, that was it for me as far as my friendship with Frank was concerned.''

"I wonder..." Sasha murmured. "Do you suppose he wanted out of the engagement? Sometimes people get themselves into situations only to regret their impulsiveness. Lacking the courage to face things directly, they force the other party to do the dirty work. It allows them to conveniently be victims and say, 'I told you so.'''

"Well, Maureen didn't mind confronting him. She broke his nose." Gray managed a brief, tired smile. "He forgave her, but he's been on my case ever since."

"Ah." Sasha nodded, and for an instant recollection animated her face. "I heard the mocking 'Saint Gray.' It never crossed his mind that you turned him in because of his betrayal. He thinks you wanted Maureen all along."

"His competitive streak really went into overdrive when we showed up for basic training."

"Marines, I take it? Did you leave your drill instructor with anything to do?"

Once again Gray appreciated her ability to catch up, as well as her wit in such a difficult time. "Not much. And we didn't make life easy for the rest of the guys, either. But the worst was how pissed Frank became when I was picked for special training and he wasn't."

Sasha stopped nodding. "Define 'special.'''

There was no way he was going to dump that experience on her tonight. He shorthanded his explanation to a dismissive shrug and muttered, "Covert Ops."

If Sasha was disappointed at his intentional withholding, she was too considerate to pursue it. She only said, "So that's where you learned those slick moves. And it explains Elias's remark about training."

Her ability to gauge words in and out of context warned Gray to choose his more carefully. "There was plenty of that. It just wasn't my idea of how I wanted to spend the next twenty years, if I could survive that long. So as soon as my enlistment was up, I took my discharge and came back here."

"To become a vet like your father."

"Square, huh?"

"Compared to what? I know how I've been sounding, but I love animals. The question is, do you? Really?"

Working with animals had been a joy, despite the cases where you couldn't help, or the ones that required you end an animal's life out of kindness. It was the relentlessness of needs both human and animal that got to him. And to have to say goodbye to so many souls in too brief a time.

"Maybe I'm not cut out for the work," he said simply.

"Bull. I watched you with Jessie. You gained

her trust as fast as anyone could. And considering my first impressions of you—''

"What were they?" his curiosity drove him to ask.

This time the ghost of a smile touched her lips. "I thought you were something hatched at Stonehenge. For someone like you to win over a frightened dog like her, that took more than skill. You have a natural gift."

Gray wasn't buying the compliment, but the comparison amused him. "When I first saw you, I thought J.M. had sent me a late birthday present."

She lifted both eyebrows. "Sorry to disappoint."

"You didn't. I prefer who you are."

Sasha returned to stroking her mug. "I think you're determined not to finish your story. At least tell me when you and Maureen realized you were in love and wanted to marry?"

That was the most difficult to answer. The impulse—a stretch in definitions if there ever was one—crept up on them, as everything else had, yet nevertheless felt natural, like high tide, like mold on bread—cause and effect. "I had to get through school and she went through the police academy. In our free time we hung out together to lick our wounds over what a skunk Frank had been. As I said, we were friends."

"That sounds...comfortable."

"You mean unromantic."

"I mean solid. Nice."

She *meant* hardly passionate, and she was right. But at the time real friendship was what they seemed to need from each other. "Maureen was there for me when my father died and I became more aware of my own mortality."

"What about your mother?"

"We lost her while I was overseas. A stupid slipup in prescriptions, a bad allergic reaction."

"How awful."

"Everyone encouraged my father to sue, but he couldn't bring himself to do it. Something in him shut down, though. Not long after he passed, Maureen started staying here. Her folks and younger siblings had relocated to Arizona, and when Maureen mentioned something about finding a place in Sonora, I guess that motivated me into action." He groaned. "God, did that sound as pitiful as I think it did?"

Sasha said nothing.

"Well, it seemed to work. As busy as we both were, we made the time together fun. It was like an affair more than a marriage, never talking shop or making plans except for the weekends. No wonder we became strangers instead of mates."

When he realized Sasha continued to hold her peace, Gray waved his hand, signaling he was through talking. "Forget it. I blew it. We blew it. It's ancient history."

"That's why I haven't sought a deeper relationship," she said, meeting his gaze directly. "I want what my parents had, or at least to feel that kind of passion once. I'm sorry things didn't work out for you.''

Her calm, nonjudgmental tone allowed him to finish. ''That last day we'd just had another squabble. How's that for a sign? She'd go nose-to-nose with an umpire at a softball game, but we never really summoned the enthusiasm to fight for our marriage. After the call I knew it was over. Why drag things on until we lost all respect for each other?

''Little did I know that she'd ended the call because some fool in a Corvette was driving through town like a bat out of hell. Speed—it was like a magnet to her. That's where she and Frank had too much in common, speed and danger. Anyway, she lost control of her car and crashed.''

Exhaling, Sasha leaned her head back against the wall and gazed up at the ceiling. ''And you blamed yourself.''

''No, I blamed myself for not letting her go sooner. For…oh, hell, what difference does it make now?''

''It must. You're still hurting.''

''She lay in a coma for six months before she died, probably hanging on to tell me what a son of a bitch I was for asking her to be who she wasn't.''

''You're not the one who made her chase him.''

''No, I just collected on her benefits. You mentioned your father's insurance policies? I received my share, too. I tried to give it to her folks, but they didn't need it. So I sat here with all of this death wealth—my parents', Maureen's. Outside my door was Frank hating my guts and everybody else feeling sorry for me and wanting to fix the problem with food.''

Sasha rose, set her mug on the coffee table and sat down on the arm of his chair. "What happened was sad and a terrible waste. Destroying yourself out of guilt would be a bigger one, Slaughter.''

"I know. I've been seeing that every hour, every minute you've been here.'' Gray took her left hand and pressed a kiss into her palm. "You've been one helluva lesson to me, Sasha Mills. You made me want again, more than I can remember wanting anyone or anything in my life.'' Gray reached up with his other hand to stroke her cheek, then he slipped his hand behind her neck to her nape. "Sasha, I want to kiss you so badly it—''

She pressed her finger to his lips. "Just do it.''

But as he began to ease her across his lap, careful of her side and her other bruises, a burst of gunfire shattered the silence.

34

Thrust into total darkness and deafened by bullets, Sasha could only cling to Gray as he swept them to the carpet in an equal eruption of energy. The force knocked the breath out of her. The aftershock made her moan.

"Christ, are you hit? Sasha!"

"Winded." But she moaned again as she worked free the gun digging into the small of her back.

As soon as she could, she twisted around, angling for a view. Gray settled close behind her. Outside, tires squealed, followed by another burst of gunfire and an explosion of breaking glass, punctuated by a roaring engine as a vehicle drove away.

Sasha slumped back onto the carpet and met Gray's grim gaze.

"Don't say it," he muttered. "You warned me."

Behind them, Jessie whimpered. Sasha saw her belly-crawl trying to reach them. Concerned that the dog would tear her stitches, she immediately rushed to her. "Stay put, baby. Jessie, come back here." Keeping low in case the sounds outside had been deceiving and the vehicle hadn't moved on, she urged the dog to return behind the couch.

Mission accomplished, she called to Gray. "Is the coast clear?"

"Yeah. Frank's moving out into the street. At least I think it's him."

"I have to give him backup."

"I'll be yours."

Jessie protested her withdrawal, but Sasha could only give the dog a reassuring pat and command, "Stay," before racing from the house with Gray lingering only to shut the door in case the dog decided they provided more comfort than bullets caused fear. Together they ran toward the lone dark silhouette in the street.

"Elias?" Sasha called as they approached him.

"I'm okay."

But his voice sounded strained, and once they were close enough to see for themselves, he looked as ill as Sasha had earlier. There was good reason. At his feet were two bodies, uniformed men with limbs askew from being thrown from the vehicle as it raced through town.

And as terrible as that was, it wasn't all. The town was in a complete blackout, which explained the explosions. Even without checking, she surmised the phones were no longer working, either.

In the distance there were voices, shouts and hysterical cries, and at one house in the second block, she saw the beam of a flashlight at a second-story window. Hoping that the sound of a vehicle racing away really meant withdrawal, she backed to where Gray was checking on the fallen men.

"It's no use," he said. "They're dead."

And not all that recently. Sasha had seen immediately that they were already showing signs of rigor mortis, but she let that detail pass for the moment. They needed Elias coherent and effective, which might not happen if he was focused on how long those bastards had held the bodies before delivering them.

She inspected his bloody face. "Were you hit?"

Gaunt-faced, Elias wiped the stream of blood from his forehead. "Flying glass from inside the station, I guess. These men...they're the guys I was expecting from Sonora."

"They had to have been ambushed outside of town," Sasha replied. "That explains why there hasn't been any help since the EMS people."

Assured by the prolonged silence, people began to emerge from different buildings and houses. They carried flashlights and old-fashioned lanterns, and more than a few had a shotgun or pistol in their other hand. Too many, as far as Sasha was concerned. Here it was the weekend, late...if people had been drinking, there could be some itchy trigger fingers in this bunch. All they needed was one odd sound, and serious accidents could occur. She kept one eye on them as they formed a cautious circle around the bodies. The women, curious when at a distance, either turned slightly away from the gruesome sight or pressed their faces against their husbands' or boyfriends' chests as they drew nearer. The men did their best to look stoic; however, Sasha suspected the majority would retreat willingly at the first command to clear the street.

"Shot them in the back of the head," someone whispered.

"Executed 'em," another corrected.

"Who's doing these horrible things?"

The frail voice rang out like a prayer into the night, but the heavens remained silent as though they, too, were stunned at why twisted, angry men were bent on creating such terror.

A stocky man clad in striped pajamas pushed to the front of the growing crowd. The way people willingly yielded to him had Sasha concluding he was the mayor or some other local official.

"Frank, snap out of it, man. The phones are out, too. What are your instructions?"

Out of respect for the position, if not the man, Sasha remained silent, giving Elias the opportunity to address the people he served. But Frank had all he could deal with twisting away from hands reaching for him as though he were some touchstone, while others waved tissues at him for his bloody forehead.

"Get back, will you. Leave me alone." Ducking out of the reach from one side of the circle, he ended up in the clutches of the other, and ultimately roared at Sasha, "Goddamn you, this is about you anyway. Say something!"

Before she could reply, his car radio crackled with static. Then a smooth male voice asked in an accent, "Are you there?"

"Borodin," Sasha whispered.

Both Gray and Frank glanced from her to the patrol car, but it was Frank who voiced their thoughts. "I thought he was in Vegas."

Yes, why wasn't he? Sasha wondered. What could have compelled him to take such a risk and come here? He had to know that this deflected all guilt off her and ruined any chance he had of staying in Nevada, or the country for that matter. Maybe her DC had found something her mother left behind. Or could Gloria have had a change of heart?

Whatever the answer, Borodin was here and had control of a police car radio. To understand what to do next, she had to know how he'd arrived. "Where's the nearest airfield?"

"What difference does that—well, it all depends," Frank replied, yielding to her stern look. "There are private strips at ranches, municipal ones...uh, Sonora, I guess. There's one in El Dorado, but that's another dozen or so miles up the road."

"Which is long enough for a corporate jet?"

"*Sasha.*"

Borodin's voice had taken on a familiar edge, and knowing time was running out she yelled, "Which one!"

"I don't know, I'm no stinking pilot!"

"Sonora," someone in the crowd replied. "But there's no tower or anything."

"You don't need one these days. The landing lights are probably radio-controlled," Sasha replied, thinking out loud. "His pilot turns them on and off from the jet." One good thing about that, though, there would be no attendant, either. That meant one less body.

She started for the patrol car, her mind racing. They still had one form of communication left, but with Borodin being able to listen in on a police radio...

Frank must have realized how many eyes were on them because, as Sasha opened the patrol car door, he rushed up and grabbed the handset from her. "This is Frank Elias," he announced. "Chief of police."

"How very nice for you. But I want to speak to Sasha Mills if you don't mind, Chief."

"Who?" Frank asked, chin jutting.

Silence followed and stretched. Sasha shook her bowed head, knowing this was the wrong man to be playing for a fool.

"You there?" Frank demanded.

"Oh, very much so. And you'd be wise to understand how close. Don't make this more difficult on yourself than it needs to be."

"How could it be worse?" Frank muttered under his breath. Into the handset he said, "What do you want?"

"Cooperation. You're cut off. We control both the east and west sides of your pitiful town. The men who just delivered my warning also took care of the electrical transformer and several telephone junction boxes. They'll apply the same precautions on the other end of town."

Sure enough, several bursts of gunfire won gasps and shrieks from the crowd. The cacophony was followed by another explosion and a few more shots. When it quieted again, another crackle sounded on the radio.

"This is merely an inducement for you and your fellow townspeople to cooperate," Borodin continued. "You have nothing to fear as long as you do as you're told. Do I make myself clear?"

"What are you going to do?"

"Finish my business. Tell everyone to return to their homes and stay there. If they comply, no harm will come to them. Try to use this radio to call for additional assistance and I give you my word you will pay a high premium, beginning with the most innocent."

There was a gasp from the crowd, and then a young woman cried, "They're going to kill our babies!"

Frank yelled, "Everybody shut up! I need to hear."

"Do I make myself clear, mister Chief of Police Frank Elias?"

Frank swallowed. "Yeah."

"Excellent. Now let me speak to her."

He all but shoved the handset into Sasha's hands.

"My hero," she muttered with a withering look. The thought that Maureen could ever have cared for this spineless wretch left her dumbfounded.

She keyed the handset. "So?"

"How delicious to hear your voice again, my spirited Sashitska."

Wanting badly to tell him she wasn't his dear anything and where he could go, Sasha remained silent, aware that small annoyance would be the best she could achieve for the moment. She was also painfully aware of how many eyes were on her.

"I see you're in no mood for pleasantries. No doubt you remain heartsick over the loss of your mother."

Dizzy with hatred, she shut her eyes. The bastard. If it cost her everything, he would pay.

The handset was pulled from her grasp. Opening her eyes, she saw Frank about to speak again.

"Just tell us how long do we have?"

Borodin's laughter was soft. "To hide? My suggestion would be not to waste time. Goodbye, Chief. *Do svidaniya,* my Sasha.''

As Frank dropped the handset onto the driver's seat, Sasha felt a hand on her shoulder. About to shrug it off, she glanced back and saw Gray.

''You okay?''

She didn't think she would ever be okay again. ''We have to get those bodies off the street. Do you think they'll open the market and let us put them in their cooler?''

''Without electricity to run the compressor, it won't do much good, not if this drags on for long.''

''You have a hardware store across the street. Surely they have a generator?'' She turned to the crowd. ''Doesn't anyone have a generator?''

''Sasha, you need something far more powerful to keep those industrial units operating,'' Gray told her.

The people nearest who could hear reacted in horror. ''Did you hear that? She wants to put the bodies in with the food.''

''You heard what's going to happen. Your other choice is to watch them turn into roadkill,'' Gray snapped. He said to Frank. ''What have you got in the station to wrap them?''

''Blankets. I'll get some.''

''Get a bunch of garbage sacks, too, and rope.''

''Frank.'' The man Sasha thought was the politician blocked his way. ''You're taking orders from him?''

"Why are they doing this?" someone else asked. "If it's her they want, why can't we just give her to them?"

Sasha knew that since her mother's body's discovery, news had spread fast and furious about her. She didn't blame people for being upset, but there were more productive things to do than waste time on petty squabbling.

Turning to the crowd, she raised her hands, requesting their attention. "I'm Officer Sasha Mills, Las Vegas Police. The man you just heard on the radio is responsible for killing these men and for murdering my mother, so you see, I understand your anguish. As frightening as he seems, he and his people *can* be stopped. By uniting as a group, together we can show them that there's no place for their kind of terrorism here."

"Why should we risk our necks for you?" an unseen man called out.

"That's a fair question, and the truth is I'm not asking for that. But these two deputies here were probably neighbors or family to some of you. Do it for them and each other."

Although a few people seemed agreeable, their voices were drowned out by the majority's resentment. "This isn't our problem," was the line she kept hearing. And there was increased mention about loss of property and questions about who would pay for its replacement than concern over lives.

A gray-haired woman came forward. "We pay your salary, Frank. It's your job to keep the peace."

Just as Sasha recognized her as the librarian, she saw Gerri Rose struggling with her husband at the far edge of the group. With a fierce wrench, the young woman freed herself from her husband's hold and ran forward.

"Frank, what do we do if they don't keep their word and start shooting their way into our homes? I want to stay with you."

"Gerri Rose, damn it." Tim Pike followed her and took hold of her again. "Let's go home. You'll be safe there."

"And what are you going to protect me with, your TV remote?"

Slapping away his hands, Gerri Rose wrapped her arms around Frank's waist and pressed herself closer to him. In that moment, any questions about how far their liaison had gone were put to rest. Although Sasha didn't know Tim except for his efforts at the fire earlier, she felt a strong spasm of sympathy for his having to endure such a humiliating moment.

Unfortunately for Gerri Rose, Elias didn't seem happy with either her timing or her conduct. "Let go. Damn it, what got into you to pull this now? I've got work to do," he snapped.

He tugged her arms from around him and pushed

her so hard she stumbled and would have fallen if it wasn't for Tim's quick response.

"Frank—" she gasped, her pale young face stricken. "I'm here to stay. I want to be with you."

"Are you blind as well as stupid? Get lost."

"But I have to talk to you. It's important."

Turning his back on her, Elias strode into the station. Sasha watched the pretty blonde's mouth fall open and then Gerri Rose burst into tears. Looking near tears himself, Tim embraced her as she sagged against him, then lifted her into his arms. Shooting an angry look at Frank's back, he carried her away.

A few people seemed to think Pike had the right idea and left, too, but the majority wanted an outlet for their anger and fear. It was soon clear that Sasha was it. They made their demands in no uncertain terms. The fact that she was a peace officer didn't seem to make any difference, more indication to Sasha that Elias hadn't cultivated respect for the law around here.

"I say if the chief won't resolve this, we should."

"Yeah, take her!"

Reaching into the back of her waistband for her gun, Sasha's view was suddenly obliterated as Gray stepped before her. He drew his own automatic and chambered a round.

"Anybody who wants to try that has to come through me."

35

Gray didn't know if it was his reputation, size or the gun that intimidated, he was just glad it halted the momentum of the crowd before things got out of hand. The danger was far from over, though. While the group backed off a few steps, their unity made them more confident and the mutters and expletives resumed.

"What's got into you now, Doc?"

The question came from Don Sargent, the market's manager, who had just arrived.

"For the last couple of years you've been acting like you got a bee up your butt one minute and a foot in the grave the next," the man continued. "Never had the interest to exchange a simple hello. Now you're gonna tell us what we should and shouldn't be doing? It appears to me your head's been turned by her."

"It's Officer Mills to you, Don. And you can stop acting as though she's to blame for this. The fact is that I am, and so is Frank. But that's irrelevant at this point. What you need to ask yourself is if turning into the same kind of animals who murdered these men and killed Mrs. Mills is something you want on your conscience. Well, is it, Don? Now listen to what Officer Mills has to say."

Sasha tucked her automatic back into her waistband and stepped forward. "I know I'm a stranger to you, and have no right to ask for your understanding, let alone forgiveness for what I've brought to your community. Nevertheless, please understand, I tried to avoid this.

"The men outside Bitters are organized-crime figures, part of the Russian mafia. And because I'm the last person who knows what they've done, who can put them behind bars, they want to silence me, too.

"It's natural for you to feel fear. I admit," she said, pressing a hand to her chest, "I am. That's exactly what they want. Fear to control us, to divide us in order to make their problem easier."

"Ain't no problem if they got what they came for."

Gray stared hard at old man Riley from the junkyard across from the convenience store. Of all the times for the wild-haired recluse to be roused out of his ramshackle hut. The town had been trying to get him off the place for years. It was an eyesore, and for the commercial value of the property so close to the interstate its removal could help turn the economic tide for the town. As a result, Vern Riley saw a conspirator in everyone and offered his allegiance to no one. But what he had to say at the moment was music to a number of ears.

Sasha met his gaze levelly. "Let me get this straight, you'd aid in the murder of a police officer?"

"Huh. Ain't met a cop or lawyer yet that didn't deserve being put against a wall and shot." With that, the man spit a wad of tobacco at her. It arced and landed just short of her right shoe. He shuffled away.

A murmur made its way through the crowd and Gray heard words like "quack" and "crazy hermit." Sadly, no one appeared offended by the man's offensive behavior.

Someone patted his back and he turned to see Shep Connors from the hardware store. He nodded to Sasha and said, "I'm sorry for these men and your loss, ma'am. But I got kids." Shaking his head, he, too, left for home.

Mary Crispin, a retired nurse who taught Sunday school and served as a volunteer delivering meals to shut-ins, spoke up from the other side of the crowd. "Are you saved, Officer Mills? I would be proud to pray with you before returning home."

"Thank you," Sasha replied. "But I'm afraid if God hasn't heard me yet, he's going to have to allow me to see what I can do to resolve this. It would be best if you go on home now. And all of you people with children," she added to the crowd, "keep them away from the windows and doors until further notice. Close shutters, blinds, shades and curtains. Don't light candles or use your flashlights if you don't have to. That will only draw attention to you. Most importantly, stay *off* the road.''

That warning achieved a full-fledged retreat. Watching the anxious and the indignant, Gray wondered how he could be so wrong about people. This was the town where he'd finished growing up. These were people who had been clients of his father's as well as his. They had attended both of his parents' funerals, as well as Maureen's.

Not one of these people even offered to help move the dead.

It was Sasha's expression that cut at him the most. He only caught a glimpse of it before she turned away, but the disappointment and increasing awareness of her vulnerability gripped his heart. ''I'm sorry,'' he said as she passed him. He never meant an apology more, not even when he'd stood over Maureen's grave the day of her funeral.

''Well, the reliable thing about human nature is that it's predictably unreliable.''

Yes, her faith had been badly damaged. How did you protect, willingly risk your life, for the very people turning their back on you? Of course, any thought of protection had to be out of the question now. He had a moment of concern, though, when he saw her reach into Elias's patrol car and bring out the car keys.

Following, he closed his hand around her wrist. "What do you think you're doing?"

"Checking to see what's in the trunk. He's taking a long time to— Wait. Here he comes." She dropped the keys onto the seat. "If the cooler idea is a no-go, at least we can get these poor souls off the street and ready for transport once it's safe for the EMS people to return."

The three of them worked fast and in grim silence. Gray experienced a stomach-lurching moment when he turned the first man and recognized him as a friend of Maureen's who had played on the softball team with her. The other deputy had just had his picture in the county paper with his wife, celebrating their twenty-fifth wedding anniversary. Both men were larger than average, and it took the three of them all their strength to transfer the wrapped bodies into the station where they were laid just inside the front door.

Winded and still visibly shaken, Frank kicked away more of the broken glass to avoid eye contact. He *looked* as if he wanted to be anywhere but where he was, Gray thought. Eventually gazing through the blown-out front window, he built up the courage to ask, "How long do you think?"

"I wish I knew," Sasha replied.

Although her reply held no negativity, no emotion of any kind save fatigue, Frank didn't take the answer well.

"Guess, damn it."

Fed up himself, Gray started toward the jerk, but Sasha reached out, staying him. Then she glanced outside, herself, only to turn around and scan the station. It struck Gray that she was trying to remember where the clock was. Finally she checked her watch at the same time he did his. "Dawn's still, what—two hours away, maybe a little less? I think they'd prefer being able to maneuver with some visibility. I'd say they'll be here at first light."

"They don't know where to find you."

"They knew where to dump them," she replied, nodding to the deceased.

"Yesterday a Suburban drove through town. I figure they spotted me leaving here and heading for the clinic. They must have hung back hoping I would make a run for it. Because of you, I didn't."

Frank stiffened. "Hey, don't blame your mistakes on me."

Sasha took a step toward the door, but in a sudden burst of fury, spun around and went after Frank, shoving him against the wall before he could react. "My mistakes? My mistake was to let a gentle woman make decisions she was in no condition to make. My mistake was letting a bully with a badge keep me from getting her out of harm's way. My *mistake*—" Stopping as quickly as she'd started, she backed away from him. "Hell, you're not worth the energy."

Gray held the door open for her and fell into

step as they returned to his house. They'd gone beyond the end of the station yet hadn't drawn parallel to the corral and pens when they heard vehicles to their left and saw two cars driving off between the convenience store and café.

"Where are they going?" she asked, coming to a halt. "I thought... Isn't that just a dirt driveway?"

Grimacing because he knew, and because of the choking dust the vehicles were kicking up, he replied, "I should have guessed. It's a back road. Pretty rough and treacherous in the dark. It eventually links up to another dirt road going out to some of the remote ranches."

As he explained, another vehicle started down the road, and then another.

Escape. Gray saw the hunger for it in Sasha's eyes as she watched the unorganized and impulsive convoy.

Expecting some of the same passion she'd displayed with Frank, he was amazed that her only reply was, "It's just as well, I suppose."

She continued into the house, and Gray followed, troubled by her sudden apathy. "What does that mean?"

She didn't answer because she was immediately greeted by Jessie, who showed her pleasure by wagging the entire back half of her body. Sasha crouched down and gave her another of those all-encompassing hugs.

"Sasha."

"Poor Miss Mess. I'm afraid you're going to get even more scared before things are done. Slaughter, you have to do me a favor," she added, although all her concentration was on the dog. "Take her back to the clinic. Maybe if you shut the door of that room and don't actually force her into a cage, it'll be less traumatizing."

The gut feeling he was getting was anything but pleasant. "Why?"

"Hopefully she'll be safe there."

"She'll be safer in my truck. With us."

When she didn't reply, merely continued stroking the appreciative dog, Gray realized what she intended to do.

"No way. You can't seriously be thinking about staying?"

"There's nothing to think about. I am."

"Bullshit. You don't know how many are coming."

Drawing a deep breath, she rose and glanced toward the picture window, but her gaze was turned inward. "Well, there were two to start, and if Borodin flew in on his corporate jet, it would hold six—he took my mother with him once on a dinner date to L.A.—so I'm figuring…eight. Nine maximum. But hopefully he's leaving someone behind to guard the plane besides the pilot, who's contracted and probably not part of the team."

"Eight, nine, make it an even dozen already, and

undoubtedly coming loaded with enough ordnance to film another *Terminator* movie, right? And you think those are good odds?''

''I don't want to fight with you.''

''Then get in the truck.'' Once again she didn't bother responding. It infuriated him. ''Christ. I can't believe you had the nerve to make that crack about Little Big Horn.''

''It's different for me.''

''How?''

''I'm through running.''

''There's no shame in being sensible, to live to fight another day.''

''I'm not leaving my mother.''

''You're not. She's in Sonora.''

''You know what I mean. It ends here.'' As he began to speak again, she touched her fingers to his lips. ''Gray, enough. Just get Jessie over there.''

He went because he didn't trust himself around her at the moment. Scooping the dog into his arms, he carried her outside. As soon as Jessie realized where she was going, she began protesting, yapping for Sasha and squirming like a sixty-pound catfish.

''You think you've got a beef,'' he muttered, ready to put the dog down as she wanted and let her fend for herself. Survival of the fittest—wasn't that what this whole mess was about? However, once inside the clinic, his manner grew more soothing. ''I know, I know. Being alone sucks. It's for your own good, though. Even when I talk sense into her, you don't want to be in that truck bouncing around. You think your belly ached before..."

He opened the window to ease the stifling heat that would soon build in there without the air-conditioning and refilled her water bowl. Then he got out because her soft cries were already getting to him.

They grew louder as he locked up, and tormented him all the way back to the house. Once there, he sensed something else was wrong.

Sasha wasn't there. Going first to check in the kitchen, he heard something, not exactly a sob, more like a shudder.

Following the sound, he entered the guest bedroom and saw her sitting on the edge of the bed, her face buried in her hands. The way she was shaking she looked to be in the midst of her own personal earthquake, but he knew what was happening. She was simply, desperately, trying not to fall apart.

36

"Sasha."

It wasn't her intention to let him see her like this. That's why she'd come back here—that and to get the other clip for her Smith & Wesson. Embarrassed, she immediately turned her back to him, pressing her palms against her eyes to dam the geyser emotion kept trying to push to the surface. To her dismay, Gray wasn't thwarted by the move.

Settling on the bed behind her, he swept her onto his lap. "Don't turn away. Let me hold you."

"I'm okay."

Nevertheless, she hid her face in the hollow of his shoulder for fear that he would see what a joke that was. All the while, she repeated those two words over and over in her mind. They were a litany she needed to repress the images of the day, and the finality of her future, assured now by the town's rejection. Rejection might not always be personal, but when you *knew* of the injustice in it, it stung without discrimination like a razor across the heart.

"You're better than okay. You're beautiful and

brave, and I can't stand watching this, seeing you get hurt over and over."

She could do without him admitting deeper feelings. This all would have been easier if she'd never been introduced to the tender side he repressed, self-medicated and otherwise tried to eradicate to punish himself. She had no use for it now, no use for anything since her future held nothing, certainly no chance to wake in his arms to a day without threat.

Yet, despite that internal conflict, when he pressed his lips against her neck, she arched into the caress, and when those caresses streamed down her throat into the V of her shirt, she wrapped her arms around him with the avidity of one parched and starving.

She didn't know or care which of them pulled open the snaps of her shirt, just that it happened. She craved the hot night air and his hotter, humid mouth on her breasts, his strong fingers mastering the clasp of her bra...craved to fit a lifetime of sensation into this waning ember of her life. In no other context could this make sense, but nothing else that had happened did, either.

When he cupped her in his hands, she pressed herself into his mouth. As the fire within spread, she straddled his thighs.

Although his hands continued to caress, Gray spoke with doubt. "I didn't intend..."

No, he would desire but resist. Mr. Sacrifice.

Saint Gray. For once Elias had it right. But she couldn't go on without this moment to sustain her.

"Kiss me again."

He didn't need a second invitation. Sinking his hands into her hair, he locked his mouth to hers. There was no time for flirting, no time for modesty. Passion ruled. Their kiss was bold and greedy, and with each stroke of their tongues, their hands gripped harder, grew more frantic. Sasha couldn't keep any part of her still and rocked against him, pressed her breasts against his chest. When that wasn't enough, she tugged at his T-shirt so that they could at least touch flesh to flesh.

It just made it worse, the soft mat of his hair teasing her sensitive nipples, her lushness against his hardness. Gray groaned and lay back on the bed, taking her with him.

"God, I want," he breathed between kisses. "I want this more than I want air."

Sasha loved the words. They melted her from the inside out, even as his touch did the opposite. But she couldn't answer in kind. She didn't trust her own voice. So she showed him.

Me, too, as she ran her teeth and tongue along his neck until he shuddered. *I want you,* when she did to his nipples what he'd done to hers.

But being able to touch and not have was as much torment as pleasure. And so, breathless, she sat up.

She waited for him to meet her gaze.

The veins in his temple and neck throbbed, but when she unfastened the snap on his jeans, he sat up, too, and did the rest. At her first stroke, as she held him hot and hard in her hand, he urged her to her knees to slip down her jeans and panties.

"You have to let me get something," he said, bending to nuzzle the dark curls he'd just caressed.

"No. I've never been with anyone this way...just the two of us. Just...us."

Realizing what a revealing remark it was on so many levels, she resolved the issue herself by taking him inside her all at once. As ready as she was, it was too much, too fast. Her gasp had Gray attempting to ease her off him, but she tightened her arms as well as her inner muscles.

Losing control, Gray groaned and crushed her to his pounding heart. "Forgive me. I can't let you go."

"Don't."

His hands were unsteady as they stroked the length of her back, drove into her hair to urge her to meet his gaze.

Knowing what was coming, she kissed him and murmured, "No more words."

"Damn it, you'll listen for once. They're not just words. I know it's supposed to be impossible—"

She pressed her fingertips to his lips only long enough to replace them with her mouth. "Kiss me...and come. Come inside me. Please." Each whispered word was a caress all its own, augmented by her rhythmic rocking against him.

Careful of her wound as he was of his size and strength, Gray nevertheless gripped her hips and helped intensify the ride. Time was their enemy—there was no denying it—but so was desire. Feeling its capriciousness undo him, Gray groaned into her mouth, "Ah, God, not yet. Not yet," as the pressure built.

But Sasha's body had never been so ripe, full of heat and him. And she wanted the rest. Repeating the subtlest tightening of internal muscles she felt him lose control, and the power of it sent her with him over the top.

The tremors lingered, and she yearned to prolong them, to repeat what they'd shared. But reality could allow only spare minutes, so they clung tightly to imprint what sensations they could. Before the first flush of passion receded fully, she ran her mouth along his collarbone, collecting a bit more of his essence. The fleeting caress spawned another spasm from Gray, so very present inside her.

Sadly, however, the sounds of the outer world were invading their dark oasis. The exodus seemed to be resuming in bits and spurts, and after what had been a brief respite, Jessie was barking with new insistence.

They had gambled with fate all they could dare.

With a last kiss, Sasha eased off Gray and began reaching for her clothes.

He, however, couldn't stop touching her, her beaded nipple, her kiss-swollen lips. "This has only made it worse," he murmured.

"I know."

"I want— Sasha, sweetheart, let's get Jessie. I'll get us out."

Here we go, she thought. "I can't. That's not an option for me."

"Everyone's going. Can't you hear them?"

What worried her was that Borodin could be observing it, too, and, as a result, initiate a change in plans.

When she failed to respond, Gray began adjusting his clothes. She could tell by his brisk movements that he was upset with her.

"You can't still be thinking of staying."

"Yes."

"You *can't* win."

"I'm not seeing this as a contest. It's what needs to be done."

Weary from the pace she'd been keeping all week, on top of the emotional strain of the last twenty-four hours, she picked up her gun and extra clip and headed for the living room. At the door, she eased to the side, unlocked the dead bolt, then swung the door wide.

All that greeted her was Jessie's louder barks. Her eyes were well adjusted to the darkness by now, and as she stepped outside, she studied her surroundings. Everything seemed as it was, but it didn't take light to gauge the amount of dust in the air due to the fleeing residents of Bitters.

A sudden cry had her ducking into a defensive position.

"Frank, don't leave me. I need you."

Recognizing the voice, she looked toward the police station where she saw a shadowy skirmish going on. Two people were wrestling, and then one fell to the ground. The other dived into the patrol car and keyed the engine. Gears grated and tires screeched as he backed recklessly into the street and then sped away.

Sasha ran, but by the time she made it to the front of the station, she could see Elias's patrol car turning sharply at the dirt road and following the last car.

Unbelievable, Sasha thought. Worse yet, he'd left behind Gerri Rose.

She went to the sobbing woman lying in the fetal position on the ground. How had she managed to get away from Tim, or did he even know she wasn't in their house? Sasha could only hope the girl hadn't done something really insane. There was no time to deal with another crime scene right now.

"Come on, Gerri," she said, touching the woman's shoulder. "You have to get away from here. It's not safe."

"I don't c-care. I can't live without him an-anyway."

"Trust me. It'll be easier than you think. Come on."

The girl allowed herself to be assisted, but continued weeping. "How could he? I told him that I loved him, a-and he acted like— He left m-me."

"Yeah, he's a regular prince. Now that you know, maybe you'll wake up and figure out he's not the answer to your problems, not to mention your dreams."

As she steadied the younger woman, another vehicle turned out of a side street by the library, but rather than head up the dirt road, it turned toward them. Sasha was about to reach for her gun when she recognized the engine's characteristic cough.

It was the white pickup. She stared in amazement as it pulled beside them and a young man, a heavier and blonder rendition of Tim Pike climbed out.

"Ger?" he called in a childlike voice. "Tim says it's okay for me to bring you home. He said it's okay to pick up ice cream if we hurry. You want a cone, Ger? I got money."

Gerri Rose pressed her hand to her mouth, either to stem her sobs or hold back a hysterical laugh. Nevertheless, aided by the young man, she slid across the bench seat of the pickup. When he settled back behind the steering wheel, he waved cheerfully at Sasha.

"Bye-bye!"

He cut a slow, wide U-turn and drove away, leaving Sasha to stare after them. Dear heaven, she thought, wrapping her arms around her waist.

"That's Tim's half brother, Lonnie Metcalf," Gray said, coming up behind her. "He's a little slow."

Things were moving way too fast for her. Sasha purged a deep breath trying to make sense of it all. "In all honesty, I don't care if he has the IQ of a gnat," she replied. "That's the truck."

37

Gray did a double take. "No way. Lonnie? He's a simple, sweet guy. Mrs. Metcalf had him late and there were complications with the birth. He doesn't even have a license, but everyone knows him and just kind of looks the other way. As slow as he drives, there's not much danger of him hurting anyone, and he only uses the truck in these few blocks to run errands for his mother. She's pretty much an invalid now."

"Maybe it wasn't him driving the other night," Sasha replied. "But that's the truck. Not that it matters anymore," she added, glancing at the eastern horizon. The telltale hint of light had her heading into the police station.

Gray followed. "What do you mean it doesn't? What are you doing?"

"Frank's gone."

"That bastard. That cinches it for sure now. Without—whoa."

He followed Sasha into the station, to the gun case, where, after testing the lock, she positioned herself sideways and kicked at the lower right corner. It took three tries, but finally the heavy sheet of Lexan popped out of its aluminum frame. She finished pulling it free, then reached for a .12 gauge, opened a box of shells and began loading.

"Want something?" she asked him.

"I have one, remember? Got it the old-fashioned way, too."

"I don't plan on keeping it, Slaughter. One way or another, they'll have it back in a while."

She then grabbed up a full box of shells and exited the station. Outside, the horizon was definitely growing lighter. It was time, Sasha thought with a sense of finality. She increased her pace, but the dust kicked up from the road hung over the town like fog and kept gagging her. On the plus side, it might help with visibility.

"You can't do this," Gray said at her elbow. "Without Frank you don't stand a chance."

"Nothing he did or said ever gave me the idea that he would be much help anyway."

"Do you hear yourself?" He gripped her above her raw elbow and spun her around. "You don't stand a chance."

"There are still people here," she countered, pointing with the shotgun. "You know that some are too old or infirm to leave even if they wanted to. What you *don't* know is Borodin. He's capable of making them pay if I run like Elias did."

"And if you stay," he snapped, "you'll *die*. Don't you get it? You're alone."

She met his angry gaze. "Am I?"

The hint of dawn added a glint to his fierce eyes and accented the grim lines bracketing his hard mouth. But she was not intimidated. He looked intense and passionate when he made love, too. The memory left her all the more aware of his essence still warming and wetting her. How could he think she would feel alone when she carried him so close?

Dropping his hand, he slowly shook his head. "You are the most courageous, stubborn, foolish— I won't stay. I'm not going to watch you commit suicide."

Although inside something withered and died, she replied with amazing calm. "I know. I saw it in your eyes before you said anything. The truth is, I don't want you to either."

As she resumed walking, he was like a great, growling mastiff. "Do you want me to beg? Fine, I'm begging. *Come with me.* I know those rough trails better than anyone born here. We don't have to go as far as the ranches, I can get you to high ground where we'll get a signal and call the sheriff. Hell, we'll call the FBI."

"Borodin will be gone by then. Out of their reach or that of any U.S. authority. I can't allow that to happen."

"Fuck him. For every Borodin that goes down

there are two to take his place. You know that. At least you'll be alive.''

''Alive and living with the memory of what he did to my mother.''

He must have seen the resolve in her eyes or heard it in her voice, because suddenly he swore and whipped her around again. This time he captured her face between his big hands and kissed her. ''Then think of this,'' he rasped against her lips before kissing her again, this time all but stealing the remaining breath in her lungs. As Sasha began to feel light-headed, she reached to steady herself by taking hold of his wrist, only to bump him with the box of shells. That and a subtle shift in the air had her succeeding in breaking the contact. She lifted her face to the waning night.

Dawn's promise caressed her like a ghostly hand.

Sasha gently pushed against Gray's chest. ''You'd better get going while you can.''

He stared at her as if she'd just struck him, then he let his hands drop to his sides and curled them into fists. ''Damn it, Sasha.''

She used the back of the hand with the shells to stroke his chest just over his heart. ''I know.''

This time when she walked, she walked alone. Before she reached the guest bedroom, she heard his truck start up.

38

The box of shells hit the dresser top with a thud. He was really going to do it. Sasha hadn't believed Gray could bring himself to leave. The sound of his truck left her both weak-kneed and angry. At the same time, she didn't want to be responsible for his death any more than she could bring herself to hate him for making the wiser decision.

She looked at the bed. The bedspread was rumpled and bore the imprint of their bodies. She leaned over and smoothed the cover until there was no more sign of them.

Knowing she had to get out of there, she picked up the shells and her suitcase and made a final, cursory inspection of the room before exiting. She had no idea where she meant to go yet, if she could indeed find a good spot to put up a decent challenge. She just wanted to get away from here to protect Gray's property from damage if at all possible, and to get away from the rest of the residences. Hopefully, if she physically disassociated herself from them, maybe Borodin would leave the townspeople alone as he'd said. In any case, he would never expect her to come at him.

However, she was at the doorway when a patrol car pulled up on the street between the clinic and police station. It was the deputy sheriff's vehicle. For an instant her heart lifted with hope, only to see the passenger window ease down, exposing...Borodin.

The vehicle gunned forward, cutting a sharp right, causing it to fishtail as it sped into the yard. That added to the sand and gravel already in the air and left Sasha feeling as though she was inside an hourglass.

*Sand...time...*hers had run out.

Backing into the house, she slammed and bolted the door. She knew locking it was a joke, but she was buying herself a chance to get some cover. Tossing her suitcase out of the way, she rushed to the couch, pushed it farther from the wall and dropped behind it.

Within seconds there was a short burst of gunfire, a violent kick. The door flew open and the room exploded with a series of shots. Lamps shattered, tables splintered and upholstery stuffing flew as though a grenade had erupted in a chicken coop. Grimacing at the flying debris as much as the deafening blasts, Sasha crouched as low as she could, knowing a few coils and the wooden frame wouldn't deflect all the bullets for long. She waited for the inevitable pause.

When the moment came, she gave a warrior's yell and brought the .12 gauge around the side of the couch and fired, pumped and fired again. The massive form silhouetted in the doorway jerked, then stumbled back into the yard. Before he hit the ground, she was charging down the hallway.

39

God, no.

Gray was halfway down Main Street, about to cut a sharp U-turn and return to the house, when a movement drew his gaze to the rearview mirror. It was a patrol car. As it hesitated back by the clinic, then tore into the yard, he saw the bold print Sheriff on the side of the white vehicle and comprehended the magnitude of his mistake. No way did that vehicle carry legit cops. His last-ditch effort, that desperate brainstorm to scare Sasha out of this hopeless idea, had failed. Not only was she too noble to run, his underestimating her courage was forcing her to face those Russian thugs alone.

Unwilling to sacrifice the precious seconds it would cost to make that U-turn, Gray jammed the truck into Reverse and slammed his foot on the gas pedal. The truck seemed to move in slow motion, until he hit the brake pedal just as hard and tires screeched and skidded in protest, proving otherwise. Without a second's thought to the abuse he was delivering to the transmission, he rammed the gearshift into Drive again and drove his foot to the hilt on the gas pedal, once more charging into the yard after the Russians.

What he saw ahead of him chilled his blood. The patrol car stood at an angle in front of his house. Three of the doors were wide open and he saw three men dividing up. As the biggest one turned his front door into kindling, a bald-headed guy circled to the side of the house.

Gray aimed straight for the patrol car, hoping to draw some attention away from the house and Sasha as much as to make sure neither vehicle went anywhere again. Bracing himself, he hit the rear tire on the driver's side. The rubber deflected some of the impact, but he still shot upward, sending his head into the roof and smacking his chest into the steering wheel. Flashing lights distorted his vision, and a searing agony stole his breath. In the surreal moment he saw the giant reemerge from the house, teeter and crash backward onto the ground.

"Attagirl," he gasped.

Buoyed by hope, he struggled to overcome the dizziness and pain. That's when he glimpsed what the man's bulk had hidden—another man crushing the crepe myrtles as he pressed himself against the wall. From Sasha's description of the snake, he knew who he was seeing.

Borodin.

Reaching for Maureen's old service weapon, he found an empty seat. Swearing, he saw that the gun had fallen to the floorboard during the impact of the crash. Gray swore again as his body protested his bending to reach for it. A split second later, in a deafening roar of gunfire, the truck's windshield exploded over his back.

Borodin was coming after him.

Not wanting to be trapped inside the cab, Gray grabbed up the automatic. Forced to abandon the shotgun on the gun rack, he dived out of the truck. That's when he realized not only was the gunfire coming from in front of him, but the shooter was using an assault rifle, not the handgun he'd spotted in Borodin's grasp.

Baldy had given up on the kitchen entrance for the moment.

As quickly as it started, the firing stopped. Gray ducked to look under the deputy sheriff's vehicle and saw nothing. Ignoring the fire in his lungs and his bruised ribs, he eased up to look over the hood of the patrol car and saw the bald guy go back to testing the kitchen door.

He must think he'd got him, Gray thought, aiming at the same time Baldy fired at the kitchen-door lock. Gray shot, but in that same instant the Russian lunged forward and disappeared into the house.

A sound behind him had him glancing back, and he saw why both he and Borodin had given up on him. The Suburban was barreling into the yard.

Virtually a sitting duck where he was, Gray hoisted himself to his feet and launched himself over the wreck of the patrol car and front end of his truck. His bruised or cracked ribs rebelled and he landed badly, immediately suffering a wave of nausea. But knowing he couldn't afford to acknowledge the pain, he righted himself. Just as the Suburban was about to pass him on its way to the side of the house, he rose and started shooting into the passenger window. One of his bullets hit the guy bearing yet another Glock shimmering in the morning light. The Russian jerked backward, the momentum carrying him into the driver. The Suburban veered wildly out of control and hit the corral corner post hard before jerking to a stop.

Gray breathed shallowly, his gut twisting at the sound of new gunfire in the house. "Come on, come on," he said to the Suburban. He knew the right thing was to wait out the men inside, to let them make the first move, then pluck them off one by one. The problem was, Sasha was under siege inside the house.

About ready to try his luck at retrieving his shotgun and charging the bastards, he heard rather than saw a door open.

The stocky Russian driver emerged from the rear of the black vehicle and started blasting away with another rifle, this one a bull-pup type, spraying Gray's pickup and forcing him to duck from the flying glass and metal as much as from the bullets. He crawled to the back end of his vehicle. When the second volley ceased, he rolled clear and opened up on the man who was squatting to peer under the truck as he had moments ago.

The ungainly position and the speed of the two shots striking in virtually the same spot knocked the man off his feet. Gray didn't have to check to know he was dead before he hit the ground.

With no time to spare, he returned to his truck for the shotgun, knowing he needed more ammo than what was left in the .9mm. But as he turned back into the yard, he endured a horrific instant as his gaze locked on the man in the Suburban aiming at him.

The Glock was gone and in its place the thug held his own assault rifle. Gray registered the man's bloody hands just as the Russian opened fire. The blood explained why the first shots went wild. Knowing he couldn't delay, Gray pumped the shotgun and fired. But as he pumped again, the wounded Russian's gun went haywire, and in the deafening roar Gray felt a sudden punch that slammed him against the truck, knocking the shotgun from his grasp. As he slid to the ground, he could only turn his head aside as the ground exploded around him.

40

Trapped. Sasha had wanted to avoid facing Borodin in the house, but it couldn't be helped. Borodin and his other man, the baldheaded one who'd appeared out of the kitchen and was waiting for her just inside the guest-bedroom doorway, had been forcing her deeper into the house. Now she was all the way in the back of Gray's bedroom. There was nowhere else to go, save the closet, the master bath that had no window or out the floor-to-ceiling window behind her. And who knew how many of Borodin's men waited for her out there. She'd heard more gunfire outside. Could someone have gotten hold of the sheriff's department or state police after all? She had to stay alive to find out, and that meant getting out of here.

Knowing that they were waiting for her to make a move, she rose to her knees behind the bed and tested the window. It wouldn't budge, so she quickly stretched and flipped open the lock. Making a point to be as noisy as possible, she pushed up the window.

As she suspected, or at least hoped, the bald one

guessed she would be trying to escape, would have her back to him. He charged out of the guest room and into the master bedroom, shooting toward the window. But Sasha had shifted to the far corner by the headboard and ducked low.

The instant the blasting ceased, she straightened and greeted him with a steady shot from the .12 gauge. The trajectory and force of the blast lifted the slightly built man up off the floor, slamming him high against the door and staining it stark red before he slid to the ground.

Certain that Borodin was not far behind, Sasha dropped the shotgun and reached for her Smith & Wesson from the back of her jeans, needing speed and ease of movement now. She threw herself through the screen and her stiff and sore body hit hard.

With tears blinding her, Sasha cursed the baked Texas earth, but also the man responsible for causing her so much pain in the first place. Things had grown strangely silent out front, as well as inside the house. Dreading the worst, she scrambled to her feet and started running. Borodin would not be going anywhere. If she did have an ally, she owed him or them what protection she could. Her heart said "Gray," but because her eyes had seen what they had seen, her mind rejected the possibility.

She experienced a new jolt when she spotted the Suburban, but the man slumped half out of the open passenger window eased a little of her anxiety. She found his partner next. What had her almost crying out, though, was the sight of Gray's truck.

He hadn't left her after all! But where was he?

It had now been too quiet for too long. Not even Jessie was making a peep. Poor pup, she had to be quaking in terror.

Increasingly uneasy, Sasha stooped to check under both the truck and the patrol car before easing her way around the destroyed vehicles.

Where are you?

Where was Borodin? And how many more men were there?

As she came around the pickup, she saw Gray.

He stood by the front door, leaning against the jamb. At the sight of the red stain spreading over the side of his arm and chest, saturating his white T-shirt, she lunged forward.

The slightest negative motion from him had her stopping in midstep and readying her weapon. Before she could speak, Gray was pushed forward. Borodin emerged from the house pressing a gun to the back of Gray's head.

Dear God, she thought, no more. Not Gray, too. Hadn't Borodin stolen enough from her and her loved ones?

"What an expression on your lovely face, my Sashitska. After all this time, has the ice princess found a man to defrost her? In that case, it will give me all the greater pleasure to have you watch him die before I send you, too, to your eternal sleep.''

As aware of Gray's intent gaze willing her to take the shot as she was of Borodin's smirk, Sasha knew an instant of doubt. Her hands were too wet, her eyes were tearing from grit and emotion, and every muscle in her body was warning her of complete betrayal at any second.

''Take the shot!'' Gray ground out.

She ignored him, focusing instead on Borodin grinning against his own discomfort in this ghastly environment of dust-clogged air and perspiration bleeding into his eyes. There wasn't even time to draw in a fresh steadying breath. All she saw was the sweat and understood what had to happen.

Then he blinked...and she squeezed the trigger.

The bullet found its mark precisely where Borodin's men had shot her mother. Sasha continued to hold her breath as the momentum jerked back his head, as the hand holding the Glock twitched. There was an echoing shot as the gun discharged. Then he and Gray both went down.

''No!''

Sasha ran. By the time she reached Gray, he was struggling to sit up and distance himself from his would-be killer. Borodin's bullet had missed, but there was enough blood on his side to scare her to death. Digging into her pocket, she pulled out the handkerchief her mother had embroidered for her years ago that she always carried for good luck. It was ridiculously inadequate, but she stuffed it into Gray's bloody hand, directing it up to his side. "Press. Damn it, you have to press it to stop the flow," she ordered, her voice shaking. "Oh God, was it a side shot?"

"I'm fine. Radio."

Afraid to believe that it was over, she first checked the house to be sure, then used the deputy sheriff's radio to call for help.

Returning to Gray, she momentarily stared down at the Russian who had caused so much tragedy. "I guess Gloria neglected to tell you that I was on the precinct's shooting team," she murmured bitterly. *"Do svidaniya, Gospodin Blat."*

Epilogue

Bitters, Texas
Sunday, August 27, 2000
10:12 a.m. CST

"We're ready to go when you are, ma'am."

Sasha nodded to the FBI agent poking his head through the doorway. Drawing a deep breath, she gave the living room one last inspection. There hadn't been much time to repair the damage, especially once the DPS and FBI agents arrived and the interviews started. But one trooper based in Sonora had relatives in the construction business and had been great about getting several members of his family out here fast to replace the front and kitchen doors, cover the shattered windows and do whatever necessary to protect the place from vandalism. She couldn't have left in good conscience without at least taking care of that.

Much of the blood was gone, too. Of course, the house would need a major paint job after the Sheetrock and plasterwork was done, and the carpeting would need to be replaced. She felt so responsible for the damage, which was part of the reason she'd worked late into the night doing what she could. But even in the dim light, she had to admit Gray might be better off razing the whole house and starting from scratch.

"Time to go, Miss Mess." She stooped to clip the leash on Jessie's collar. The agents liked this contingency least of all, but it was one she'd been most adamant about. Once she'd radioed for help from the deputy's vehicle and got some towels to put more pressure on Gray's wound, she'd freed Jessie, who hadn't left her side since. Much to the nurses' displeasure, Sasha had even snuck her into the hospital to check on Gray, and back at the house Jessie had slept on the bed with her when she'd finally turned in. She didn't trust anyone here to care for the dog, so taking her had become a moot point. Sasha had even gone so far as to arrange for a first-class seat for Jessie on the flight to Las Vegas. She was paying the fare herself to keep some independence from the bureau boys, who were already trying to dictate to her. Besides, using Borodin's money gave her another small sense of retribution.

At the door she hesitated. She wasn't leaving Gray a note. She knew it was cold not to, but who knew his plans? He might hire someone to come in and do more work while recuperating, and she didn't want a personal message intercepted by a stranger. No, that wasn't honest. He hadn't had much to say last night, and she was beginning to think that risky shot she'd taken had planted a seed of disappointment or even resentment in him.

In any case, it was time to move on. She pulled the door shut, ducked under the police tape and tested the lock. Discreetly caressing the cascade of overgrown crepe myrtle one last time, she remembered her first moments standing here. Finally, she headed for the silver Ford sedan. Out by the street a car pulled in, a white SUV that Sasha recognized and informed the wary agents was someone she knew.

J.M. emerged. In the busy aftermath, she'd almost forgotten about him. He'd cleaned up well, and except for the leather sandals, was dressed like an attorney heading for a morning round of golf. As far as she was concerned, he could have done that and skipped this visit.

"You probably don't want to speak to me," he began.

"We do have a plane to catch."

He nodded and cast the two young agents a respectful look as they monitored his every twitch. "You've become quite the heroine. Now that the phones are working again, the lines are buzzing with talk about you. Sasha Mills...a big-city cop, no less. Very exotic."

"A metro cop. Hardly TV chic."

"Small towns like their celebrities, too. It's already been suggested we name a street in your honor."

"No doubt the one with the truck-eating potholes."

With a delicate cough, J.M. continued. "I suppose it is too little too late, but I wanted to come and tell you that I didn't learn about what happened until almost noon yesterday. And then I was at the hospital. I confess, I succumbed to the temptation of excess libation after being called away from the meeting with the investigator Thursday."

"Friday."

"Well, there you go. Um...I've already filled in Gray. He told me about your mother. About... I'm very sorry."

Sasha knew she was being hard, but she'd had no time yet to grieve let alone find understanding for all of what happened. She'd been busy with interviews to help the police and government do whatever else they could to take out more of Borodin's network and begin confiscating his assets. The jet at Sonora had put smiles on faces. The Suburban towed out of here along with the patrol car might buy the local boys a decent barbecue. It would take longer to repair her attitude, to get used to the hollowness in her heart left by all she had lost. And she wasn't sure what it would take to reconcile her feelings for the citizens of Bitters.

"At least some people have the courtesy to keep their distance." She nodded to where Elias stood

at the front of his station looking sheepish and very
left out. The DPS officers had informed her that
the mayor was already looking into the legalities
and cost of breaking his contract. As far as Sasha
was concerned, the mayor needed to be informed
that someone was apt to run against him, too.

"Would it interest you to know who started the
fire that got you stuck here in the first place?"

Sasha shook her head. "I discovered that myself,
not that it matters at this point. Lonnie Metcalf."

"Gray said you recognized his truck. You're
wrong, though. It was his half brother, Tim Pike.
My nephew-in-law," J.M. intoned, adding a roll of
his eyes.

Her mind was reeling with names, dates and stories; however, Tim's jumped to the front of her
mind without a problem. Not just for his attempts
to help with the car, but his humiliation suffered at
the hands of his wife and Frank Elias. "No way."

"A man in love can be driven to do desperate
things. You're right, firemen are among the first we
consider heroes. Problem is, you can't be a hero
without a fire. Truth is, we don't have that many,
and those that occur, we tend to let burn themselves
out so as not to waste water."

"Come on, J.M., that was the church where he
married Gerri Rose."

"I'm not saying there wasn't a little anger mixed
in with his desperation. But it *was* an outside fire,
not one started inside the attached Sunday school

addition or the church itself. I feel containment was always his intent.''

"Now you sound like a defense lawyer.'' Sasha didn't say it as a compliment. "You can't excuse his actions. What if I had identified that truck sooner and his brother had been arrested? Would Tim have let him go to jail? To prison?''

"No, of course not.'' However, J.M. did look momentarily doubtful. "All of that is irrelevant now anyway.''

"Don't tell me the insurance company cut the check and everyone's going to keep their mouths shut because there's enough for expansion?''

J.M. eyed her over the vague line of his bifocals. "Don't become hard, Sasha. Leave me one ideal, please. It's not the fire, it's because Gerri Rose is pregnant.''

"Great. The new American family—Daddy's doing time and Mommy's having an adulterous affair.''

"The child isn't Tim's.''

Now Sasha was willing to listen.

"Yes. Words escaped me, too. And I'm afraid I showed my true colors yesterday when I let you down by leaving the church site to soothe my hysterical sister. Between her asking me to talk sense into Gerri Rose and Tim insisting on DNA verification, and Gerri Rose— Well, suffice it to say, I tied on a good one and was of no use when you needed an ally most. I'm so ashamed. When I get home, I'm pulling out the phone jacks from the wall and making myself a monster pitcher of Bloody Marys and seeking oblivion until Monday, when I'm expected to come up with divorce papers for my near-catatonic niece.''

''At the risk of sounding as dysfunctional as the rest of you, I almost feel sorry for Tim.''

J.M. gave a brief bark of cynical laughter. ''Save the compassion for someone with both oars in the water. Tim, bless his myopic heart, is willing to keep trying to make things work. Even as Gerri Rose fantasizes that Frank will want to make an honest woman of her.''

Sasha thought of the scene she'd witnessed between Gerri Rose and Frank Elias before the panic set in. ''Stranger things have happened. I give her 8–1 odds.''

''Oh-ho, you may still be a softy after all. I thought 20–1. Then again, who knows? It would be a relief for future Elias offspring if all this has put some metal in Dad's spine.'' He glanced over at the station. ''If little Bubba ever gets to know good ol' dad.''

For the child's sake, Sasha rather hoped not. This was one instance where growing up with only one parent couldn't hurt. But to J.M. she said a polite, ''Thank you for explaining.''

''Have you seen Gray?''

She couldn't deny the dismissive tone in her response and was a little frustrated with the attorney's determination to keep chatting. They really did have a flight and it was at least an hour's drive to San Antonio's airport.

"Briefly," she replied. Gray was a subject she definitely wanted to keep private. She was, however, equally protective of his health. "He needs rest. I hope people will give him some space."

"I thought maybe you'd be seeing to that."

"I can't stay here, J.M."

Although the agent at the driver's door cleared his throat meaningfully, J.M. checked his watch, glanced back toward the road and made a face. "Oh dear. You've no intention of coming back at all, do you?"

Jessie began to pull on her leash, sensing cooler air inside the sedan. "I'm going to be pretty busy. Once I finish with the depositions, I'll be taking my mother back to Minnesota where my father is buried."

"Of course. Well, I've kept you long enough. If you're ever in this part of the country again... Sasha," he said, suddenly serious, "Bitters may have stubbed its toe on the definition of compassion, but this isn't a bad town. It's simply been too long since we saw your brand of dedication."

Sasha could only bow her head.

"All right then." He began to turn away and then murmured, "Oh. I almost forgot. Gray asked me to find out something for him. In the end, what you said to that Russian—he was curious."

"Do svidaniya, Gospodin Blat." Sasha nodded remembering. "It means, 'So long, Mr. Networker.'"

J.M. looked intrigued, then with a crooked smile patted the hand she rested on the door of the sedan. "Safe trip."

As he drove off, Sasha let Jessie into the back seat. But before she could get in herself, she heard the screech of tires again. It triggered a reflexive gasp in her and had the two agents drawing their weapons and ducking behind their doors.

A taxi careened into the lot. As it drew up before them, the left rear passenger door opened and an arm holding an IV sack emerged, then a tired voice called out, "Hey, Junior. Give a guy a hand?"

As the agents exchanged glances, Sasha assured them, "He's talking to me." Hurrying to Gray, she scolded, "Are you trying to kill yourself? You sent J.M. ahead to delay us, didn't you?"

Between her and the cab, he managed to stay upright. He didn't look any stronger than when she'd seen him last night, but there was a glint in his eyes she knew better than to ignore.

"I had to come," he said. "But as you can see I'm not totally without aid."

She eyed the IV bag he carefully held higher than his heart and the bandages wrapped around his chest exposed by the open doctor's jacket. She didn't want to know how he'd acquired either, or how he'd conned his driver to be his accomplice. "You have to go back, Gray."

"Hell, this looks worse than it is. The bullet just took enough flesh between my side and inner arm to hurt like hell for a while. But this is good for another several hours," he said, nodding to the IV.

"It's still too much of a risk. I would have called."

"No, you wouldn't. You'll be busy and then get busier. Tomorrow will turn into next week, and finally you'll decide you're better off forgetting about this place—and me."

She focused on the bag. "You know that's not true."

"Then tell me what you plan to do once you finish up in Vegas?"

"Take some time off. I'd like to actually see Anna's cottage in Louisiana. As for long-term plans, that'll take more time and consideration."

"What would you say if I came along to do some of that myself?"

Too emotionally battered to risk putting much faith in romance, let alone in happily-ever-afters, she put pragmatism first. "What about this?" she asked, nodding to the clinic and house.

His gaze didn't leave her face. "Guess I can hire someone to cut the grass. Look, I know we both have enough loose ends between us to make a hairball big enough to choke a lion, and you want quiet time to deal with your loss. And yeah, it's too damn soon for this conversation, and no fun at all to be having it with an audience.'' He shifted to touch his forehead to hers. ''But hear me anyway, will you? While I was lying in that hospital bed thinking about you leaving this morning, something struck me hard.''

''I didn't pay my vet bill.''

He growled and glared into her eyes. ''You fought off a small army and you're turning coward now? Sasha...the guy in the bed beside mine, the one in a coma? He had a visitor after you left last night. She read him something. Told me a friend sent it to her from off the Internet. It went, 'It only takes a minute to get a crush on someone, an hour to like someone and a day to love someone, but it takes a lifetime to forget someone.' Sasha... sweetheart, I don't want to spend the rest of my life forgetting you.''

Sasha closed her eyes for a moment, feeling a surge of relief and joy as great as when she'd first seen that he'd survived. When she opened them again, she shot a quick glance at the agents, who had the courtesy to turn their backs.

Then she framed Gray's face with her hands and kissed him.

''One thing,'' she murmured against his lips when he finally let her speak. ''If you think I was hardheaded before, wait until I go into my nurse mode.''

As she climbed into the car beside Jessie, Gray grinned. "I can't wait for my first sponge bath."

He handed the nearest agent his IV bag as he eased in beside her. After handing it back, the agent shut the door. Seconds later, the sedan rolled out of the lot and out of town.

Helen R. Myers

66796	DEAD END	__ $5.99 U.S. __ $6.99 CAN.
66572	LOST	__ $5.99 U.S. __ $6.99 CAN.
66504	MORE THAN YOU KNOW	__ $5.99 U.S. __ $6.99 CAN.
66436	COME SUNDOWN	__ $5.99 U.S. __ $6.99 CAN.

(limited quantities available)

TOTAL AMOUNT	$_____
POSTAGE & HANDLING	$_____
($1.00 for one book; 50¢ for each additional)	
APPLICABLE TAXES*	$_____
TOTAL PAYABLE	$_____

(check or money order—please do not send cash)

To order, complete this form and send it, along with a check or money order for the total above, payable to MIRA Books®, to: **In the U.S.:** 3010 Walden Avenue, P.O. Box 9077, Buffalo, NY 14269-9077; **In Canada:** P.O. Box 636, Fort Erie, Ontario L2A 5X3.

Name:_____
Address:_____ City:_____
State/Prov.:_____ Zip/Postal Code:_____
Account Number (if applicable):_____
075 CSAS

*New York residents remit applicable sales taxes.
 Canadian residents remit applicable GST and provincial taxes.

MIRA®

Visit us at www.mirabooks.com

MHRM0202BL